Dorset Libraries
Withdrawn Stock

For you Han.
Always
x

Echo

Come to me in the silence of the night;
Come in the speaking silence of a dream;
Come with soft rounded cheeks and eyes as bright
As sunlight on a stream;
Come back in tears,
O memory, hope, love of finished years.

Oh dream how sweet, too sweet, too bitter sweet,
Whose wakening should have been in Paradise,
Where souls brimful of love abide and meet;
Where thirsting longing eyes
Watch the slow door
That opening, letting in, lets out no more.

Yet come to me in dreams, that I may live
My very life again tho' cold in death:
Come back to me in dreams, that I may give
Pulse for pulse, breath for breath:
Speak low, lean low,
As long ago, my love, how long ago.

Christina Rossetti

Where you used to be, there is a hole in the world,
which I find myself constantly walking around in
the daytime, and falling in at night.
I miss you like hell.

Edna St. Vincent Millay

Pomegranates

Pomegranate season was her favourite time. She liked the way the fat balls would hang from the trees, dangling their temptation over the walls of gardens, enticing you to quickly swipe one as you strolled back from school. All her friends did it too, and although a few owners would come out and make a comment, most of them did so good-naturedly, disappearing back into their gardens with a small smile and a wry shake of the head. School kids.

She liked the perfume that they left on the breeze, the stickiness of the juices as you cut through to the little scarlet gems – and the intricacy of mining out those jewels.

She walked home without her parents now she had turned 11 – that still gave her a little thrill – a feeling of independence just around the corner; the awakening of something she couldn't yet grasp.

As they turned the final corner before her home, she smiled when she caught sight of her little sister Laila stomping around the garden on her chubby legs. Laila squealed as she saw Eve, her leg-speed increasing to a pace that her coordination couldn't yet keep up with, sending her stumbling onto the grass. Eve swooped in, school bag

7

slung across her shoulder, and, still laughing, swung Laila around, eliciting the bubbling brook of giggles to which toddlers alone hold the secret.

"Look, Laila – for you, sweetie." Eve offered up the ripe pomegranate that she had stashed away for her baby sister.

"Pom pom," gurgled Laila, grabbing the fruit, and setting off determinedly to the kitchen where, she already knew, help would be on hand in the form of a sharp knife and a willing family member.

Eve glanced around the garden before following Laila inside. Everything was ripening – the figs hung heavy on the trees now, and little pockets of sweetly scented jasmine air were everywhere. She liked helping her parents in the garden. Not so much the cutting back and pruning – she actually rather preferred the wild abandon that the honeysuckle, hibiscus and bougainvillea strove for. But she loved seeing things that had been planted many weeks or months before shyly peering out into the world for the first time.

She heard the strains of her mother's piano playing as she turned back towards the house, and she smiled again as she wondered whether Hugo was home yet: he'd promised her a trip down to the beach with him and his friends once he got back from school. Eve ran up the steps to the verandah, and into the house to find her snorkel and mask.

The house was always full of music, whether drifting out from the cassette player, or from her mother's hands at the piano. Right now, her mother was playing the Enigma Variations again, the notes echoing around the house. She smiled warmly as Eve came in, allowing her hands to continue drawing the beautiful melody from the keys.

"Oh I love this one, Mummy! Tell me again about why this one is special!" Eve said.

Her mother smiled, knowing that Eve already knew, but that there was pleasure in this repetition, these little rituals. She managed to keep the music flowing as Eve ducked under her arms and clambered up onto her lap. Eve was getting too gangly really for that now, but her mother always just opened her arms a little wider, and made it possible.

"What is so special, Evie, is that the parts at the end are saying, on paper, the exact same thing that was said at the start. But the magic is that they sound completely different; when they are played out loud, they say a completely different thing!"

"That's not possible, Mummy!"

"That's the magic, Evie – they are saying something different to you, because you can now hear them differently. The music has taken you on a journey, and without that journey, the start and the end would sound the same to you. But with that journey, you can hear the difference. Magic! Life always finds a way."

Battle

The fug of death filled my nostrils, permeating me from the inside. The air was too thick to breathe in. It was a moment strung out like the unending stammer of the machine gun. A soldier ran at me, wild eyes screaming, his ragged breath close enough to share my air. The pop of small arms fire, and he lurched sideways – a red water-bomb exploding on the side of his head. My feet slipped on the heaving mass of failing life carpeting the ground. I was standing in the middle of the battle.

And then I was floating. A witness. A survivor. Invulnerable yet impotent. No bullets could pump into me up here, but I had breathed in the insidious death. My hidden wound would do its silent work.

The sergeant in charge was drunk on blood: ordering suicidal attacks and brutal butcheries. A little girl ran off into the woods. The sight began to unpick the seams of my own sanity. My brain distended painfully to accommodate a new comprehension of normal, like a balloon bulging too far, too fast. He couldn't be judged. And then it went quiet.

There was now only one soldier left. Him. Only him. Me. Only me. A witness. And a perpetrator. My wings unable to beat strongly enough to keep me above all of this, away, I floated slowly down to corporeal reality. The world around me was cloaked in silence. Unbearable silence. Incensed fumes, perfumed with death, wafted upwards, an incantation to some god, somewhere. A tiny gnat danced in a smoky beam of light.

I was taken to a side door – brushed stainless steel. Clinical, cold. I took in the raised platform that the entire carnage had been enacted upon. A stage, a modern-day gladiatorial arena to entertain and amuse. Stage hands were humming to themselves as they knelt underneath the creaking structure, tinkering with this and that; one taking time to sweep the floor.

The soldier was led down the wooden steps. Broken, confused, blood on his hands. The sergeant shook his hand, and I felt the callouses. "I hope we'll be seeing you next time, boy; you did good out there!" He hit my shoulder hard, barked a laugh, and left me there. Alone. I was free, but floundered under the weight of what I had done. Had it been me? The wrench from one reality to another was agony. Dislocation from oneself. And no quick push to shunt the joint back into place.

I stumbled out of the theatre of war, past the old façade of crumbling gargoyles and plasterwork – posters already advertising next week's show. A crowd of screaming women were ordered away by uniformed men: the women's distress clashing painfully with the expressionless eyes of the guards. Their tidal wave of grief crashed over the building, and left *behind the flotsam of despair and loss. Thousands of bits of crumpled paper stranded on the coast between hope and reality. The papers jerked in the breeze, so fragile, so vulnerable. I knelt slowly to pick some up. The heaviness of their meaning made them difficult to lift. Letters, photographs: moments and faces lost forever. That abrupt lurch one takes from existence to non-existence in the space of a breath.*

Shadows

I'm going to see a psychotherapist. I still find that fact slightly amazing. I've never felt the need before, but now I do. I just can't keep everything together at work, and these nightmares; they are clinging on to me all day, restraining me in another place, another time. I'm feeling stuck – as if my feet are caught in thick treacle, just yards from where I actually need to be. I can't move them.

She has come highly recommended, this therapist – Claire – with all sorts of accolades to her name. I just need her to get me moving again. I have so much on at work, and I know that people are beginning to see me slip, to be nagged by creeping doubts when I'm asked to take on important pieces of work. I hate that – I want them to see me as they always did – as competent, capable. If that is what they see, then that is what it is easier for me to be.

But these nightmares are relentless now: I had another last night. I sat up in bed abruptly, like a free diver kicking desperately to regain the surface. The shroud of the nightmare still clung to me as I clutched at my throat and gasped to refill my lungs. The legacy of the dream dripped off me in glistening droplets that lurked in the shadows of the room. I turned and clicked on the night-light beside my bed. Most of the shadows then retreated, but the soft glow of the lamp was not enough to obliterate them all. Some simply tucked themselves behind the chest of drawers, the stool and the pile of clothes on the floor. They always do. I see them. They never leave me alone. The dark places in the shell of who I am.

Turning to the small notepad and pencil beside my bed, I wondered how to make sense of any of this on paper. Still, I started to write. Hesitantly at first, trying hard to grasp at the fleeing remnants of my nightmare. After a few moments I stilled my hand, letting the dream come back to me, claim me, inhabit me. When I opened my eyes again, my hand sped across the page, the limits of human mark-making frustrating me, as the images started to pour out.

Should I tell Claire about this dream? She had advised me over the phone to write them down, but last night's was so graphic that I feel uncomfortable about sharing it. I'm not sure I want her to see so much.

I climb out of the chill of my bed, kicking off the sweat-stained duvet that never keeps me warm enough, and wander to the shower that never seems to wash me clean.

Window

I had the strangest sense that as I looked out of the train window into the night, another world, another reality was somehow just there, just beyond the glass, millimetres from my fingertips on the pane, hurtling along just as I was, keeping pace in an entirely different realm. Was it looking in on me here, pressed to the glass as I was? Was this invisible barrier between me and the night also the boundary of something beyond?

The window was the strangest thing. Something you usually can't even see, which light passes through. And yet, when the light levels are so much darker on one side, you can not only not see through, but also everything around you is reflected back to you – an illusion of the fullness of this reality, this room, this life.

Abundance

As Eve dived down into the water, she felt at home. With the water cocooning her, holding her, she looked for the fish. They soon found her, collecting around her in a small shoal, clicking their curiosity through the muffling liquid. She grinned over at Hugo, a stream of air bubbles escaping from her snorkel and wiggling upwards. Hugo smiled back, and then took out the little bag of breadcrumbs they had brought with them for the fish. Within seconds, the space around them was alive with flashing colours, eager streaks of vibrancy. Gentle clown fish – curious, but never wishing to stray too far from their protective anemones – the grumpy-looking groupers, striped zebra fish, the darting lyretail anthias in their orange swarm, and the stately emperor angelfish. The parrot fish always ignored them unless they got too close, preferring to carry on breaking off tiny bits of coral with their beaks – a noise that could be heard reverberating through the water.

She loved this – loved watching this dance of nature, coloured in such spectacular palettes. She had always liked the contrast between the stark sandiness of the landscape outside and the overwhelming burst of colour that came as you put your head under the water. A kaleidoscopic garden. The way the fish just hung there suspended in front of you, free of gravity in this other world. And she loved these times with her big brother.

They did it over and over again – coming up to the surface to take in enormous gulps of air, and then kicking downwards to rejoin the colourful throng below.

With the breadcrumbs finally finished, she saw Hugo turn the bag inside out and shake it. Everything looked so comical and slowed down that she grinned again. Hugo glanced over at her and gestured to the surface. She nodded back, and they pushed off from the bottom and rose back up to the air.

They lay on their backs on the sand, drying off in the bright sunshine, laughing and discussing which fish they had seen that day. Eve was learning all their names from Hugo, and could identify most of them now, but there were always one or two new ones. He knew so much about them all – their feeding habits, where they laid their eggs, whether they preferred living alone. She always listened intently to him as he taught her about them, but what really captivated her was simply watching them all dance.

A Golden Age

Once, a long time ago, there was a prosperous, peaceful land called Enanti. It knew nothing of terror or darkness. It was a place of light and learning. Its main city, Albedo, was glorious, filled with fountains and open squares, and famed far and wide. This was a Golden Age. And the land was twice the size it is now. It traded freely with other countries, and the people lived in harmony and peace.

Outside the main city, the land was richly wooded, with rivers full of bounty, and settled with many towns and villages. People travelled easily between all parts of this land, forming a cohesive, unified community. The leader at the time, Eferon, had a council, whose members were wise and fair. Everything was in balance, and life was rich.

The dark mist

Something was causing increasing numbers of deaths around the world – festering and growing like an infectious disease. News footage showed a loose ball of dark mist rolling along the ground, and simply absorbing any people in its path. It was terrifying. It would appear and form from nowhere, kill, and roll onwards.

As it developed, this vapour took on more form, killing more and more. It started to be shaped like a strange, dark, lizard-type creature – immense – that would open its jaws and swallow people up. As it ate, its thick tail rose upwards in ecstasy.

The mist was growing in strength by the day. It was targeting certain people: it consumed those who had lost hope or were in despair. For some, it seemed just a mere day of those feelings was enough to conjure up the mist, which would appear and consume them.

I was in a dark bedroom that I shared with another girl. There was a packing case on the bed, and we were staying there to attend a school assessment day. The room had a big, wooden, built-in wall of heavy-looking wardrobes, with dense velvet red curtains. I was sitting on the floor, my friend lying on the bed. The mist started to appear behind my friend – looming out of the darkness. She couldn't see it. The atmosphere plummeted. My friend started to speak: "Everything is going wrong..." and the mist loomed higher behind her, drawing itself up for attack. But then she smiled, and added, "But I really don't mind – it will all get better at some point."

In an instant, the creature disappeared, but it left behind a tangible sense of dread and spiked adrenaline. We had found out how to thwart the creature, and we raced up the stairs to inform others.

The setting above ground was vastly different – an old-fashioned tea-party was in full swing. Parents were being fêted by the school and staff, all grating smiles and simpering. Soon it was time for the parents to leave, and just we children remained to be assessed.

There was a dark feeling beneath this school façade. My skin prickled and I smelt the bitter tang of danger. It was some form of research/experimental/torture facility. With their eyes blind, our parents had left us here, and we were alone.

Under a canopy of stars

"But I'm scared of the dark, Daddy! I don't want to do that!" Eve said, loudly.

"But Evie, sweetheart, that is exactly why we are going to try it. We will all sleep outside in the garden together, look up at the stars together, and show you the dark is OK. Together. OK? And if it gets too much…we'll just all come inside," her father replied.

"Can I sleep next to you?" she asked back.

"Your little camp bed will be jammed up so close to mine that nothing will be able to get between. Promise". He smiled back at her.

"And can we have hot chocolate?"

"We can do better than that!" he laughed.

And they really did. That evening they set up all the little camp beds in the garden, and built a fire in the middle which cast flickering light out over them. And they did have hot chocolate, which Eve's mother heated over the fire in a little pan, stirring occasionally and tasting. And Eve's father gave them each long sticks they'd collected from the garden earlier, and then produced a large bag of marshmallows to toast.

"You've got to have marshmallows with hot chocolate!" he exclaimed, "and it is actually the law to have toasted marshmallows when you have an open fire."

Eve grinned up at him, and shook her head in mock exasperation. He tried to tickle her on her side, and she collapsed in giggles.

This was wonderful, she thought, as she sat there in the night with her family. Laila had given up trying to wander into the fire at every given opportunity, and had now climbed up into their mother's lap and fallen asleep, her flushed and peaceful face shimmering in the fire glow. As their mother's arms had cradled little Laila, Hugo had taken on the hot chocolate duties. As he poured the steaming liquid out into their little camping cups, he smiled down at Eve.

"Given our little sister couldn't make it to the performance, I think you can have a little extra, Evie."

She knew that they were all being extra kind to her because they wanted to help her have a happy night, here under the night sky. And that warmed her in a different way to the fire. She was happy, here with them all. She felt safe – she didn't get that familiar adrenaline rush that she got at night when she woke up and the house was all dark. Sitting here, surrounded by the dark, actually within it, she felt held and at peace. Because she had everything she needed. There wasn't anything to fear here. In fact, she thought, as she looked up at the night, it was stunning. The sky was alive with stars. They seemed to pulse and glow, arching overhead like a protective shield. Little bits of light to accent the darkness.

"You know, Evie, the stars are still there in the daytime," said her father. "Did you know that?"

"Are you sure? How come we can't see them then? I thought they set like the sun."

"Because the rest of the sky is too light to reveal them properly. They are there but you don't notice them. So you don't stop to wonder at their beauty. Sometimes you need a bit of dark to show up the special bits – a bit of contrast. So, that's why I like the dark: it can show you the stars."

Eve loved that. She snuggled closer into her father's shoulder, and his arm came around her, flooding her with warmth.

Still somewhere else

I sat as still as I could in the waiting room, retreating into my shell. I didn't want my body to betray my nerves. I was glad we were meeting in an office, actually – it was far less intimate. As I was shown into Claire's room that first time, I saw books jostling for position along one entire wall. I liked that – it seemed a funny contrast to the clean lines and orderliness of the rest of the small room.

She was probably about 15 years or so older than I, and she smiled as she indicated where I should sit. I liked this chair. Its vintage shape had been re-upholstered in a beautiful pink and grey felt, which was slightly worn on the arms. I liked the slight abrasion under my fingertips as I stroked it. I wondered how many people had sat here, rubbing it as I was, wearing it away by degrees.

I think we were speaking of my issues concentrating at work, the disappointment I felt from my immediate boss, why that bothered me – that kind of thing. I could feel my mind was wandering, trying to calm itself by looking around and finding other things to focus on. I squirmed in my seat.

And then I mentioned that I wasn't sleeping well.

"That sounds important, Eve," Claire said, waiting for me to go on.

I felt a rush of frustration. Why couldn't she just ask some simple questions I could answer more quickly – which would help me more quickly?

Without thinking too carefully about my next choice of words, I said: "I'm having bad dreams at the moment. They are happening all the time, and I often wake up and find it hard to get back to sleep." Then, more quietly, "They are more like nightmares, really, and they can hold on to me for the rest of the day."

"That must make being at work extremely hard – when you have a lot to do, but you are still somewhere else," Claire stated.

I looked up at her. "That's exactly it. I feel I am somewhere else. That is just how it feels. But I should be used to that."

Creeping chill

"Not today Evie, I'm afraid", said her father. "You and Hugo must stay at home in the garden this afternoon."

"Why, though? Why can't we go out?" Eve asked. "We were going to go diving for shells today!"

Her father pushed his hair off his forehead, looking down. He looked worried and unsure. She couldn't remember seeing him look like that before, and it jarred.

"What? What is it?" Eve asked again, an edge to her voice now. "Why aren't you at work today, Daddy? What is happening?"

"Probably nothing, sweetheart. Just some people in high-up places having a bit of an argument with each other. I'm sure they will sort it all out. But until they do, we just want you where we can keep an eye on you. That's all. Where we can make sure you are safe. Why don't we all do something here at home today? What would you like to do?"

Normally Eve would have loved a day at home with the whole family. It was a rare treat to have her father home during the week. But something felt wrong. It tasted metallic and cold on her tongue, and it made her throat feel tight.

Cracks

All had been peaceful in Enanti for as long as people could remember. But there came a time when discord crept quietly into the land.

It came when the council fell into disagreement about whom the leader, Eferon, should marry. He was already in love with Quella – a beautiful, wise woman who had been by his side in the Citadel for several years. Everyone knew they were lovers, and that their bond was deep and precious. But a proposal of marriage had come from across the sea: the King of Teo was offering his daughter to the leader of Enanti, and, with this union, advantageous trading terms and diplomatic ties. The council was split: half advised him to marry his lover – a proven aide – while the others urged him to accept the proposed marriage from afar.

A disputatious campaign ensued, with each side constantly needling Eferon to accept its own recommendations, while warning him against those of the other camp. The pressure told on him. He started to behave erratically. His judgement faltered. He felt the opposing pulls of being a man in love, and the leader of his nation. And he remained caught in indecision.

Eventually, those in the council who opposed his relationship with Quella conspired to make Eferon believe that her love for him had died and that she had abandoned him. They took her captive, and rode with her for many days, to the very edge of the land, where they chained her to the wall of a cave by the sea, at the foot of a long flight of rocky steps. They left provisions there for her, enough for at least a week, and one of their number to guard her.

They knew Eferon would take her absence hard, but hoped that by forcing his hand, clearing his line of vision, they would be helping Enanti to move towards a bright future.

Eferon was devastated by her disappearance. Wracked with anger and grief, he tore apart the Citadel looking for her, desperate for answers. Quella consumed his mind. He was tortured by visions of them together, entwined, fused, urgent. He wondered if she had meant any of it. Doubt crept into his mind.

Crossing the field

I was recuperating from something serious, in a live-in facility. There was a large open field outside, fringed by woods. There was a war going on. I had just put some henna in my hair when we were told we had to go – we were to be evacuated immediately. The building was being attacked. I wasn't allowed to take anything. But as we scuttled through the bushes, watching the explosions happening around us, I felt I was carrying more and more, and kept stumbling.

We were going to try to get to my sister's house, through the woods. She was visiting me, along with my brother. We started to cross the field to the tree line. Little red, white and blue bombs kept dropping down from the sky, and we had to keep looking up to dodge them all. When we reached the tree line, there was an enemy marksman. We fell to the ground, pressing ourselves into the mud. We became smaller. But my brother stood up and walked into the wood so that they would follow him and we would be safe. We shouted at him, screaming for him to come back, but he disappeared into the trees.

And then the world changed...

"Evie, Evie – wake up." She started to come to, aware that someone was shaking her, whispering in low, urgent tones. It was Hugo. She pushed him off grumpily, but he continued. "You must wake up Eves – please." Something in her brother's voice made a slow icy line start to travel down her back, and she turned to him and sat straight up.

"What is it?" she whispered back.

Hugo took her hand, still warm from sleep, and led her silently over to the window. She could feel his hand trembling. He pulled the curtain back a tiny fraction and she gasped. Right there, in front of her house, tanks were rolling up the street, scraping against the bougainvillea tendrils, bristling with guns. It was only now that she started to tune into the other sounds that were alien – the crunching of heavy vehicle gears, the distant whine of aircraft and the ominous throb-throb-throb of helicopter rotor blades. She shrank back against her bother. 'What's happening, Hugo? What's happening?"

Dislocation

I told her then. I told her about the war. I told her about it taking my family, and my home. How I had come here and started again. I'm not sure why I told her; I never really told anyone. Why would I? I couldn't bear the awkwardness that came with it. Of course, I had to roll out some prepared statements sometimes – like why I had no parents, why I lived with my aunt and uncle. And of course, there were the scars on my back – ugly and ridged.

That explanation had come sooner than I would have liked as a girl – at school in the showers after a hockey match. I'd been so elated over a home win, and the feeling of being a proper part of something again, that I had actually forgotten about the scars until someone had gasped in the shower next to me, and pointed them out to everyone. I hadn't been ready for it, and it had felt as if I had been stripped bare, far below the skin. I think I had stammered out some workable response that had said enough, but it had ruined things. I remembered that.

The nascent camaraderie I'd been building with these new friends now became more guarded. The irony was not lost on me that they, by knowing more about me, were now allowed to see far less. I wasn't ready to give them more.

And yet, down the years, I'd sometimes wished the scars were scratched right across my face – that my damage was visible to all. I would not have had the option to hide it away, conceal myself. Hidden wounds were a toxic burden, holding me apart from the world around me – a world that carried on in blissful ignorance. Why couldn't they see what the world was really like? My physical scars meant nothing to me; just the tip of an iceberg.

Even my own appearance reinforced my sense of isolation from the world playing out around me. When I looked at myself in the mirror, I looked as if I belonged exactly where I was; right here. Perhaps if I had looked like an outsider, the sense of dislocation I felt would not have jarred so much. But nothing marked me out – from my slight frame, to my father's pale complexion.

It was only my eyes that I felt could betray me, their grey-blue depths speaking of other worlds, other lives. I saw it when I looked in the mirror. There was occasionally something unknown, wild and alien in my gaze. It captured the distance that the wild keeps in front of humans. But, even then, maybe it was something that could only be seen if you knew what you were looking for, or if you had been there yourself. Perhaps no one else could see what I saw in that glass.

I sighed deeply. Perhaps it was just easier that way; easier to blend in, live anonymously.

When Claire had asked me what I did that helped, I told her that, too. I thought it would shock her, but it didn't seem to. The drinking, the empty sex. I told her about the people I pick up in clubs – people I will never have to see again. That helps. And for some reason I needed her to understand that it helps.

"Why do you think it helps?" she asked.

"It reminds me who I am, what I deserve."

I feel like one
Who treads alone
Some banquet-hall deserted,
Whose lights are fled
Whose garlands dead
And all but he departed.

Thomas Moore

Life raft

I'm so tired, tired all the time. These nightmares keep hold of me, dragging along behind me through the day. They cast a pall over everything – everything. Like a black blanket, heavy and suffocating. My whole body feels on alert, on edge, waiting, waiting. I want a different kind of sleep – heavy, drugged, oblivion. I want to go back to the nothingness.

I find the nothingness sometimes still. I can find it momentarily, in drink, in sex, in focusing on a piece of work for hours on end – but then it all comes screaming back. Why? This never used to happen. What is happening to me? I used to be so good at keeping all these feelings away. There was no point in holding them – they were just too painful. I want to detach, detach, detach. I used to be able to…

Now I feel at war with myself.

I spoke with Claire about the need for crutches – skills that I had needed before, but which now seemed to be losing their power.

We had an exchange that stuck in my head long after the session ended. It cut something inside that was still bleeding.

"You fought hard for those skills, Eve, they helped you to survive. But they are a legacy of the past and they are not helping you now. Perhaps you don't need them any more, in this reality. When they are controlling you, stopping you moving forward, that can only serve to reinforce any feelings of displacement and impotence.

"It sounds as if you are still in that war zone, that you never really got the chance to leave. That no help was available to welcome you into another place, another reality. So you've been left somewhere in the middle, a foot in either place, and no place to rest. A permanent limbo," Claire told me.

"Yes," I said. "I know that is true. And I so want to stop all this. But how are you meant to abandon ship without a life-raft to jump on to?"

"What about just diving into the sea? Nothing separating you from the world around you? Have you ever just gone diving into the sea?"

Had I ever just gone diving into the sea? Those words felt like a hot iron pressed against my skin. How could she know?

The flooded maze

I am outside, under the scorching sun. The heat and light are searing. Stunted white walls, coming up to my mid-thigh, carve off in every direction. They are not brick, but something more clinical, with cleaner lines – detached and somehow sinister. Gazing at the walls, I see that they form an infinite maze, with endless dead-ends, geometric patterns, swirls and small staircases, leading to…more of the same. There is no possible solution to this maze, but you must play the game nonetheless. I will wander through this maze endlessly. I know that.

Coming up to just below my knees is clear water. A flooded maze. Nowhere, except the tops of the walls, is dry land. You must constantly wade through the hopeless trap of watery paths, searching without hope.

My eye can travel for miles. I can feel the white light of the sun above, the heat on my shoulders. I am a prisoner here. I am a grown man, wearing a loin cloth, staring resolutely ahead at my challenge. I have been sent here to be punished, but there is no crime to my name. This punishment seems just – quietly expected. I am not broken. I am a gentle strength.

The white light is blinding, remorseless, knifing through me. I have no sense of panic, just a calm resolve to try, and a strange sense of dignity.

I am exposed. The brightness reveals me. My lack of clothing strips me down to the elemental glare. My prison could not be more infinite, expansive or glaringly white, yet there is a horror to it, a claustrophobic oppression of hopelessness. Nowhere to protect myself, nowhere to hide away, to regroup in a cool, dark place.

The water is cool, the sun warm on my shoulders. I am in no physical pain, distress or danger. But the prison for my mind is absolute. It is a masterstroke of cruelty and torture.

Complete, permanent isolation. Never meeting another person or animal, never seeing a growing thing. Withdrawal of permission to engage with the living world – separation and remoteness. Removal from normal life.

Everywhere is emptiness. Infinite, bright emptiness. Such sterility and nothingness – as if all the richness of life has been sucked out, to leave this vacuum of basics: water, air, light. It is terrifying. That such a trio of basics can be so horrifying is a surprise. But I feel resolved. Resolved to walk this maze, endlessly. I start to walk.

The separation of lives

I often found myself standing on Marni's doorstep after work. With my cousin I could let down some of the façade I had to wear all day, rest a while. While Peter, her little boy, slept, we would often sit and talk for hours – occasionally joined by Sebastien, her husband. Often there was something beautiful in the simplicity of our chat – it was about nothing and everything, relaxed and intimate, covering school places to issues at work. But today, I wanted to talk about something else – something personal.

"I've been seeing a psychoanalyst," I mentioned, as I sat at her old oak kitchen table, running my fingers over its whorls and knots. Each ring here shows a phase of life, I thought, as I stroked it. I saw how Marni's hand stilled momentarily as she filled the kettle under the running tap, allowing the water stream to hit the edge of the kettle and spray over the counter. She quickly readjusted and pushed the kettle fully under the stream of water.

"How long? Tea or coffee, Eves?" she managed to say, without effort, and without turning her head from the tap. I felt a burst of gratitude towards my cousin – always so easy to talk to, always so gentle in her approach.

"Tea, please." I smiled at the back of Marni's head. "Several months now. She's really good. I think it's been really good."

I waited for her to finish making the tea, bring it to the table, and settle down, and beamed her a smile of thanks.

"So – good, huh?" Marni took it on.

I started to tell her about our recent discussions about the unconscious, about the parts of me that I had shut down. I wanted her take on it. I trusted her completely, and more than that, I really admired Marni's mind. A fluid, imaginative mind, with great awareness of the human condition. Although her gifts were natural rather than taught, I felt confident she would quickly see the truths and realities behind the more academic discussions I'd been having with Claire.

"Do you think I hide too much of myself?" I asked, directly.

"I think you hide an awful lot of yourself, but I'm not the person to say if that is too much, Eves. I suppose the litmus test is how it works for you."

"I thought it was working for me," I said quietly. "But now I'm not so sure. I sometimes feel like a caged animal. Like I designed and made the cage, but now realise I never made a key – I don't really know how you open it all up."

* * *

Back at my own flat that night I thought back to that day, so many years ago, that I had first moved in with my aunt and uncle, and my cousin Marni. My aunt, Vi Lanner, was

40

a well-meaning woman – she hadn't hesitated to open up her home to me – but she had wordlessly insisted I leave all my 'baggage' at the door. Everything would be bought new. New clothes, new toys, new life. Least said, soonest mended, in Vi's view. She was a firm believer in life forging on ahead as a remedy for all ills, and underlying that was an acute awareness that she was out of her depth with this one, and that what I needed above all else was to see her as a stable influence, not flailing about in the horror of what had just happened.

So that is what she presented to me, from that first night when Paul had collected me from the airport and brought me to their front door. Vi had visibly quailed at the sight of the little scrap flickering on her threshold, dark smudges under her eyes, her wavy dark hair loose around her face, looking a lifetime older than her 11 years. But Vi had rallied herself, given out a breezy smile, and stepped back graciously to invite me to enter my new world.

I had sensed the landscape here rapidly, and had fallen into the line set out for me – no fuss, no deviations, full of gratitude. My cousin Marni, several years my senior, had been brought home from boarding school as a special dispensation, to allow me to find my way in this new environment, before I accompanied Marni back to school.

I didn't have time at the start to have any feelings about the school – feelings were a luxury for those not in shock. I was too dislocated from the leaps between different worlds that had all happened in such a short space of time. Five months before I had been a different person, a different girl running around the garden with her brother and sister, a different daughter running up for one last hug from her mother as the bell rang for school, a different friend, called for after homework time to go out and play under the arching flame of the forest trees and jewel-like bougainvillea. Not only was she not there anymore, that 'there' no longer even existed, and sometimes I wondered whether I did – exist, that is. Who are we, really? What gives us form in the world? What holds us here? What is left when so many pieces have blown away?

Because I didn't know the answers to any of those questions, I decided simply to blend in with my surroundings until I could find a better answer. At least that way, I had reasoned, there would be something left of me, something that would be pulled into the future, in case a way forward presented itself. I think I approached it rather like someone who cryogenically freezes a terminally ill spouse just before death, to have some tiny candle flickering in hope for a day when science may just provide a solution, a new reality.

So, I had 'knuckled down', studied hard, 'done myself and my parents proud,' 'not allowed the tragedy to affect my life.' And in earning those accolades, I tasted the ashes of that victory – the people saying those things to me really believed them. I had done it, pulled it off. I was now adept at working undercover.

Of course, there had been times when I had wished it were otherwise, wished it so hard that I thought my feelings themselves may somehow have the power to form things into being. There had been times, with Auntie Vi sat on the end of my bed, tucking me in at night, that I had wanted my aunt to reach out and take my hand, ask me to talk, ask

42

me to let it all out, wanted her to be a safe pair of arms to fall apart in. I could almost see her fingers creeping across the flowers on my embroidered duvet cover, inching closer to mine, to gather me in – I could have sworn I saw those fingers start on that journey a few times, but then they faltered. With an abrupt change of pace, Auntie Vi would briskly announce it was time for bedtime prayers – with a fervour that suggested that she fundamentally believed they would ward off all the darkness in the night. That was one of the hardest parts I had to play. I resented that faith, resented the god that hadn't saved anything I had loved from the darkness, that had allowed that shadow to sweep through my life, consuming all I knew in its suffocating blanket of ash. The words weren't just meaningless to me, they enraged me: "deliver us from evil".

Paul was different – a quiet, humble man, who had allowed his wife to dictate the terms and pace of their conjoined lives many decades ago. His attempts to soften some of her more graceless attempts at unrelenting cheerfulness were quickly quashed by a sharp look and a clear message that he was meddling in affairs he knew nothing about. He was a kindly, but distant uncle, both in terms of the time he spent cloistered in his study, and also in his emotional availability. I sensed that very early on in his marriage he had sought out the path of least resistance, resigning himself to a partnership built around the space for his wife's firm beliefs and opinions, at the expense of any of his own. A garden can only contain so many plants, and some are simply too rampant and hardy to be competed with. So, from him, too, I learned that the lonely path can also be the easy path.

Or was it the other way around? Either way, it was simply easier to move along under the radar.

Although it was Paul who was my blood relation – the elder brother of my father – he left the upbringing of his niece squarely in Vi's camp. If that made me feel abandoned by him, I was never aware of it at the time. I had no feeling of belonging anywhere enough to have recognised an abandonment.

Marni was what I had lived for in those days; Marni, with her shock of red hair, her bold freckles and her warm heart. Marni, who, in those early days, hadn't waited for me to ask to climb into her bed, but who had simply climbed in beside me herself, whenever she had sensed the need. Her love was patient, often silent, never probing, but it was there like a living thing, pulsing and glowing like a wonderful undercarriage to my teenage years. Marni was a happy person, not in the emotionally blinkered, desperately cheerful way of my aunt, but in a genuine, see-the-balance-in-everything sense. And because it was so genuine, it never grated on me. In fact, I positively delighted in it. Just as Marni could bump into me in the corridor at school, glowing about something that had happened to her that morning, so she could glow with pleasure for any of my own successes. And it was never done in a way that made me feel the pressure of living up to my billing, 'not to allow the tragedy to affect my life'. No, it was done in such a sensitive way that I could feel that Marni fully understood what it may have cost me to get here, to do this, to win that.

Hiding

Eve shook as another bomb fell in the distance. It had been unrelenting for days and days now, and still it made her flinch every time. She looked around at the faces of her family; they all looked so much older, heavier.

Her parents kept everything going as best as they could, working hard to stay positive and cheerful, but Eve was old enough now to see the cracks – and to know in the pit of her stomach that they were just as scared as she was.

They were running low on food, but her parents still made family meals – with everyone sitting around the table as they had always done, trying to chat about the future, and what they would all do when this was over, when they were able to go out again, and breathe the air, and no longer feel like cockroaches trapped in the pipes.

"Just a few more days, I think. I really think so," her father had said one mealtime. Eve's mother nodded gently at them all, to lend credence to this fantasy, as she held Laila in her arms, trying to soothe her as the staccato noises invaded from outside.

45

Hanging

I was condemned to death with a group of friends – none of us knew what for. The terror of knowing I was to be killed consumed me. We were getting dressed to be taken to the hanging place by the guards. One of the guards commented that we shouldn't be wearing our 'good' clothes. This callousness enraged me.

We were standing in a line now, all on stools, with nooses around our necks. I tightened mine as much as possible so that I would die quickly. I was waiting for the awful jerk that would break my neck.

But suddenly, I was just watching from the crowd, my friends still all lined up to be executed. My voice was gone, and I couldn't move my body, couldn't stop the killing. I had to stand and watch, with the rest of the crowd. I felt strangely sad that I wouldn't experience that neck-breaking jolt. I had betrayed them.

The guilt. The overwhelming guilt. I couldn't breathe.

We, the Drowned,
Hold our hollow hearted ground
Till we swallow ourselves down
Again, again.

Lisa Hannigan

Bubble

"You coming, Eve?" John poked his head around my cubicle partition, hanging on with one arm. I didn't like these partitions. His head looked ridiculous just hanging there like an expectant schoolboy, and anyone could walk almost right up to you before you became aware of their presence. It was unnerving, especially when you were deeply involved in your work and not tuned into the world around you.

I stifled a jolt. "Umm – yes, I'm coming. I just need to get this written up. There's not much left to do, but I'm going to comb though it once more. I'll be along really soon."

"Sure? OK. We're setting off now then – the advance party." John smiled, pleased with his pun, slapped the partition wall abruptly, twice, and then his head disappeared.

The noise level receded as my remaining colleagues headed off to the team drinks. It had been a tough year for the firm, with changes in legislation meaning fewer people sought out their services, so we had to make those cases we did have really count. Mistakes, slips, misses: all stood out more glaringly now. This had not been the year to start having trouble sleeping again.

I refocused, applying myself to the screen in front of me, and began to read through once again. It was a great brief; I knew that. Clear, concise, well-argued, well-structured. But I just needed to check again, check I hadn't missed anything, hadn't omitted something that could make all the difference. I had been missing so much recently.

Today was the anniversary of everything; the day the world had changed. I had worried a bit when the date for the team drinks came through, knowing I would rather not be there that night, just in case. But, it's just a date, like any other – meaningless, really.

My reluctance to go now was just tiredness talking. I'd be fine. Closing the file on the case-notes, I knew I couldn't postpone it much longer. I pushed myself up and wandered to the staff lounge, carefully altering my persona from work mode to semi-work mode. It was a subtle shift, but one I had perfected years ago.

There was a bite in the late afternoon air. The days were shortening, and most of the heat had been sucked away by the end of my workdays now. I walked briskly down the pavement, taking care to step around the obvious patches of forming ice. 'It's the black ice you need to watch out for,' I heard my mother's words suddenly in my head, from another age. 'You never see it coming.' I gasped from the sharp hit of pain I got from the memory, and hugged my arms tighter around myself.

I was standing outside the bar now, looking in through the pane that was gathering condensation on the inside, the sweat of all the energy being released, running in droplets down the glass. I watched as one droplet after another was born, bulked up, and began to descend down the window, tentatively at first, then gathering speed, until it reached the bottom and disappeared.

I could see their table from here, nestled in the corner, cosy and inviting. It was already covered with various drinks and plates of tapas. John was just finishing some anecdote, whereupon they all laughed loudly, John slapping his thigh and elbowing the man next to him, trying to eke out a little more acknowledgement.

I saw Maria, who had joined the team only a few months before, sipping from her flute, and eyeing John over the rim, using her long lashes to full effect. As she caught John's eye, she lowered her gaze, smiling coyly. Her sights had been well and truly set for the evening. If I entered now, John would be thrown. He'd made no secret of his interest in me, and I had made my lack of interest equally clear. But, he would still have found it impossible to openly pursue anyone right in front of me, just in case.

As I watched the vignette through the glass, the beer sloshing casually around the tumblers, the genuine relaxation of the faces of some, the expectation clearly written on others, I knew I couldn't go in. Not tonight. I wasn't capable of that tonight. I watched for a few more precious seconds, peering into a world I envied in its bubble. And then I turned away.

Wreckage

Raul cast his eyes around the ruins of another village – pillaged in the night, torched and left as embers. He knew that they would find few survivors here. It was the same story all over Enanti. Anyone found alive was captured by the forces of the Shadow Beast, and pulled off screaming to damnation. He closed his eyes as he felt the terror here from the night before, his heart heavy with sorrow.

He knew that the forces of evil were on the move, raiding further and further into Enanti, bolder with each passing week. The Free, those who lived still beyond the control of the Shadow Beast, were retreating increasingly into the woods, pushed to the very margins of their land in order to hide and survive. This was a Dark Age for Enanti – a land at war, its people clinging on to the edges of life, fleeing the forces of the Shadow Realm.

Raul sat around the snapping fire that evening with his friends. It was a glorious night – stars thrown wide into the pitch sky, silhouetting the trees that surrounded them. But the lack of clouds meant the temperatures were plummeting, and he was glad of the fire tonight.

51

He had to see Minerva. He had to know when this woman, Eve, was going to come. There was so much at stake here now, and she was crucial to this fight. He needed her. She had to come soon. Minerva would know – she would be able to see in her visions when this Eve would arrive.

How often have you sailed in my dreams.
And now you come in my awakening,
which is my deeper dream

Kahlil Gibran

Haunted

I walked through the damp avenue of trees that lined the main path of the graveyard. I didn't come here often – and if I did, it was always alone. The only person I could have handled being with me would be Marni, but I preferred the solitary option.

It had been my aunt's idea – the stone memorial here to my family. It contained none of their remains, obviously, but Vi had felt it appropriate to mark their lives with this more permanent headstone – a place to come and remember. Everyone remembers such different things, standing facing a grave. It is such a personal thing, that re-ignition of your inner memory receptors – all firing up at once, making connections that were long forgotten, allowing space to feel the past.

I never remembered them best at this memorial, but I did occasionally feel the pull to come here and just stand a while. Maybe Vi had been right about that.

I thought back to that small service, when we had stood around the stone, solemnly committing their souls to God. I had felt disturbed by the lack of any mound with earth heaped over it. I didn't know how I noticed the lack of it – perhaps because it was always like that in films. But the earth was smooth and untouched in the shadow of the stately headstone. It chilled me. Not only was it a reminder that they were not really there, but it made me angry, too – angry that the passing of their lives, my life, had not been noted by the earth. Nothing had changed here, no soil was rent or split in empathy with this loss. All was as it had ever been.

I'd felt cheated then, standing there beside this hollow grave, furious that the earth itself was not screaming out my pain for me. Marni, standing next to me, had instinctively known not to try to hold my hand – I needed the honesty of being utterly alone. My auntie Vi had not understood this, taking my hand after the service, patting it awkwardly with her spare one, and busying me along to the refreshments waiting in the Church Hall.

Vi's was a strange need to comfort; a few pats on the hand was acknowledgement enough, and then she was determined to keep me 'too busy to be sad' – she had immediately handed me a plate of sandwiches to pass around. Marni's way was to allow me the space I needed to work out my own way of comfort, if any could be found at the time.

These images from years ago played through my mind as I approached the headstone now. More than two decades had gone by, and I had only come here a handful of times. With my hands deep in my pockets, and my coat buttoned tightly against the blustery chill, I read the words carved into the stone:

IN MEMORY:
ELIZABETH AND PATRICK LANNER,
AND THEIR BELOVED CHILDREN HUGO AND LAILA LANNER,
SNATCHED FROM US FAR TOO SOON.
A BEAUTIFUL FAMILY, WITH SO MUCH TO LIVE FOR.
WE WILL ALWAYS REMEMBER THEM.
SURVIVED BY THEIR DAUGHTER AND SISTER, EVE LANNER

Under that it had the dates of each of their lives – the brief snatch of time each one of them had lived on this earth. But I had always found the wording hard to read; if this 'beautiful family' had been snatched away, where did that leave me? This had been my family. Had I been snatched away too – in any sense that mattered? It made me feel as if I didn't really exist - that I was just a flickering hologram that remained, forever lacking the voltage to snap into proper focus. A family can't be just one person, can it? So this Lanner family had gone – and I had never really known where that left me. Somewhere between the ether of being and not being – an archive of family memory and witness. But no longer a member of anything. I was reading my own gravestone. They might just as well have carved my own name on there at the bottom. Some nights I had ached for that; had asked the forces of the universe to make it so. But they hadn't. They had kept me alive, like a conscious body part, where the rest of the body had died off. I was still attached to something that wasn't alive any more. What are you meant to do in that situation? Drag it along behind you?

I didn't kneel at the headstone; rather I used the time

simply to stand and think. To think of happier times, and agonising times. To think of those who had known everything about me – had watched me take my first breath, my first steps, enjoy my first party. I obviously hadn't thought it consciously at the time, but I was fully known then, and I ached for that. I knew I never would be again. Those shared moments of childhood are irreplaceable. I had assumed that my brother and sister, at least, would be there always, travelling through life with me, bringing something precious out of the past into the future. I yearned for that familiarity, for the way my brother used to ruffle my hair, the way my sister had pressed into me when she'd sneaked into my bed in the night. I yearned for my mother to put down my favourite meal in front of me at the weekend, not needing to ask what I liked. Just knowing. Teaching me that I was known. Just knowing the most mundane things about someone can actually be the most intimate knowing; a knowing that is one step ahead, never forced, just aware, due to the intimacy of shared life.

And I thought especially of little Laila here. Was I the only one left to remember now? At least there's me, I thought, fiercely. There's me, Laila, and I will always remember.

As I stood there, I felt my skin prickle. Glancing up I saw a little girl standing in the gathering gloom under the mass of an old oak, behind the headstone. She was small and slight, with dark glossy curls that were blowing in the wind. She wasn't wearing enough clothes for this weather – just a thin cotton dress – but she stood completely still, looking at me. I started, physically jolted by the sight.

"Laila?" I gasped. I shook my head, for a fleeting moment thinking that my own yearning thoughts had conjured her up. This little girl was older than Laila, but looked just like her. When I looked again, she was gone.

The ice bridge

We were being attacked. The high, empty walls of the castle rang out with shouts and the clang of metal on metal. I saw figures moving in the shadows, behind enormous pillars: samurai-like, melting into the shadows. Mysterious and covered. I was trying to escape with my friend, but it was hard to know where we should be fleeing to. The fighters had breached the walls, and they seemed to be everywhere, encircling us. I crouched down in the darkness of the external courtyard, near a large gate. I carried no weapon myself. I don't know why I and the person with me were to be helped to escape. I didn't know who the person was.

I eventually saw my chance and ran for the gate. I was outside the castle now - feeling extremely exposed and vulnerable. Hunted. I had never left the castle before. I looked around at the walls and battlements, and saw the immense, fast-flowing river at its side. It was night, and the depth of winter. A canopy of stars furnished the heavens. Some of them fell down from the sky, and they sizzled a little as they rained down into the icy river, adding to the shards of ice.

I saw a very narrow bridge of ice, leading out over the river into the darkness. It was incredibly beautiful, with effortless arches and turrets like a fairy carriage, all carved in ice, glowing with soft lights from within. Ethereal beauty promising an escape from the turmoil that roiled beneath. It vaulted out over the onyx water, seeming to float just above the tumult, serene and elegant. Part of me wanted to cross that bridge, to flee to the other side, but I was worried I would end up in the icy river, which flowed fiercely, just a few inches below the bridge. It was a magical, luminous structure, promising much. Tantalising. But I knew it couldn't take my weight. I turned away from the bridge, and into the night.

Sea glass

Whenever I went to the sea I always felt a release of pressure. As if a breath I had been holding could finally be let out. I could venture out from my shell a little.

I was standing on the cliff tops, in the wind. I recalled an exchange with Claire from just a few weeks before. I had been talking about how I shut my feelings down, to survive and keep going. I had said simply:

"I have found a way to turn off the wind, but now I am starved of oxygen."

It was true, I had found a way – but it only worked for finite bursts, before the need to escape overwhelmed me. Then I would come here, to the sea, to the wind. I needed it. It was just enough to feed what was inside me, prevent it from going out. I would stand in the wind; feel its power. I understood it, and it understood me.

This was a place with a completely flat horizon - a space that allows your mind to expand and wander. No distracting landmarks or features. True calm. The contours of the land are smoothed down to a pure, unrestrained line – a sense of the infinite. Infinite simplicity. You can transpose on to the sea: imprint your own deepest feelings there. It is boundless enough to be the backdrop you need it to be, to hold everything. I needed that vastness today.

I looked out over the eternal waves. It was only in this space, this edge-land, that I felt able to unlock the powerful sentiments within myself – as if their magnitude could only be released when in the presence of something still more immense. It felt soothing to be so small. The sea was such a vast expanse that I could take my fears, my hopes, my griefs, and lay them out a little; look at them.

I always felt a particular closeness to 'other' here; the veil between worlds was stretched so thin. So thin that you could almost feel what you had lost, almost reach out and touch it. Being by the sea allowed me to grieve. Little punches of time I allowed myself to feel that enormity of loss.

I enjoy the wonderful dichotomy between the eternal you sense by the sea, and the constant daily flux. The crafted castle just waiting to be washed away, the secret beach you must leave before your way back is cut off. You are always on borrowed time; walking these magical places for a fleeting moment – a brief window into a world that is then hidden and washed anew; never entirely the same again. The constancy of change.

As I stood up there on the bluff, the wind picking up around me, I saw a tiny figure down on the shore, dressed in nothing more than a summer dress tied in bows at the shoulders. The little girl was standing still in the wind, staring out to sea. I gasped. Laila. Why was I being punished like this?

I started along the rough path that led down to the beach,

desperate to reach her. Scrabbling over the jumble of rocks and branches, I glanced in her direction. As I did so, I saw Laila turn around, look at me, and place something carefully on the sand. I hurried on, slipping a few times on the loose stones, and eventually gaining the sand. The little girl had vanished.

I reached down and picked up some sand, letting it slip out through my fingers. These fragments have been ground down over millennia, I mused, watching them fall. The power of the waves comforts me: so thunderingly powerful. Could they wash everything away? The sea is life to me. It soothes, it caresses, it ravages and cuts. It washes away some of the things you can't let go of. You can swim, or you can drown. It is life.

I walked over to where the little girl had been, and my eye was caught by a glow from the sand. I scooped up the piece of sea glass that was lying there. It was beautiful, rubbed smooth and frosted by the sea. A pale blue. I ran my thumb over its surface, and felt a deep longing. It was broken and damaged, but beautiful in its new, altered state. So tactile, such a gift. I felt the poignancy of the moment as I held it.

What happens to all those abraded parts of you? Where do they go? Is there some beach somewhere that all the little lost parts of yourself wash up on to, like all this sand? Can you ever go there?

I slipped the sea glass into my pocket. It aroused a sense of connection within me that I couldn't examine too closely. After some time, just looking out at the sea, I dragged in a breath deep enough to last me several months, zipped up my coat to the top, turned and left.

It took me much longer to reach the tops of the cliffs again. As I did, I turned to take a last look at the sea. A tiny figure was walking alone along the strand line, dark curls flattening against her head as the stinging rain began to come down. I watched in anguish as the little girl wandered along the shore, around the headland and out of sight.

Incantation

Back in London, I accepted an invitation from Vi to a choral concert. As I listened to the swell of voices, I wanted to cry. The purity of the sound washed right through me, holding me in thrall. Why had I stayed away so long? It was soothing, enlivening, devastating. It spoke to my spirit in a way that I had allowed nothing to for so many years.

I had sung in a choir like this one, before, when I was happy. I had loved the process of making a communal sound that rose and rose, becoming something far greater than the promise of the constituent parts. Our choir mistress was a formidable lady – I remember her now, her hair in a ferocious bun, jet-blue mascara magnified by the glasses she always wore, giving her a severe, owl-like expression. She did not suffer fools – a trait she was clearly proud of, mentioning it verbatim on several occasions to cowering parents who had the temerity to question her approach. I loved her passion – loved the sharp click of Mrs Hazeldean's heels on the parquet floor in the colonial school hall, her relentless attention to detail, to the blend of sound, the slim wand she wielded in her right hand, weaving her magic on the rapt choristers. I loved the rigour of it, the feeling of being forged in a fire, the alchemy of transformation. And god, what a transformation! The motley assortment of voices became something so pure, something so special to be a part of, that I lived for those moments.

I had tried being a part of the choir again at my new school, afterwards, in England, but it wasn't the same. Nothing was the same. The wonder that I found in singing turned into a blade, that cut too close to something too raw. There was not enough of a scab there yet to withstand the sweet agony of the sound. I asked to leave the choir, but my aunt was so convinced that I needed 'normality' in my life that she insisted the school kept me on. So I shut my ears to that sound, stood there robotically going through the motions for several more terms, until I managed to do myself out of a position organically. With other talented singers in the school, and competition hot for places, the choir mistress had simply not picked me.

Memories of those times moved through me, swirling gently with the ebb and flow of the voices in the church.

"They're marvellous, aren't they darling?" I heard Vi say.

"Marvellous," I nodded. They really were. Well-schooled, utterly in tune and time, they transcended themselves as individuals.

This might be something I could try - something that used to give me pleasure. Perhaps this was one path back to some of the things I had lost through the years. And it felt a safe path – I would be one among many, a voice in the crowd, but holding a part in this world.

Our abraded lives

The next evening I was back in Marni's riotous kitchen, allowing myself to relax into the colourful jumble of warmth.

"Did you have a good time at the beach? You hadn't had a break in such a long time. I was really glad to hear you'd gone down," Marni said.

"I'm sorry – I should have seen if you were free. I know you'd mentioned coming away with me sometime," I replied.

"It's fine, Evie! I mean it when I say I'm glad you took the time, and I think you needed that time on your own, not with me. I'm always here. But was it good?"

"It was good. I think I needed it. But…"

"What?"

"Well, it just affected me a little more than I thought it would. I thought I'd go down, have a bit of a break, take some time to slow down, and come back feeling ready."

"Ready?"

"For all this. Just ready, you know, to get back into the fray."

"Oh, Evie." Marni stopped fussing with the shopping

67

and came to sit down next to me, reaching for my hand. I didn't stiffen as I would with that contact from anyone else. I gently clasped Marni's hand back.

"Tell me?" Marni prompted.

"Oh, so much seemed to happen down there. I mean, nothing actually happened, it was all up here." I tapped the side of my head vigorously, almost angrily.

"With everything I've been talking about with Claire, and with you, it felt very different. I usually go down there to just stop and think, let it all out, really, but this time I've come back with more questions, more things that I want to unearth."

Marni waited as I searched for the right words to express what was going on.

"I've felt so certain of how I should be all these years – what works for me, how it all fits together to keep moving forward. But now my head is full of questions that just keep going around and around. Look at this."

I slid my hand into my pocket, and pulled my little piece of sea glass out on to the table. I tried to explain my thought process about the transformation of this tiny thing, what it meant to me, how its abraded form spoke to me so deeply.

"But I keep coming back to this question, now, Marni. What happens to those bits of us that are worn away? Where do they go?

"I've read so much about how we are all products of the relationships that we have, that it makes me wonder all over again who I am. If we really are forged by the relationships we have, what does their death mean for our individuality? If parts of us are only accessible through that relationship shared with another, do parts of us get lost forever? I know we are altered, but…lost? Am I always less now because I've lost them?"

"Eves."

"And then, well…and then I just wonder whether there is any point at all in feeling any of this, if it's so painful. It's making me question so much, but I'm not finding any peace or relief at all. I'm wondering what I'm doing, Marni, and now I'm not sure I have the choice to pack it all away again. I feel like I'm stuck on a speeding train, somehow, and I know the driver is missing, and I've got to get up there and drive this damned train, but I haven't got a clue how to. I just know it feels necessary. It's like something is speeding up inside me – an unstoppable force – and I hate that." I smiled wryly at Marni, my tears close to the surface now, but trying to pull a little emotional distance back.

"Evie, it might feel like this for now, but it won't feel like this forever. I think you've kept your feelings so hidden away for so long, that they are bound to feel overwhelming."

"But what do I do, Marni? I can't concentrate at work, I feel this restlessness running right through me. I don't know what to do."

"You don't need to do anything until it feels clear, and right. I know you are going to find this time horrendous, and really unsettling, but I am always here for you. Please let me help where I can. Even if you just want to come and stay with us for a while, Evie. We'd love that; Peter would love it, too!

"And just do what you need at work – no more – and then let it go. You've given them your sweat and tears over the years, Evie; they owe you a bit of slack. Try to stop worrying about letting them down. That is not the measure of you. It's never been the measure of you."

"I've been thinking of doing some other things again, just seeing how that feels," I said hesitantly, wondering what Marni's reaction would be.

"That sounds like a good plan. Do you have some ideas?"

"Well, I loved the concert that Vi took me to actually. It made me think about joining a choir again. And I thought I would start swimming again. Something different to the gym – and I used to love it so much."

Marni nodded her encouragement. "Why not come along when I take Peter for his swimming lesson?"

"Yes, I might just do that," I said, feeling drawn to the idea.

Metal monsters

Aliens lived among us, vicious and calculating, taking pleasure from killing. They were chilling: masters of disguise, roaming the streets, looking like any human most of the time. But just before they killed, they assumed their real form, with whirring metal appendages, and sharp integrated blades. All these elements were permanently attached to them; part of their being. They butchered people.

I was part of a team trying to stop them. But we had no useful weapons, and no real sense of how we could stop them. We heard that they were planning a massacre at a crowded theatre – more like a football stadium. For some reason we allowed the game to go ahead, and we mingled with the crowd. I watched as people poured out of the town below, winding up the hill towards their death. I felt helpless, but strangely resolved to try. The theatre/stadium had rich red velvet seats, and a ceiling of sorts.

I suddenly spotted one of these camouflaged creatures sitting a few rows ahead of me, off to the left. He knew who I was. This amused him, as he knew we had nothing with which to stop him. He deliberately looked over to a young, blonde woman seated several rows behind him. She caught his eye, and smiled and flirted with him. I suddenly saw a flash – a telepathically-transmitted message from the creature – telling me what was going to happen to her in the next few minutes. She would be brutally slaughtered, and her head severed, her arms torn out from her shoulders. Blood would be everywhere. This world of people, all excited about the match, would change in that beat of time, into a hell of blood, terror, agony and unspeakable sadism. The shift of life to death.

The creatures, led by the one who had communicated with me, left their strategic points around the room, and started to move. They were to spring into action at a pre-arranged signal, and annihilate everything. And they were going to enjoy it – their metal, jagged-edged faces hysterical with pleasure and blood-lust. They thought it was very funny.

I don't know why we hadn't sent everyone out of town. There was a sense that we had a plan, but I had no idea what it was, or what we were going to do when the creatures attacked. I felt an overwhelming responsibility and impotence, mixed with deep sadness and anger. Outrage, and a desire to protect. I knew deep within myself that the creatures could not hurt me in any way. I was definitely human, so I was unsure what was protecting me, but I knew I was untouchable by them. Yet I was rooted very firmly within this unfolding tragedy; very much a part of it.

Exhaustion

"I wish grief could be more like a marathon," I said to Claire one morning.

"Can you tell me what you mean by that?"

"I mean, it already feels like a marathon, but it doesn't have an end. You wake up each morning, and the grind just starts again. I see those runners crossing the finishing line; I see the elation and the sense of release that they have earned themselves. And I wish for that; a feeling of crossing the line, being able to stop running, that the ordeal is done. I feel cheated, as if the effort I put into every day never brings me to a finishing line – never brings me that moment of fulfilment.

I'm not exactly sure what it would look like, but I yearn for it just the same."

"I can hear that – like a need to rest, to have a defined ending."

Yes – exactly. But it's ludicrous, I know, because grief won't suddenly disappear. Yet that doesn't stop me wanting it to – so much."

"I think it is a very normal longing. Like the need people have to hold a ritual to mark a death – it provides a defined moment to attempt to express the inexpressible. It works as a socially accepted moment to feel release."

"Yes. But then those moments dry up, and there is an endless desert ahead of you that you need to keep trudging through, with no more of those moments, no more of those rituals ahead that you can push on to for another pause."

As I walked home, I could feel that things were changing, shifting, moving into new positions. An army reassembling, waiting to advance. I knew what I would do that evening; I would look through the box of memories that I kept locked tightly away.

Conduit

It wasn't something that I did very often – just a few times, actually, over the decades. Enough to keep it torturous: not enough to take the sting out of it in any way. The fallout from it affected me deeply for the next few days. But occasionally, I felt a pressing need to prise open the lid of that box, and sift through the contents.

I kept it in a drawer, under piles of clothes, so that even getting to it was an effort, and there was never any chance that I would catch sight of it inadvertently. Acknowledging it was always a premeditated, controlled choice.

With the door locked, I felt prepared. I knelt down to rummage through the bottom drawer, my hands blindly seeking until I made contact with it. I withdrew the box and sat back on my heels. Simply looking at its carved exterior was enough to start my mind reaching for those dark places. I wondered whether I should be doing this at all, and I very nearly put it back out of sight, where it couldn't hurt me.

Then I moved abruptly, decision made, and brought my legs forward, crossing them in front of me as I had done each day at primary school. With a decisive click, I undid the little metal catch on the box. It felt as if I had opened myself.

There wasn't much in the box – everything I had had at the time had been lost – but there was a collection of photos that my aunt and uncle had kept. Christmas shots that my parents must have sent to them each year, occasional pictures of proud moments of our lives that my parents had wanted to share: a fancy-dress party we had all been to, me covered in rosettes on sports day, my brother leaning out of the window on his birthday, beaming widely at the camera and waving. Priceless stills of a lost life.

My fingers read them as much as my eyes, stroking down the shiny images, the shiny faces, the shiny life, tracing the paths that I hoped my parents' fingers had made as they had looked through the pictures, chosen the ones to send, packaged them up for England, and sent them on their way. I could close my eyes and imagine the smiles on their faces as they looked lovingly on the moments of life that they had captured. And now, decades on, my hands were where theirs had once been, and that meant something to me.

The box also contained a few precious letters and cards written by my parents when I had come over to England for a few weeks one summer. I hadn't wanted to go, but they had thought it would be a good opportunity for me to feel a little grown up, a little independent, and I had actually hugely enjoyed the trip. I had stayed with my aunt and uncle, and while they had seemed very old to me, they had taken my visit to heart, and made a huge effort to take me around all the local sights, even making a journey to London with me that had set my senses reeling. My parents had written to me every few days, and each letter also included scribbles from little Laila, and a few brief lines from Hugo. I had always felt confident in Hugo's love for me – basked in it as I grew – but he was no letter writer.

There were other things in my box; darker places. A coroner's report on each of their deaths. Although we had lived abroad for many years, we had remained UK citizens, and these things had to be done properly. So a land that did not know us, and had no comprehension of what had happened to us, signed their epitaph: 'unlawful killing'.

Then the newspaper cuttings. Even once I had left and come here, the war followed me. On the news every day, it had saturated my day and my mind, despite Vi's attempts to rush the newspapers into the recycling, or swiftly switch the TV off when any coverage came on. At first I used to creep out of my bedroom at night to the recycling bin, to cut out and preserve parts of my life. The need for some form of connection was strong. This petered out over time; there hadn't been a definitive moment when I felt I no longer needed to do it any more – it was more a question of a squirrel filling its stash for the winter months ahead. There comes a point when any more just becomes pointless. The paper the stories were printed on was too fragile to provide any sustenance.

I had also uncovered a place in the library where my aunt or uncle – I was never sure which – had filed away news reports of me, of the time I had been brought over here to live with them. I had felt furtive, stumbling across something that I shouldn't, but which was all about me, my life. Although they had probably sought to shield me from the pain of it all, the fact that one of them had hidden these things away here, secretively, reinforced my feeling that these things were best left unspoken, closeted away. I had taken some of the cuttings, added them to my stash. If my aunt or uncle had ever noticed that some pieces were missing, they had certainly never mentioned it. Again, I was never sure if that left me feeling resentful, or grateful.

There was a grainy image of me in one of those cuttings – shocked by the flashing bulb, taken as I had arrived in this country. I found it hard to look at. That girl looked hollowed out; a shell. She had not yet learnt to hide her vulnerability, and the level of exposure in the photograph appalled me. She looked so raw that the slightest touch would leave her screaming.

I quickly moved on, not wanting to fully absorb that one. I returned to the photos of before, seeking some relief. But the laughing faces and crinkled eyes cut deeper than the documents of officialdom. The pictures were a far more final death knell to the enormity of what had been lost. 'Unlawful killing' didn't stand a chance in the tsunami of emotions that the images created.

Suffocating with that wave, I was wracked with sobs that shook my whole body. It was burning, a pressure inside that I could not get out enough to relieve the pain. I clutched my chest, terrified by the beast growing inside me, pushing outwards. Even my ribs ached as I fought to regain control.

Later, much later, I lifted my head from the floorboards, pushed myself up to sitting, packed it all away again carefully, snapped the box closed and went downstairs to obliterate it all with drink. Tonight I would get dressed up, go out to some anonymous bar, and go home with anyone who asked me.

Numb

I had been there several times before, had even lived there for those few weeks of holiday one summer. But the whole place was alien to me. I didn't understand that at first. It was as if I saw everything through a piece of broken glass, at a distance, slightly dream-like with muffled sound. Even my aunt's voice sounded muffled to me, as if it was reaching me through layers and layers of foam. I was always half surprised when I turned towards the faint noise and did indeed see my aunt's lips moving in time with those sounds.

I remembered the music that my mother had loved to play in our home. There was one piece in particular that I often thought of now: the *Enigma Variations*. My mother had always had a certain look, a certain awe and reverence when she explained the power of the Variations – the magic of them – but now I saw that it could also be a poison – the same things could be severed from you, rather than enriched – depending on the journey.

Perhaps that was what was going on here. It wasn't that Vi's house had changed at all; it was just that I saw it with different eyes. The house was exactly the same as when I had visited as a child – perhaps too shockingly the same. I half-imagined that everything should be different, that things should have profoundly changed, in acknowledgement of the vast shift in the world. The fact that nothing here had fundamentally changed felt wrong. It made me doubt which reality was real – made me even more aware that I was the one out of step here, the outsider. I didn't know whether I felt as if I was looking into this safe world that was wrapped in a bubble I couldn't break through and enter, or whether I was the one trapped in a bubble, and couldn't get out. I resented, and yearned for, this bubble world in equal measure.

Collapsing house

We had a house with one large kitchen-type room, and all the other rooms downstairs. We all had to pack a bag. Then our house collapsed. Only my room survived, and you had to crawl to get in, as the ceiling (kitchen floor) had fallen at an angle. We had to leave.

Years later, I was on a walk, and we stopped for lunch where our house used to be. I went in and it was all so strange. Everything was cobwebby and sad; mine but not mine.

Into the wild garden

The dream had been so real. I shuddered. They were not usually so intense, so tangible. The morning was kissed with sunshine and I decided to walk to the park. I had a slow shower, hoping to clear the worst of the fogginess in my head, then dressed, wincing with shame as I remembered the vacuous sex from the night before, the cold wall of the alleyway behind the club pressing into my back, the urgency of trying to be in this world.

I shouldn't have gone out last night. I knew it was a mistake even as I'd got dressed up, put on all that make-up – I knew how awful I would feel this morning. But I'd needed to be close to something, to someone, even if it was all an act. All that ridiculous grunting and heaving; why do people feel closer to someone after that? I had never felt further away.

The weather was fresh and blustery, dark clouds racing through the sky, allowing bright shards of sunlight to gleam through. The threat of rain was ever-present, but I liked the challenge the brooding sky laid down. I felt a ghost of something I felt always at the sea – a glimpse of the pain and pleasure that was being alive. I sucked it in.

I walked briskly to the park, winding past puddles where fallen leaves were congealing and changing form. The thin November sunlight was just enough to catch at the remains of vivid colours, but it was an altogether bleaker scene than just a few weeks previously.

Inside the park, the regimented ranks of handsome London plane trees that line the neat terraces and semi-detached streets of my part of West London morph slightly into more organic clusters of much older trees and shrubs. Unlike the elegant uniformity of the avenues outside, here, these different trees offset each other; yellows thrown forward by a deep red backdrop, clashing oranges and pinks, purple highlighting greens.

I slowed to admire the remnants of the display of one fine French oak, ragged at the edges now, as if her play had been staged for just a few too many evenings. But the tree was reluctant to lose her finery, clutching the last few leaved branches to her chest, as if it were a well-loved dress, shy of the nudity to come. Soon, the tatters of her dress would carpet the earth, trodden down by passersby. And she would stand there all winter, exposed. The final curtain of winter was relentless.

I watched quietly as my mind moved to other images, other conversations. Last week, I had told Claire about a tree. It meant something to me, this tree, and I had found it oddly important that Claire should understand.

* * *

I always looked out for it – felt the oddest sense of affinity

84

with it. It was nothing, really, just a dead tree in a field that I saw from the train window every time I went to visit Paul and Vi. It was in a row of trees that lined the boundary between two fields, a natural cluster that had survived down the years of modernisation. The whole line was vibrant and thrusting, except for this one tree. I had first noticed it many years ago, standing out starkly from the green life around it. It was an old oak, its twisted branches looping back on themselves as if having continual second thoughts. It must have seen much as it had grown. And then it died, lost its glossy green adornment, and now stood there, bleak.

The sight had jolted me that first time, and I had deliberately looked for the tree ever since, snatching a glance from the speeding train. It had changed a lot over the years. Within a year or so, its crown had been removed, pruned back into a safe shape, head slashed open to the rain and skies. The millions of villi it had used to sense the world had gone. And each year it had wizened further, hardened into this new state, darkening with each harsh winter. Yet somehow, as it withered further back into the backdrop of green running riot around it, it stood there, more pronounced, more quietly defiant. It moved me in a way I couldn't explain. If it had stood there completely alone, I doubt I would ever have noticed it – just an old dead tree in a field. It was the jarring juxtaposition with the life around it that gave it such a sense of pathos. The sap, its essence, cracked and dry, not flowing, but retreating to a secret place within, hidden. The idea of holding yourself deeply apart. Each winter, the trees around it would join it with a temporary death, branches reaching in supplication to the thundering winter skies. For those few months, the line of trees would all look the same. And each spring I would hold my breath, half expecting the stumps of the old oak to start to show the same buds of life as the trees around it. But of course they never did, and I would slump back in my seat in the train, feeling a bone-deep weariness.

It somehow retained an immense dignity for me, that old tree. I saw it there, standing proud and dark against the fresh green, unable to be a part of what was around it. But still there, still valid, a sentinel of so much that could remain unspoken. It was the memorial to my family, to me, to my life, that I needed. I found far more of what I needed in that brief flash past in the train, than I did from an hour standing before the headstone in the leafy graveyard.

* * *

I decided to walk right around the park. Most of it was reasonably groomed, with manicured borders lacing down the sides of paved paths, protecting the lush lawn beyond. Suddenly the air chilled further and I caught sight of a cloud of dark curls running away down the path. The little girl wasn't dressed for this autumnal weather, and my skin prickled in empathy. "Laila?" I called out, then louder "Laila!" as the little girl ran on. I ran after her, stopping abruptly as I turned a corner and realised that I had lost sight of her.

This part of the park was unfamiliar to me. It had been deliberately allowed to go to seed, to provide more habitat for native wildlife. As if even the life that lived here had been squeezed to the very edges and left dispossessed. And now that injustice had been noted, and work was underway to provide it with a home again. I liked that.

The area was immediately more vibrant, uncontrolled, with tangled stems clutching hold of ramblers that had been allowed to fend for themselves. Late-flowering roses studded the confusion of branches and limbs, mingling with winter jasmine. The grass, too, was higher here, tall enough to hide my shoes, tall enough for the wilderness to start claiming me back.

I wandered through under a heavy bower of roses that threatened to pull down the old wooden support arch that I could still just make out beneath it. Through the arch, a riot of undergrowth and foliage rambled in every direction, highlighted by shots of colour from late-flowering plants. My hand tingled as I trailed it casually over the vegetation at waist height. There was something glorious in this abundance. Something that moved me in a way the manicured borders had failed to do. I found that a little alarming. I thrived on order and the idea of control; I found it safe. But places like this still drew me in, and I had the oddest sense of someone calling out to me, trying urgently to get my attention, banging on the glass. Little snatches of memory – of wild jasmine tendrils, abundant bougainvillea, jacaranda and lush pomegranate trees. I found it profoundly unsettling, but curiously invigorating. I felt the same thing at the sea, and it was what kept drawing me back, giving me the oxygen I needed. But I didn't go too often; the emotional landscape it opened up for me was too vast and painful for me to look upon that frequently. It felt like opening up my chest at home. As I thought this, I had a sudden sense of that same action also holding true of opening up my own chest – and my hand inadvertently flew to my rib-cage, feeling it tighten.

Before I left, I was taken with the urge to bring something from this place back home with me. I carefully picked a few of the wild roses from their mantle, forming a little posy of fragrance in my hand. They basked in my hold, little jewels, each one of them, creamy white petals blending to the warmest yellow in the centre.

I took them home with me, placing them carefully in a little vase, which I set in the centre of the immaculate granite kitchen island. They looked odd there, cast adrift on this stone mound floating in the middle of my seamless white floor.

But they made it more like home, surely? I recalled Claire's request at our last meeting that I put down some thoughts about what home, and family, meant to me.

What did family mean to me? It meant everything I had lost; how could it be otherwise? It meant everything I no longer had. It meant my mother and father, laughing in delight as I capered around the garden after my little sister Laila, it meant the gentle, reassuring arms of my beloved Hugo. It meant feeling safe, feeling a belonging to something more than myself. Feeling I wasn't alone; that some protective ring kept me close to the fire of the familiar – of family.

My mother had always said that home 'is wherever your family is'. That had soothed my child-like concerns at the time, but where did it leave me now? Where was home? Was I forever homeless, until I made a new family? Or did it not work like that? Home seemed such a simple need – a primitive form of knowing your anchor-point. Once lost, can you ever get it back? Can you bang down a new steel staple into the sea-bed, and run up a line with a new buoy bobbing cheerfully as a surface marker? Or is it more like childhood: once gone, it is gone forever? I wasn't sure. I only knew I existed without my anchor-point; cut loose from the line. The line had not been allowed to fray in the natural way of things; it had just been abruptly cut. Sometimes I looked at the blunt rope end that trailed behind me and wondered whether it would ever connect to anything again... Sometimes I thought it resembled nothing more now than a silent noose, tempting and repulsive.

And home? My flat was no more than a place to live, rest, dress and eat. It wasn't home – not in the real sense. Yes, I needed the refuge it provided, the peace and the privacy, but I could leave it in a heartbeat and move to another. It wasn't a sentimental place. It was modern, not overdone – quite conventional, really. Enough to conceal more than it revealed. Like the still surface of a lake, with sunlight reflecting off it. Everything had its place, and was clean and organised. No one would ever have guessed at the state of the clothes and bits and pieces crammed into the chest of drawers and cupboards in my bedroom; squashed in, hidden away from view. No one would ever see it, so it didn't matter if it all needed a good sort through.

Hours later, as I moved towards the curtains to close out the night, I jumped as I caught sight of the little figure reflecting back from the dark glass, just over my shoulder. I didn't even turn around to look – I knew no one would be there. I knew I had just a precious few moments to look on her small face before she disappeared.

"Laila," I whispered, and stroked the glass where the image was. Like fingers drawn through the surface of water, the image shook, rippled and broke down into a thousand pieces, leaving nothing.

Torn fabric

The vast canvas stretched from the floor of the art gallery to the ceiling. It was unbleached cotton canvas, not expensive, but with a tactility to it that appealed to me. It had been cut into two, from the top to the bottom, completely rent apart. Skilful hands had sewn it together, but the scar was ugly and uneven. The sides of the canvas were wonderful, lyrical, dense, but the scar was deeply troubling and drew the eye. I understood that it was the separation of two lives within one body. An unbridgeable gap. A shift, an immense unfathomable divide. I could tell that the fabric had been cut before the work was done on the second side: the colours were different, the patterns and whorls, all different. The cutting had come mid-embroidery. Life stuttered, then gradually took hold again, on the other side. But the link back to before was gone, making it dangerously distant. I understood that I needed to bridge it.

Passages in the mind

"Can you tell me about this little girl?" Claire asked. "You've mentioned her before, and it feels as if she could have an important part in all this."

"I couldn't save her," I whispered. "My sister." I clutched at the arms of the chair, desperate for traction. "I tried to, but I couldn't save her. I should have been able to. I was right there, and she was all alone."

I shook as I went back down the passage in my mind to the horror. I could hear the whining of the shells falling again, the dust rising everywhere, the crack and pop of small arms fire getting closer, and the smell of death.

Ashes

The shells were falling again. They seemed to be falling almost constantly these days, and the dust hung permanently in the air. The family had spent weeks now, cowering inside, waiting for it all to be over. Eve huddled with her siblings on the sofa, listening to the noises getting closer.

Her parents were in the kitchen, trying to scrape together some food and drink for them all. Her brother was sitting with his arms wrapped right around her, his chin resting on her head, reassuring her with his presence. Suddenly, Laila got up from the sofa beside them and darted towards the kitchen. That was when the bomb hit. There was an enormous noise. The end of the world in a second. She remembered a wave rocking through her, followed by a blast of dust and brick. Shards of reality went shooting off into the abyss. The air became a desert, hung with dust. Her eyes misted over and she fell into blackness.

When she opened her eyes, she couldn't breathe. She felt the cold sweat dropping down her body as she gazed in shock at the devastation. She struggled for a moment, before realising that her brother's arms were still around her, but slumped now, and heavy with death. She lay there for several hours. Her back felt hot and sticky, but she couldn't focus on that.

The kitchen didn't exist, obliterated by the explosion. There was sky above her head that shouldn't be there. Her home, cracked open. After some time, she heard muffled cries coming from under the rubble near where the kitchen used to be. Laila. Oh god, Laila.

Pulling herself free of her brother's arms was the hardest thing she had ever had to do. Once upright, she clambered in among the wreckage to find her sister. Her own hearing was muffled and whiney; a high-pitched white noise was running through her head.

Pushing away the chunks of rubble, she gently uncovered Laila, trying to wipe off the whitening dust that covered everything, settling on a new reality. The little girl was hurt, her leg at a funny angle. Eve clutched her to her chest, trying to whisper some soothing words.

"It's OK, Laila. It's OK, sweetheart. It's me, I've got you. Come with me, sweetie." Carrying Laila in her arms, she started down the stairs. Then she saw the soldiers in the street. They looked straight at her, raising guns to their faces. "They look like strange beaks" was the only thought that could enter her head. Eve had not known real fear until that point. Now she could taste and smell it.

The soldiers came right up to Eve, two disappearing up the stairs behind her to check the building over. A moment later, they came back down the remaining steps, and stayed behind her. Eve felt the cold push of a rifle tip in her back, nudging her forwards. One of the soldiers pulled

Laila from her arms and held her out at arm's length. Eve remembered their words precisely: "We have no use for this one. Leave her here."

"No!" Eve shouted, before receiving a warning blow in the chest from a rifle butt.

"She's mine – she's my sister! She needs help. Look at her leg! Please! Please!" she sobbed.

"She's staying here. Come."

The soldier dumped Laila on the ground in the rubble of her home, twisting hard on Eve's arm to pull her away from her sister. Eve knew that Laila's screams would never leave her.

They didn't rape her straight away. She was made to walk for several minutes before they came across a piece of open land with a wall on one side. She knew that it had happened, but she couldn't recall any of it now. She had often wondered why her mind had remembered so much in such agonising detail, and yet had chosen to cover over some other parts so completely. She knew that inside her it was laid out somewhere, waiting for her to lift the blanket away, but she never had.

A few weeks before she had been playing tennis against this wall with her siblings, laughing as they tried to keep their tally up above ten each time. Now, she heard the soldiers' laughter instead. "It doesn't matter," she told herself. "It really doesn't matter." Whatever the soldiers were looking for inside her, couldn't they see that there was nothing left there any more? Nothing at all.

The shearing of worlds

When, after several weeks, they saw Eferon's grief undiminished, the council members who had organised Quella's disappearance realised their mistake. Fearing his anger, they rode out of the city at night, fleeing to different corners of the world. They left a letter telling Eferon how he could find Quella. He set off at once, galloping through the night, changing horses at every inn along the way.

Meanwhile, Quella's guard in the cave, Eferon's handsome but vain younger cousin, had plans of his own. Resentful of his older cousin, and consumed by jealousy for Eferon's beloved, he had backed the plan for his cousin to marry the princess of Teo in the hope that this would deliver Quella into his own arms. When she continued to rebuff him, he told her that Eferon, far from being distraught at her disappearance, had been relieved that his moral duty to her was over, and had readily agreed to marry the princess from Teo. He claimed that all Albedo, and the Citadel itself, was humming with joy and excitement at the impending nuptials.

When this news, too, failed to give him his desired outcome, something in his mind snapped. Angered at living in his cousin's shadow for so long, he strode down the steps into the cave at dusk, and raped Quella.

Once his rage was spent, he looked down at her, and realised what he had done. As he clambered off her, he took the chains from her wrists, before fleeing into the night. Some say he became the first of The Craven, although not all agree.

When Eferon finally raced down the stairs into the cave, Quella had gone. He found her body, lying vacant and lifeless, rocking in the surf that washed into the cave entrance. Unable to bear the agony of what his cousin had done, or the pain of knowing her lover was marrying another, she had chosen death as the release she craved. And she had walked out into the waves.

Eferon carried her pitiful body to the top of the cliffs. In his anguish, he screamed at the sky. Then, taking his sword, he hit the earth with such power that it trembled, and cracked. Right across Enanti, the crack snaked rapidly through the ground, shearing trees in half, and sending huts tumbling into the void. Eferon himself, began to fracture in two. Wind whirled around him as he was cloven clean in half. He fell to the ground, dead. From one half of his broken and lifeless body arose a great swirling rush of ashes, which formed into a vortex, then coalesced into a vague shape of darkness. A second swirling cloud rushed upwards from the other half of his body, rising high into the air, and then falling as coloured petals on the land on this side of the crack. As they fell, they settled on the ground, forming rich clumps of sea pinks.

The crack widened, and the sea roared in. A new limit

to the land was anointed by sea pinks and erigen, which kept vigil over the growing strait. Part of Enanti was being carved off, drifting further and further out to sea, carrying Eferon's prone, split body lying next to that of Quella. And above them both loomed the haunting cloud of dark ash, moving and swirling with menace. Soon this fragment of the land had disappeared from sight, somewhere far out to sea. Out of sight, but not out of severed memory. That land is now known as Tenebro, or the Shadow Realm. It is where the Shadow Beast reigns. It is from there that the attacks are launched that have ravaged Enanti. And it is there that he holds Alette captive.

Shame

I often wondered how much Vi and Paul knew about what had happened to me – what they had been told. They never spoke about the loss of my family, yet I knew they knew all about it, which cast a question mark over whether they simply treated my rape in the same way, or whether they just didn't know.

I found it very hard to accept that they might know something so private about me. And if they did, then the fact that it was never spoken of made me feel dirty somehow, ashamed.

In the first year or so, with my limited understanding of how these things worked, I had a vague fear I might have become pregnant, and then be found out. Whenever I showered, I would press my fingers to the pulse in my stomach, and chill with dread as I wondered whether it was my own heartbeat, or that of a child. After a year and a half, I managed to convince myself it was no longer possible – and set about firmly banishing any thoughts or memories of the incident from my mind. And the mind is an astonishing thing. Right through my teens and early 20s I would have been genuinely surprised to be told that it had ever happened. I had worked so hard to disassociate from that event that even being shown CCTV footage of it would barely have convinced me of it.

But now it did come back to me sometimes – in sharp flashes of memory that made me wince. The blanket I had thrown over it all was starting to slip off.

Lost

"Do you know what Vi said to me?" I whispered, so low that Claire nearly missed it. She waited for me to continue.

"When I had been with her a few months, most of them spent at boarding school with Marni, she came into my room one night after I'd had a nightmare. I wanted to tell her about my dream; I needed her to know what I had seen. I started trying to tell her. She stopped me. Not unkindly – she isn't unkind – but she stopped me, and just said, 'The war is over, Eve.'

"But it isn't, is it? It's never been over. I knew that then, because I felt the pain of her words, the pain of not being seen. But I suppose I'd forgotten about it over the years. Kidded myself that, yes, my war was over. She must know, I thought. It must be I who am wrong. She must know, because she is the one looking after me."

Room

I was in a small, white room. Every time I opened the door, the people outside were speaking in a strange language that I couldn't understand. I couldn't talk to them, so I kept going back into the room. But then I realised that, as I was alone in the room, I couldn't talk to anyone at all.

Punishment

Another Friday night, another nightclub. I pressed my painted nails into my palm, fists clenched, as I made my way through the pulsing crowd on the dance floor – following him outside. Adam was it? Or Callum? I hadn't quite heard it over the throbbing music and the alcohol coursing through me, but it didn't matter; it made everything easier. He hadn't even asked my name. And if he had, he wouldn't have been given my real one. That was something I kept out of it.

He paused ahead of me and looked back, sending me a wink, checking that his luck was still in. Of course it was. He wanted me – and that was enough. I couldn't expect anything more.

"Taking your time there, honey? Come on." He reached out his hand to stroke down my arm. I shuddered at the contact – part revulsion, part compulsion – and smiled back at him.

"You don't give much away do you?!" Adam/Callum joked. "That's OK. As long as there is one thing you are giving away tonight, I'm happy."

I felt the familiar wave of disgust wash through me at his

comment. That was all he saw in me. But that was all I was. All I was. That he could see it so clearly was devastating. This is how it had to be. And I stepped out into the cold alleyway behind the club.

He pressed me against the cold metal of the door we had just come through, pushing his tongue crudely into my mouth, grabbing between my legs. He knew there wasn't any need for further finesse, so he didn't provide any.

He shifted me slightly to the right, and I felt the rough bricks of the alley wall through my flimsy top. My blood chilled at the echoes of other bricks at my back, all those years ago. I whimpered, and tried to move away.

I think he mistook my noises for encouragement. "That desperate, are you? Come on then."

So I tried again: "Not here, please; not here," I managed to stammer out.

"Here is as good as anywhere, baby. It's not like I'm going to get us a room now, is it? Bit late for that." He pushed in harder, speeding up. And I let him. Because it was easier that way.

And all I could see as it happened was the faces of those soldiers. And all I could hear was their laughter.

It didn't take long. Almost like knocking back a shot, the build-up was always more of a pull than the event itself. He, satisfied and looking pretty cocky right now. Me, devastated, and mind awash with more than I could grasp hold of. I felt cheated – I wasn't sure of what. I had wanted oblivion, and had only got some scratches on my back, and a dark heavy feeling sitting in my stomach. I leaned over to one side and retched.

Oracle

"What do you think? Will it be soon?" Raul looked questioningly at Minerva as he awaited a response from the seer. She closed her eyes and linked herself into those ancient communication channels that she traversed so fluidly.

"It will," came her quiet reply. "Very soon. I would look for her at the ripeness of the next moon. Things are shifting now, on the move, and it will not be long before she comes."

Raul tugged his furs more tightly around him. The lengthening spring days still had a sharp chill in their evenings. "And where? Where should we look for her?" he asked.

"That is even clearer to see. It will be one of the deeper, cloudier Shifting Pools. There are only two with the necessary sediment and murk to admit entrance to one who has yet to consciously choose these things for herself. Two with enough depth to immediately link to the subconscious mind over the conscious. And one of those is unlikely – far off in the Hinterlands. You should go and wait at the other – the one in the deep cave on Drumlin's Hill. That is where she will enter our Lands."

Raul knew better than to question Minerva's belief. And more than that, as always, he sensed the truth of what she said as he listened to her soft, purposeful voice.

"It needs to be soon," he added in his own quiet voice. "Things are changing. More and more villages are being laid waste. We can't pinpoint where these new attacks are coming from; they seem to be all around us, moving silently among us. We have fallen back to the forests now, and we are safe there for the moment. But it is only a matter of time. The Craven are on the move – and their numbers are increasing by the day. We need her. And soon."

"She is nearly ready," replied Minerva. "I can feel it. She will come very soon."

Shadow Beast

The dark mist was filling the room again, suffocating me. The air was dense and drugged, and I couldn't get enough oxygen. A deep chuckle reverberated around my room, seeming to come from every direction at once.

"What are you?" I shouted into the Darkness.

Another rumble of deep laughter.

"You know me, Eve."

I gasped. "Yes." I did. Somehow, I did.

I watched as the dark mist started to take some form in the corner of my room, sucking in shadows from behind every surface. It built and built in density, looming high over me, until I could make out some edges of a form. The shadows overlapped, transposed, adding more and more depth to the Darkness. That vast, dark, horned lizard, raised up over me, sucking me in with its bottomless eyes. He had found me, here in my bed. I'd locked all the doors, but he'd come walking in the

107

night, straight into my head.

He raised himself up, higher and higher, as my ceiling disappeared, and it was just me on my bed, and him reaching up into the night sky — impossibly tall, like a column of pitch cloud. Coming for me.

"You belong to me, Eve. You are mine."

"No! No!" I screamed, as he reached for me.

The world of dream is psyche yearning
for consideration...
We are visited at night, and we get to hear
other voices.
They are not ours; we are more theirs.
Dreams are a gift from the dreamtime
that opens our vision.

Kathee Miller

Unlocking

I have the oddest sense that something is about to happen. Something momentous, something I have no control over, but which feels good, exciting. I've no idea what it is, why I'm feeling that – it's really strange.

Things are shifting around inside, like an army mobilising its troops into position, before…what? I don't really know, but I get the sense that things are on the change, life is altering, and I need to keep up or I won't survive. Something is quickening in me, gaining momentum. Sometimes it feels more like something bulging, something I can't contain for much longer, something wanting to break out. Break free maybe? I feel….well, I feel, I feel…

This other side of me, this person underneath, is starting to wake up, starting to stretch, starting to need some changes made to the room I find myself caught in.

I tried to explain it to Claire.

"Tell me more about that room," Claire had asked.

"It's small. It feels really neat, and white, but really small. And there's nothing in it; just me."

"Anything else?"

"I don't want to stay in it any more. But I don't know

110

what is beyond the door. I want to get somewhere else, but I don't know where. But this room is feeling too small. I feel as if I am getting bigger, and it isn't comfortable any more. And the door, and the frame, and the handle; they all look as if they are pulsing – throbbing and changing size. I don't like that. I'm not sure whether I want to open the door, or whether there is something the other side, trying to open the door and get in."

"That sounds quite scary. What you are describing sounds as if there is some change underway, whatever that may be, and change can be scary. And it is especially scary when you've constructed everything around you so carefully, and for such reasons as you have."

"I am scared. But it seems to be mixed with something else, too; something like anticipation, or curiosity – or something."

Dream

The field of covered bodies

I had to go on an adventure — through endless fields. I didn't want to but I had no choice. I was with my parents. It was harrowing, with steeply sloping hills that made our horses lose their footing, and long hedge-lines. My horse was tired. Were we looking for something or just wanting the end?

Towards the end, in a snowy field, I realised I had dropped my jumper. I could just have let it go, and left this terrible place, but I felt a desperate need to find my jumper first. I told my parents to go to the end, that I would catch up with them. Turning my horse around, I trudged back through the fields. Some were like large, high-walled rooms — a little like squash courts.

At the very bottom of a sharply sloping field, I stopped in the corner by the hedges. Looking for my jumper, I pulled the surface of the field aside at this corner, as if it were a sheet. Underneath was a jumble of dead bodies, arms and legs sticking out at hideous angles. I knew they would be there, knew about them, but pretended they were not, and covered them all up again, still trying to search for what I had lost.

Drowning

The following Saturday morning, as I floated in the pool while Peter had his swimming lesson in the shallow end, I tried to let the tension flow out of me. I hadn't been swimming for 25 years. The water felt achingly tender on bruised skin. Marni was sitting on the side, reading, and we were all going to have lunch together after the swim.

I heard the teacher at the other end of the pool teaching Peter's class what you needed to do to drown. How strange, teaching children how to drown, but perhaps that is the best way to teach them to float. Demystify the process; take away the fear. The more I thought about it, the more it appealed to me.

And as I floated in the water, this was the thought that played in my mind – more of a wondering. All I had to do was to raise my arms above my head in surrender, and exhale. Let my breath leave my body. And down I would go. I would never have done it, never have taken so much away from those who loved me, but it was strangely comforting just to know that I could. It made me realise that every day was a choice not to.

I still wanted to experience the enveloping that only

113

water can give, so I let myself sink down into the water, feeling it cradle my head, and hold me. So still, so silent there. I had a sudden vision of ducking beneath the water with Hugo, all those years ago.

Then suddenly I was violently sucked down, a stream of noiseless bubbles spilling from my mouth on a voiceless scream.

Our banquet of dreams is spread each night.
We can choose to eat.
We can choose not to eat.

Jill Mellick & Marion Woodman

A shift of worlds

I abruptly found myself in a cave, damp walls setting up a constant drip. The swimming pool had disappeared. I reached out and touched the rivulets on the dank walls, and their rhythm altered immediately. It reminded me of my own skin after a nightmare. My body was at its peak of alert, and my mind was scrambling. A familiar icy chill ran through me. I know what happens to a mind as it struggles to comprehend a new reality. It is just like a body seeking oxygen, but forgetting to take in deep enough breaths. The mind takes pitiful little gasps, the depths remain unreachable for a time; locked down. A strange duality existed: terror at what had just happened, yet also a sense of inevitability about it, as if some part of me had known that I would find myself here, in this strange place.

Obeying the weakness in my legs, I sat down awkwardly on the floor, but regretted it instantly as the damp iced through me. I remained seated for some time, though, until my mind was able to find another gear. Peering around the cave, I sought some clues. When I had calmed myself sufficiently, I stood and turned towards the area of light to my right. It wasn't as if the cave was freezing cold, but the fact that I was already wet made me lose heat fast.

The light stung as I emerged into the open. With my vision starting to clear I saw I was at the top of a steep slope. Scrub and rocks were all around, and stunted trees blanketed the lower slopes. Beyond that, endless forest.

I heard voices, and I froze. Snorts of deep laughter, and then the soft thump of hooves walking towards me. As my vision cleared further, I looked up into the face of a man on horseback. He didn't smile, but I didn't feel intimidated.

"You should," he said softly.

Startled, I searched for his eyes, and backed away. His eyes had the intent glare of the wolf.

"Here, Eve, put this on." He held out a thickly woven blanket towards me. When I continued to back away, he jumped off his horse, and wrapped the blanket around me himself.

"How...how do you know my name?" I managed to say.

"I've been waiting for you to arrive, Eve; we all have. The signs all pointed towards today."

"What signs?"

"Sit down here, and get yourself dry. You look half-frozen," he said, ignoring my question.

I remained standing, but started to rub the damp off me, and the life back into my body. I kept my eyes on him the entire time.

The exchange was so strange, and I struggled to make sense of anything that had happened in the past hour. The man spoke more softly now: "I know that none of this makes sense to you. Get dry, and we'll return to camp. Then we'll talk."

I nodded.

"Can you ride?" he asked, as another man rode up the slope towards us, leading a spare saddled horse with him.

"A little."

I swung myself up on to the horse, acutely aware of several sets of eyes on me. Men and women, dressed in tawny furs and leather, all astride horses – about eight or so. I felt shut down, simply going through the motions until something started to make sense again. The movement of the horse beneath me was a comfort. It felt familiar, real, a rhythm that I knew.

As we rode along, the others talking sparingly to each other, I gathered that the man who had spoken to me was called Raul. He seemed to be their leader, though this was more implied than stated. He wasn't a tall man, or as obviously strong as the other men, but he didn't need to dominate physically; an air of authority hung from his shoulders with the furs that were fastened there, held with a wolf brooch. He was darker, smaller, quieter.

Suddenly, he pulled his horse up, and jumped down, his eyes scanning the area. He walked with the grace of a wild animal, setting his feet down with intent. It was hard to believe that someone so quietly powerful could be elegant, but he was. When he walked it hinted at something being held back, power coiled tight; ready, always ready. He threw back the heavy furs that were fastened at his chest, freeing his right arm, that hovered now over a sword at his side.

He was staring off into the distance; assessing the risk. Then he turned and strode back to the others. They all looked as if they lived their lives outdoors, fully of the woods, several with scars visible on their faces, but he was the king here; it was clear. The leader of this pack. His voice when he spoke was clear and direct – quieter than I had anticipated, given the obvious tension coming off him. But I had the unsettling feeling that I would not like to be on the receiving end of his anger.

"There could be Craven ahead. I sense something, but the wind is in the wrong direction, and I can't get anything. Two of us should go up and take a look. Anyone fancy it?"

A large man stepped forward.

"I'll come."

"Good. We'll have to stay very low, Silas. I don't want to risk them seeing us above the canopy if they are out in the open. If it's anything, it will probably be just some small scouting party. Stay low, close to the trees," Raul said.

Silas nodded. Then my grip on reality shifted again as I watched the two men shrug off their furs, to their leather clothing underneath. I watched transfixed as an enormous set of wings sprouted majestically on the shoulders of each man. A minute ago I had been standing in a clearing with a rough band of men, women and horses, and now I was standing with what looked like avenging angels. Their wings were huge and powerful-looking, umber browns speckled though with flecks of gold and ochre, the flight feathers large and edged with sepia.

"You stay here, Eve," Raul ordered, as he started to beat his wings. He had wings.

I just nodded, my mouth probably open. It wasn't as if I had many other appealing options.

I stared as Raul and Silas left the ground and moved swiftly up into the trees. I lost sight of them as they cleared the canopy and moved west.

The remaining men and women turned to their horses, checking straps and fastenings, as if this sort of event were an everyday occurrence. Maybe it was, here. Their nonchalance actually helped, as seeing them all being so casual allowed my own pulse rate to start to steady. To fit in here, I thought, I just need to carry on as normal, not show any shock at realities such as people with wings. And I wanted to fit in. The pattern that usually ran me, with its compulsion to remain under the radar, was screaming at me, so I bent my head and busied myself with the girth on my own horse. But I couldn't fit in here, either, I thought, as my fingers moved blindly at their work. I didn't have an incredible set of wings.

Within 20 minutes, Raul and Silas were back, landing lightly in the clearing, and folding their magnificent wings away.

"Nothing," Raul said. "False alarm. We keep going to camp."

And with that, they all mounted their horses again, and looked impatiently at me as I struggled to keep up with events.

I sensed rather than saw the eyes of the men on me as we rode silently back to their camp. I felt as prey must feel being brought back injured to feed the cubs – a hollow acceptance, a surrender, a hopelessness?

The thick tree cover eventually gave way to a large open clearing, and I saw the encampment ahead. Its lack of permanence was evident in its abundance of cloth and animal hide for building, rather than any more durable structures. A rough smudge of tents arced around to the right and back, while, on the left side, an open area held the site for a great fire, with some large felled tree trunks around it by way of seating.

Raul had dismounted, and came over to help me down from my own horse.

"This way," he said.

He led me around to the gaggle of tents at the right, nodding greetings to people as we passed.

He ducked through the flap into one of the tents, and I followed him in. As my eyes adjusted to the candle-lit glow inside, I looked around. There was a bed, low to the floor and covered in more furs and woven quilts. A little table to the side seemed inlaid with tiny pieces of shell or stone that caught the light, and in the open space between the bed and the side wall, there was a large metal tub that steamed gently. A long mirror was propped against the tent canvas on the other side of the bed. The bench next to it was covered in furs, trousers and woven cloaks, all in the same earthy browns and creams.

Within the tent, Raul appeared too large. Whatever he was felt constrained by the gloom of the tent, and he seemed less at ease in there.

"This will be your tent while we are here," he said. "There is some hot water in that bath there for you. There are some dry clothes for you to change into, and soon there will be something to eat at the fireside. It's being prepared now."

"You've got wings," was all I managed to say.

Raul smiled down at me, his eyes gleaming in the candlelight. I glimpsed something untamed there, something of the woods outside. I took a step back.

"You'll see that a lot here. I'd forgotten that that would be a little odd for you to see," he said.

"A little odd, yes."

"It's not a trick Eve, it is just how we are. It is how life is here. You will get used to it." He then continued more softly. "There is a lot more here to throw a person than a simple set of wings."

He scanned the room quickly, checking, I think, that I had everything I needed. Had he organised everything? Then he turned to go. "Get washed, get dry, and get something warm on, and then I'll see you out by the fire."

He strode back out, towards the large fire and log seating area that they had passed on the way into the camp. I followed him, unsure what else to do. If he was king here, there was no point in trying to hide. Far better to stay close enough to observe.

When he heard me behind him, he stopped abruptly and took a few paces back towards me. Outside the tent, I didn't feel the need to back up. He took hold of my shoulders, gently but firmly.

"Eve, you are quite safe here. No one here is going to hurt you. You really need to get washed and dry and changed – or you won't warm up again properly. Please." He nodded towards my tent. I nodded back at him, and turned away.

I caught up with him later by the fire. Watching him before I approached, I saw him talking quietly with his closest band. His stillness held an almost palpable power. It was in stark contrast to the more overtly physical actions and mannerisms of the men and women with him. But they naturally looked to him for their lead. Every time they raised something, they automatically looked straight to him first, for his reaction. I could see why. He was far more inscrutable, his dark eyes showing keen intelligence and a fathomless stillness. In his eyes I caught a glimpse of someone who could wait for an eternity, who knew the secrets of patience. A man who saw a far greater picture than most of us ever do. He was nodding slowly at something one of the other riders had said.

He unnerved me. Far more than the powerful men who surrounded him. I was used to masculine force: I never let it go so far as to intimidate me before popping its ego like a balloon. But I felt a different male energy from him. I felt as if he alone was able to see through to the core of things, and I wasn't sure I wanted him to. His hawk-like, tawny gaze seemed to notice everything, every nuanced look, every unconscious movement. Anyone would be unnerved.

As I sat down beside him at the huge communal fire, I didn't wait for pleasantries. "I have to go back," I said. "My cousin needs me – my nephew – they are at the pool. Please help me get back to them."

"I will. I am helping you to get back to them. But that might be in a way that doesn't make sense to you. I'm sorry for that. But don't worry about them missing you. The time you are here will count as nothing with your loved ones – they won't notice you're gone."

"Why do you think you are here?" He looked at me

searchingly.

"Does there have to be a reason? A lot happens in life for no reason at all."

"That is true," he nodded, "but there are some things that happen only for a reason, things that can only happen to us, things we are responsible for."

"And how are you meant to tell them apart?" I asked, exhaustion catching up with me now.

"You can't always, but it doesn't mean that you shouldn't ask the question. And sometimes, if there is a reason, you can only see it much later. But again, that shouldn't stop you asking the question."

"Well, if you can't figure it out half the time, then why does it even matter?" I snapped, frustrated now, and only half-listening.

"Why do you ask a question simply to make a point? If you are not ready to listen to an answer, then you are not ready to ask a question."

I looked up at him then, embarrassed.

"Sorry."

He let out an exasperated sigh. "Do you think I care about you being rude? Eve, we can all be rude. I just want you to be real. I'd be a lot ruder than you are being if I were in your position. I know you are tired, too. We can leave this for another day."

"No," I spoke more vehemently than I had intended, and held onto his arm. He looked back at me, and smiled.

"Good. That's more like it. A little more of what we mean can go a long way."

He paused then, and looked into the fire for a time. He

stared into it for so long that I began to worry that he really wasn't going to continue. But then...

"Do you know that feeling you have when you see something in a dream, that you know is personal to you, a sign that only you have the key for?" He spoke low and soft, urgently.

"It is like that, Eve, with you being here. You may not yet see it, but believe me when I tell you. It is only you who could be here; only you can play out this particular act."

"So you think that everything follows a pre-determined path, that all is set already for us?" I felt hugely disappointed. My whole being rejected that idea.

"No, not at all. Your being here has a reason, yes, a fundamental reason, but how it all unfolds is up to you. Through every tiny choice you make, a different path opens up. An unfathomable number of paths. Some of the paths link together, and some never come together again. On those paths, you either need to accept the resolution you are heading towards, or trace your steps back to another junction. At many points, Eve, you will feel as if you are in a maze with no solution. An endless maze."

My head swung around to him, astonished.

"What! You don't know, do you..?"

"Know what?" he asked.

"Nothing. It doesn't matter."

I sat silently for a moment, then his words broke in gently: "We all carry reasons for things within us, wherever we go. This isn't happening to you because of some outside force that you can't comprehend, Eve, this is happening for a reason that you have brought in yourself, within you.

When you break an arm, there is a reason to seek out help for that breakage. This is similar.

"None of us can control everything, control events, but we can all choose our own response to those events. And you can also control a lot more than you realise you can."

"Is this real, or is this a dream, too? This is just a dream isn't it?" I asked.

"Why do you doubt the reality of your dreams? They are just as much a part of you as your waking life: a vital communication between parts of yourself. There is much you can learn from listening to them. When you dream, you are sometimes more awake than when you are awake. Here we give great importance to them. Below the threshold of consciousness, everything seethes with life. Within you, under all the defences you have put up, everything seethes with life."

"That's what Claire would say," I muttered, then louder: "I don't understand. I'm trying to, but I don't."

"I know." He sounded sad. "But my hope is that you will get there."

Firelight

My upper back was sore, and felt hot and uncomfortable. A dark-haired woman of about my own age saw me shifting around by the fire and trying to scratch it. She quietly came over and sat next to me.

"Can I see?" she asked. "I think I might know what is troubling you. I'm Lara – I'm the healer here."

"I don't know how I did it, I must have scratched myself in the cave when I arrived, and I think it's infected now. I have scars there from before. It's been feeling really hot and sore."

"Come with me," she said, and rose to standing, extending her hand to me. I took it, and followed her into one of the numerous tents. She was slight and graceful, her dark hair captured loosely in a long braid down her back. I had the strangest sense that I had met her before. She pushed back the soft folds of the entrance, and led me inside.

She was extremely careful and gentle with me, and I sensed an unexpected sadness in her as she looked at the wounds on my back. She didn't say a word, but I could feel the genuine emotion that she offered me.

127

As she washed the cuts, she seemed to administer to them as if they were the most tender things she had ever seen, dabbing them carefully and lovingly, taking her time. Her tenderness caught me off-guard, and I felt deeply moved.

"Are they bad?" I asked, using words to cut the emotion off.

"No, they will be incredible. If you let them be."

It wasn't the response I had expected, but I was so exhausted now that I didn't even try to ask her what she meant. Nothing had been what I had expected, so why should this be any different?

When she had finished strapping up the wounds, she made me promise to let her take a look at them in a few days. Wandering back out to the fire, I sat down heavily, greedily sucking in the warmth. I used a stick to push a few embers back into the fire, and sat back to watch the flames.

I thought about home. Not my home in London – my temporary encampment – but real home.

It has been said that the past is a foreign country. But I see it differently. The past is my own country, my home, and I have been exiled. And now I walk restlessly through the days, trying to find my way home. My childhood has been encapsulated in a snow-shaker toy and set up upon a pinnacle. Steep cliffs fall away around it, and a vast chasm aches between it and me – a chasm filled with soldiers and death. I can see a tantalising glimpse, but I can never get there.

Had Claire been right about my being drawn to war? How war can set up a futile, life-long search in those who have lost so much to it. We are forever unable to go back to that exact arena of war, but we can go to others, endlessly searching for some of the things we have had stripped away. A heartbreaking search; a search with no end. It made a little more sense now, the drive I felt to get back to the remote snow-shaker toy on that precipice – wading through those trenches of death.

And I was tired, so tired. I wanted to go home. I wanted to curl up once again in my home; feel safe, feel connected. Perhaps the answer lay in reaching certain parts of my childhood, but I didn't know how. I could never go back there again, yet I also had a new awareness, stuttering to life in me, that vital parts of my old life are carried forward within me; they've always been there.

I pushed my stick further into the fire, disturbing the glowing embers. The flames flared brighter. This new thought was exciting, but, if anything, it just added to my restlessness, as it lacked clarity. I didn't understand what it meant, yet I felt the enormity of its potential, throbbing under the surface of my conscious mind.

I allowed the warmth of the fire to seep into me, to tempt my eyelids down, to nudge me towards sleep. My body ached and needed rest. For once, my mind allowed it without a struggle. I slept there that night, by the fire; the movement and spark of the fire before me, the unseen mass of the darkness pressing up into me from behind.

We came to a meadow full of flowers.
We saw and realised that they were there,
but we had no feelings about them.
The first spark of joy came when we saw a rooster
with a tail of multicolored feathers.
But it remained only a spark;
we did not yet belong to this world…
Everything appeared unreal, unlikely,
as in a dream…
Step for step I progressed,
until I again became a human being.

Viktor Frankl

Little Bear

There were many children running around in the camp. Some seemed to have no parents, and were looked after communally, sharing the food around the campfire, and sleeping in a few dormitory tents nestled among the others. So many people here, in this temporary encampment – and I had no idea what their story was.

There was one little girl who literally ran into me that first morning, knocking me backwards as she rushed wildly around the corner of a tent. She shrank back immediately, and cast her head down.

"It's OK, don't worry. I'm…"

I stopped short as she raised her face to me, catching me with her eyes. I knew that look. She had haunted eyes, wide and deep, that had seen too much, survived something unimaginable. She quickly averted her gaze, but the jolt stayed with me, as deeply as if she had just burned a brand on to my mind with that brief glance.

She stood in front of me, her shoulders hunched over, head down, small frame braced. So still. No one stands that still unless they have been taught by life to survive that way. No one stands that still when they are at peace. The tension in her body ran down to her fingertips and her ankles, and I could imagine her toes clawing down into the earth within her boots, like a corpse in rigor mortis. Her hair, mousy and matted, sat on her head like a moth-eaten felt hat.

"It's OK, Sula. It's OK, love." Lara had appeared close behind the little girl, from around the side of the tent, and spoke to her gently. She kept her voice low and calm, and after waiting for a few moments, she came closer and tenderly stroked her on the back.

"Come on, Little Bear. It's OK. This is Eve, and she is very kind. She won't have minded —will you?"

Lara smiled at me, and I smiled down at the little head bowed in front of me. Such a small head, weighed down with a heavy burden.

"Of course I don't mind, Sula – is it? Are you Sula?"

She didn't answer in any form, not even an inclination of the head. Lara stepped forward and began to gently lead her away. As she turned to go, Sula raised her eyes to me once more. Her gaze then shifted to the side slightly as she caught sight of the bandages peeking out the top of my jacket, just between my shoulder and my neck.

"This? These?" I asked as my hand went up to the bandages and I instinctively crouched lower to allow her a better view. With her eyes never leaving them, she walked the few steps between us, and reached out with a hesitant hand.

"It's OK – you can touch them. They are just covering up a cut I had, but it is feeling so much better. Here…" I crouched lower as her hand sought out the rough fabric, taking it between her thumb and two fingers, and rubbing it slowly. As she did so, she turned her face right towards mine and looked directly into my eyes. She must have seen something there that provoked it, as before I could catch my breath with the intimacy of the moment, her small hand touched my cheek. It didn't move, she just rested it there on my cheek – the lightest of touches, as if she knew that any movement was just an adult's misguided way of shushing away the fear, of rocking away the pain of the moment. This was far purer than that. Sometimes stillness is the most moving expression of all. It just lets you be.

And then she was gone, running off around the backs of the tents again.

"Is she mute?" was the first question for Lara that came to mind.

"Yes," sighed Lara. "She can't even tell us her real name and I don't think she can write, either. I started to call her Little Bear, which she seemed to like, which eventually became Sula, as she needed a proper name. It suited her, and more importantly, she seemed to be pleased, so it sort of stuck. She…"

We were interrupted by three people coming out of the forest, calling for Lara. Two of them I recognised as part of the band that had found me in the cave; a woman named Sorcha, and a very tall man, Arno. These two were supporting a man in the middle, letting him rest his weight on them as he stumbled into camp. His right leg was hanging limply, and he screwed up his face with each jarring step.

"Might be broken, Lara. Stupid idiot stepped in a rabbit

hole, didn't you Breven?"

"Bloody big rabbit, then," Breven managed to get out, with an attempt at a grin. "I could have made a comfortable home in that!"

Lara rose to her feet immediately.

"My tent. No, don't worry Eve, you stay here – I'm OK." And she led the way.

I stayed there for maybe an hour or so, allowing thoughts to flow through my mind. That luxury of time allows a different form of stillness to descend. Not the stillness of fear, but a stillness of the mind, after a maelstrom of thoughts has been given the proper space to whirl and ferment.

In London I had found this release occasionally after a run, or a walk; the perpetual rhythmic motion of my body somehow allowing my thoughts to be jostled and sieved, until they were able to sift down like the gentle rain of falling flour, creating a still mound. I'd never found it from stillness itself before. Life in London didn't really allow for that.

I had always been tired in London, I realised now. Well before the dreams began again. So much effort required to keep my mask up all the time. It was an excruciating life I had constructed for myself. Still, at least I had constructed it. I'd made it through another day.

I'd never really considered the cost of this until now. It had never been about that; only the fact that I had survived another day, another month, another year. I had zipped myself into those suits, churned out those briefs, painted my face, chased those accolades – all so that no one would see me struggle, and ask: 'What happened to her? Why can't she do that?' I knew enough about psychology to know that the tactic worked: if you don't want a pack of dogs to sense your fear and attack, you present them with a lack of fear.

Exposure

I didn't feel safe. I didn't want to come out of hiding. I'd always been fascinated by the idea that you 'take people as they are' – at face value – leaving any judgement of their past firmly out of the reckoning. But it disturbed me as much as I also yearned for that anonymity and acceptance of just who I am now; me, here, in this time and this place. Because I knew, beyond any shadow of a doubt, that to take people for how they present themselves can be a terrible misjudgement. It always was in my case. The Eve that people saw – even my friends – was one I could edit, adapt endlessly, perfect and then present. So I loved the fact that my friends accepted me simply for 'who I am' (what does that even mean?), but I also knew they couldn't possibly know me unless they knew my past, my life. Make of that dilemma what you will! I wanted them really to know me, but I was so glad they didn't.

I understood hiding. Somewhere in my psyche was a filing cabinet where 'hiding' had been filed under 'good'. It was what kept us alive all those years ago, kept us a family – a unit – alive, at least for a while. My last memories of my family were of our weeks in hiding, before we were blown

136

apart. We were all together. And now I am alone.

I thought back to the trip to Crackington Haven I had taken after the storms had thrashed the coastline down there last winter. It was the only time I had come away from the sea feeling worse.

I had stared out over the beach I knew so well, and felt sick. The golden sands of last year were gone. The beach was hollowed out, scraped back to the jumble of bedrock and boulders that had lain hidden for so many years, now exposed. Dark and dripping from the waves. So dark. It was a profound image; this covering carved away. I had felt suddenly revealed myself. I took it so personally. The sight of so many tiny figures scrambling all over the rocks, metres lower than they would have been last year, had been deeply disturbing. As if they had been picking over my own internal landscapes, digging and searching through the cracks and rock pools. I'd wrapped my scarf more securely around my neck, and hugged myself. The wind had had a chill to it then, and I hadn't wanted to be there.

Is this what happens to us all in the end? I wondered. The thought was challenging. Stripped bare, laid out for others to examine and judge? One storm and all that camouflage is stripped away, one storm and everything is different. Things long buried were feeling the air.

Escaping

We lived in this sort of school, set in large grounds. Something was wrong here. We were closely watched, and there was a perimeter that we could not travel beyond. There were certain things at the limits, that, once touched, sent you instantly back to the centre of this strange place. We were trapped.

The teachers said it was all for our benefit, our protection and safety. Here, we were comfortable, well-fed and looked after. Just trapped.

But our safety was unimportant to me. I spoke passionately to my group of friends. I wanted freedom – the ability to make choices, take up a hobby, travel, live in my own way.

We started to plan our escape. We knew that touching certain things would send us straight back – a lot of these things were food, and items we really needed. But we discovered that if we painted them, in whatever colour each thing was, we were safe from this instant recall. The layer of paint offered us protection.

I painted some red grapes red, and lay them in the sun to dry.

A teacher walked by, and we quickly hid the paints. She noticed nothing unusual about the red grapes beside us.

We went to a door, in the middle of the wilderness edge. It was a standard white house door, in the middle of the trees. We opened it, and there was another one exactly the same beyond it.

Suddenly we heard a teacher searching through the undergrowth for us, getting closer and closer. Terrified, we quickly opened the second door, and another, and then the next one was opened for us. We stepped into a new reality.

It felt strange for a while. We needed time to adjust. It was odd to be free. We started off by camping out in the open.

There was a protective force-field that protected us only from things from above. We saw a strange branch just hanging in the sky above us – levitating in mid air, an enigma. We realised that it had come from our old world, and that this new world was directly beneath our last one. In an attempt to trap us into returning, the teacher was dropping things down, unpainted. Once touched, we would be instantly transported back. It was a dangerous portal between these two worlds.

The forcefield kept us safe. But as the days went by, the forcefield began to ebb, and little sticks, gently, so gently, were let down to almost ground level. I wasn't overly concerned because it all happened so slowly that we had time to avoid them.

I took the train with one of my friends to London, to see life.

We found a stray dog, and put it on the train back to our camp, while we continued in London for a few more hours. When we returned, our friends told us about this dog that had arrived alone on the train, so they had sent it back on the next one. I felt an intense sadness, and pity for that dog.

Man is two men;
one is awake in darkness,
the other is asleep in light.

Kahlil Gibran

The things that fall in war

"What is this place?" I leaned forward to refill my cup from the pitcher – I was parched after a full day of helping with chores around the camp. It was good finally to sit around the campfire and stop.

"You are in Enanti," Lara replied.

I wasn't stupid enough to think that this was somewhere I could find on my globe at home, that my usually diligent geography teachers had failed to mention.

"It seems so different to what I'm used to. Where are all the towns and cities?"

Lara smiled. "You don't like living outdoors?" She grinned. "It's not for everyone – at least, not at first. But Raul has kept us safe. He did what he promised. And here we live as the Free. We move our camp on frequently, to try to stay safe, but at least we are free."

"Safe from what?"

"We do – did – have many towns here, and a beautiful city, Albedo. That was where I came from."

As Lara paused, I realised I was surprised that she had

come from another life than this; she seemed so natural in this environment.

"Some of us here came from Albedo, others from elsewhere, but now this is home. One day I would love to go back, to walk its streets again, to sit by its fountains and drink sherbet with my friends under the full moon. It was so beautiful, Eve. It was built from copper-stone, so it glowed in the sunshine. The citadel at the top of the hill was always festooned with flags, which caught the wind, and called our hunters home from miles around. We had festivals and fêtes; life felt like one long summer."

"Why can't you go back now?" I asked.

"The towns have been lost to us, and Albedo has also fallen. They are nothing but empty shells now. The buildings are the same, but vacant. Albedo still stands but its soul has gone. Death walks there. The Craven came, the vanguard forces of the Shadow Beast. He seeks to control all of this land. They came in their thousands, and ransacked the towns. No one was spared. So many were lost – even the young."

I winced at her words, stabbed through.

"I'm sorry Lara. I'm so sorry." I said quietly. I reached for her hand, and held it tightly.

Haltingly, I told her of my own version of Albedo, and she told me more of hers. Her parent had died already some time before the fall of Albedo, but she lost her husband and many of her friends when the city fell.

"I felt so useless. I was a healer, but I could do nothing for them. It was too late," she said. "But coming here saved me – and now I am the healer here."

143

"Is Sula from Albedo too? Did she come with you?" I asked.

"We think she is from Albedo, but she came here later." Lara paused and closed her eyes before continuing. "I can't imagine what happened to her in the meantime. I think she was hiding out for some time before The Craven captured her. I can't bear to think what she went through, but she managed to escape, and she made her way across country, completely alone. Raul found her one morning in the forest, and brought her here. "

My heart ached for her, this little girl who had seen too much. Her face was too thin, her eyes too old. I wanted to take that look out of her eyes.

"She hasn't said a word since arriving here. But she is settling in, starting to respond to some of the other children, and she certainly seems to like you!" Lara beamed at me. "That's the best healing; right there! And apparently I'm meant to be the healer here!"

She was being deliberately flippant, of course, but it still made me smile. Feeling that I was doing anything at all for Sula made me feel happy.

"Have you always been at war here?" I asked.

"No. There is a story, handed down the generations that speaks of our past."

And she began to weave a story about the Golden Age of Enanti – when everything was in balance, Albedo was a glorious city, famous throughout other lands – and Enanti was ruled by a man called Eferon and his council.

I listened intently as the story unfolded, as the shadows crept in and fractured the land. Clove it right in two.

Lara continued: "For many generations, the people of Enanti tried to calm their shock and return to as normal a life as possible, but with a feeling of unease creeping into our northern borderlands. A feeling of something dark coming and going from across the seas – reaching over to us from the Shadow Realm – too intangible to put a finger on. People began to disappear. Not many – but enough for stories to start to be woven about the Hinterlands, the far far north of Enanti. Albedo, in the south, tried to carry on as before, but began to sever its dealings with the northern Hinterlands, turning a deaf ear to the darkness that moved there, just under the surface. We had been living in denial in Albedo. With the capital's back turned, the forces of the Shadow Beast were able to take a firmer and firmer foothold in the northern Hinterlands – secretly gathering strength and increasing their numbers. And then with growing boldness – many generations after the cleaving of Enanti – The Shadow Beast launched his full-on assault for the whole of our land."

Lara stopped, her throat dry. "I'm meant to be the camp healer, not the storyteller," she joked. "Those are the stories passed down. Every child in Enanti knows that story, but make of it what you will… All we really know for sure is that Enanti is no longer at peace. We are a country at war."

Raul and Esker came over to join us, carrying steaming bowls of food.

Lara continued: "There is a little girl of this land, who has been captured by the Shadow Beast; Alette – that's her name. She is young, not into her teens, and she was taken a while ago. We believe she is still alive. She was taken to the

145

Shadow Realm, and is being kept in exile, in the Hall of the Shadow Beast. She is vital, she is a beacon here – of hope, of possibility. Enanti needs her. She has the pure heart of childhood, but she is more than that. The Ancient Ones speak of her as a salve to our divided lands – not a leader as such, but a hope to bring things back into balance. A talisman. There have been years of war, of lost lives. She is the key to restoring Enanti. We've fought for years to bring her back here, where she belongs, but we have heard that only one person is capable of doing that. You. You hold the key to all this, Eve, and I'm asking you to use it. There is something about your coming that was meant. We don't really understand it, but the Oracle was clear on this, and others of us have also felt it."

"Where is the Oracle?"

"Well, she is everywhere, and nowhere," Raul said.

His hands apologised for him, and he continued. "In Enanti, we don't believe in keeping information like that within one individual. We do have Minerva, a talented oracle who can see many things. She is safe; she is with another group of the Free who managed to get her out of Albedo in time. But she is not the only one. We believe that all of us have the potential to operate as the oracle; it is all to do with tuning into the world around you. In just the same way as I can tell if a deer I am tracking is about to bolt, or about to dip its head down and continue to eat the grass. That is the skill of an oracle – reading all the sensory information around you. And we also rely on dreams, on the signs we are given, and who is the carrier of those signs. All these things are filtered and analysed, usually unconsciously, but it means we know more than we think we do. In practising those arts, we are simply bringing more of that into our conscious world."

"But don't oracles tell the future?" I asked.

"In a way, it can seem like that," Lara interjected. "But it is not really the future, because the future is an unwritten work, a blank page. We are all of us scribbling furiously as we go through life, making certain scenarios more or less likely as our tales develop. But only more likely; never certain."

"So what do the oracles add – or these types of skills, at least?"

"They just give us a little more warning about those events most likely to unfold. If you have honed these gifts, you can see with more clarity – extrapolate out into the future further – not just see the eagle about to swoop down on to the rabbit, but see that likelihood even as the eagle stretches on his nest that morning. That rabbit; that eagle. It is an instinctive knowledge. You feel life as it aligns, as it collides, as it tears apart.

"Minerva knew it was likely you would arrive here on the day you did. She felt that all the necessary conditions were in place to assist you in making that leap. And Raul and I felt it too – very strongly. So we didn't know for sure, but it was a reasonable bet to be there, waiting for you. Yet you could still have chosen not to come, and we would have waited for another time," Lara said.

"But I didn't choose to come here!" I looked around at the small group. "I really didn't!"

Lara smiled at me. "Sometimes it can feel like that, I

know. But the part of you that you are conscious of is like the tip of an iceberg. There are so many parts of you down there in your unconscious who also have a part to play in making these choices, forming these decisions, driving events in your life that you can't understand. They are poorly named in a way, for labelling it 'unconscious' makes us thinks of those parts as sleeping. But believe me, they feel very conscious and sentient to themselves! It is just that we are sometimes unaware of them; we have shut them away. But they are still there, affecting everything."

"Like lost pieces of ourselves...?" I whispered.

"Not necessarily in the way you mean. They don't just disappear. They are repressed inside; they become part of what we are unaware of. They are our unconscious, our Shadow.

"It will drive our dreams, trying to bridge that chasm between itself and your known self, trying to make itself heard. And it will call loudest when there is a serious imbalance between our conscious self and our true nature."

I shuddered. It felt so invasive, the idea of this subconscious; like a creature living within me that I couldn't see, hidden down there, moving around freely without my permission.

Lara noticed. "It doesn't have to be bad, Eve. You don't need to fear it; it just is what it is, and you can get to know it better, know yourself better. Down there in the dark, we will find many things we don't like about ourselves. But we should at least know they are there – look them in the eye.

"And it is also a gathering of untold strength, energy. A treasure trove, the essence of us, a source of immense power. We need to find ways to bring that energy on board, make it part of us again. Where there is light there must also be shadow."

"But why should we listen, if we have chosen other ways over them before? If they haven't helped us before, why would they now?" I asked.

"For the same reason that a parachute is an excellent tool to help you when you need to jump out of a plane, but a damned annoying one to be dragging around after you when you land in the water and need to start swimming. At that point, it might be better to swap to a float!

"Both the darkness of the night and the glare of the suns can be blinding. You need a mixture of the two to see clearly."

"And what is this Shadow Beast?"

"He is powerful, beyond understanding. He can sap a man of his mind simply by talking to him. He can assume any form, but is usually seen as a prowling beast – something ancient, horned. But he can appear as anything; anything that can help unravel the mind. It can be different for everyone. I've known a battle in which he appeared differently to every man I fought alongside. But he is always black – a dense black that swirls and eddies. And the more you fear him, the denser he appears, the more form he is able to take. As if he feeds off your fear, sucks it in and becomes more bodily in this world."

Could I ever atone for Laila? By helping them find this child, could I fill the aching void inside me? Could this girl Alette even be Laila's lost soul – my second chance to get it right? Why else did I have a role to play here?

Newport

I was living in a strange country, where many different types of people lived among a series of cities and urban settlements, all completely distinct and with their own character. Newport was the main centre. It had long, gleaming corridors, quite sterile, high in the clouds, with windows all down one side.

My settlement was an ancient, walled city, with narrow cobbled lanes, brick and mud buildings all jostled together. This was a desert world, full of heat and dust. I had a Vietnamese friend called Tan. We were young boys, pre-teen and full of hope. We spent our days together, making memories in the dust.

There was an ominous feeling in the air. A change was coming. Our world was about to fracture. The different cities were being infused with a sense of apartheid. Over the radio, different ethnicities were ordered to convene in different cities; some of them were to be wiped out. Those in charge remained nameless and remote, but we felt their power.

I was filled with anger and a sense of injustice. I was from an ethnic group that seemed to be in charge, so I would be fine. But my friend would not.

I went with Tan to the old walls of our city. It was hot and dusty. We suddenly knew that we were under attack. A shout went up that we needed to get to Newport. Three Land Rovers started to race from the dusty open square towards the dark tunnel under the city walls, to the enormous, gaping wooden gates. Two of them made it through and out to the desert beyond. The third did not. The gates came crashing shut, smashing down from 60 feet high. We were being hemmed in. The third Land Rover crashed into the sidewall of the tunnel.

Horses were brought into the square, and home-made rockets were launched from blasters on their noses: blowing our way out through the closed gates. The Land Rover was reloaded, set off and we exploded out into the heat of the desert, through enormous, splintered gaps in the gates.

Newport wasn't safe but there was nowhere else to go. I knew I could not be hurt or killed, but I still felt the claustrophobia, the panic of those around me; the horror of their situation. I had somewhere else to go if I chose, and I felt ashamed by this.

We were then in one of the high-up, blindingly white long corridors of Newport. There was a huge gathering of people. They were all going to be killed.

Many months later, I was living in a quiet suburban house on the outskirts of Newport, surrounded by a beautiful flower garden. A conservatory on the front of the house jutted out into

151

the garden, embraced by roses, and bright, bright light.

I had visitors who had come from very far away – from another country entirely. They were mocking the coverage of recent events from here: the shocking slaughter of many thousands. They were making it clear that they thought it had all been grossly exaggerated. Because, look! Here we were in the bright sunshine of the conservatory, having lunch, enjoying the flowers. All was perfectly normal.

I felt a gulf between us that I couldn't bridge. Their failure to grasp what we had lived through burned an uncrossable chasm between us. I felt shame that I was living this peaceful life so soon after what had happened here, immense anger at my relatives' lack of awareness, and overwhelming grief at what I had lost.

Just then, we heard noises in the road. Army noises, the militant drum of boots marching. A helicopter flew overheard, beating the air. A pure, clean terror knifed into my chest as I realised soldiers were coming up the garden path to search for people. People to be killed. It wasn't over. It would never be over.

I wasn't invulnerable this time, and neither were my guests. I made them duck down behind the wooden panelled lower walls of the conservatory. We crouched there as soldiers moved up my path, centimetres away on the other side of the wall, rattling our windows. We held our breath. My guests' eyes were wide with shock as they entered into my world.

Feeling with a thousand fingers

I strode off into the woods, needing some time to myself. The strain of constantly being outdoors, in full view of everyone, was wearing me down. I wanted a place where I could shut the world out, lock the door, rest behind the walls, and come out only when I was ready. It was unnerving to be living outside, surrounded by unfamiliar noises. I felt encircled, cornered. The fresh cool of the dawn gave way to the blustery warmth of the day, then receded back down as dusk fell, as if someone had removed the plug, and the warm air simply drained away. The intimacy of living this close to nature and her rhythms was too personal.

Among the trees, I came to a small clearing and leaned down against the tangled roots. The solidity of the trunk behind my head allowed me to think that someone had my back. Living in the camp was like living with your back permanently exposed. Even in the evenings, when the night was inky black around us, we sat out around the fire. I thought they were mad, that first night. Anything could be out there in the gloom! And when it came for us, we

153

wouldn't even see it. It would find us there, sitting staring into the flames, unguarded, oblivious of what moved under cover of darkness.

No, this was much better, I thought, as I settled back against the tree. As I rested on the moss, I felt myself starting to relax. This was actually pleasant, restful. Shards of sunlight cut through the canopy and danced on my face. I closed my eyes, enjoying the changes of light that played across my eyelids.

Sensation started to climb up the hand which lay resting on one of the larger roots that snaked away from the tree. I discounted it at first, but then stiffened as I felt a faint pulse drumming through the root to me. There was a sudden screech from the forest, and my eyes slammed open. I didn't realise I was holding my breath until I started to wonder why I felt so peculiar. The next breath came in a deep rush, and with it, strange sensations on my tongue. Yew, sap, sharp tangy fir, earthy grit, bracken and the metallic punch of rock. I instinctively wiped my tongue against my cloak, and, rather than finding relief, I was assailed by pungent animal essence, chalky dust and a choking smokiness.

As I scrambled to my feet, the screech came again, accompanied by the crunch of bone splintering, ragged breathing and a low growling. The sounds were too loud in my head, as if the dying animal was breathing out its life into my ears. I heard the thumping of its heart as it slowed, felt the tearing of its flank as claws raked through it. As I listened, there was a faint gurgle, and then a rush of expelled air as life left that body. I glanced wildly around the clearing, trying to connect the savage hunt I heard with something my eyes could verify. But nothing. Then birds started calling around me, deafening me with the volume, as they rose from the trees and pulled themselves into the air.

Away! was my only thought, and I ran from the clearing. I clutched at my ears, trying to block it out. Around me the forest had erupted, screams and whoops, howling and... noise. Unbelievable noise. Like an explosion, sound waves rippled past me as I ran. I wanted to get out, get away. A small incline lay ahead, and I struggled up the rocky outcrop, trying to take myself out of the trees. I slowed as I neared the top, and spun around to see what was coming behind me. There was nothing; nothing was chasing me. Out of the trees the noise was less, but only a little. As I scanned the canopy from above, I thought I might see some immense beast tearing through the trees, or an army on the march.

The forest was vast, and stretched away from me to the horizon. I knew roughly from which direction the sound had come, so I scanned the trees a few hundred metres away, but nothing. My eyes travelled out further towards the horizon, and I let my vision blur as my body calmed. Suddenly, a movement caught my eye, and my eyes snapped back into focus. In a clearing, several kilometres away, there was a wildcat, eating its prey. And I could see it! I blinked, and looked again. I could see it; how was that possible? It was so far away. I focused on it and my vision jumped in even closer. I startled as it raised its head and looked me in the eye, then, assessing the level of danger as low, returned to its kill. I was amazed, I could watch this creature, eating its meal, over kilometres. I saw the blood on its fur, congealing now, the hunger in its eye, the shafts of sunlight on its fur. It growled low, then sought to tug the lifeless body of…what was it? I turned my attention to what it had killed, and saw the glassy-eyed stare of a rabbit. Its empty eyes stared out at me.

A wave of emotion hit me. I could feel the panic of its last few moments, taste the desperation hanging in the wind. Simultaneously, I could feel the sating of the predator's hunger, his alertness as he sought to protect his kill. As I watched, transfixed, the wildcat tried again to tug the rabbit forcibly back to the cover of the trees. With his head up, and his shoulders working powerfully, he lifted his prey in his jaws and trotted to the trees, the rabbit's legs dragging pitifully across the ground. And then he was gone. But I knew exactly where he was; I could hear every leaf that crunched as he passed, every twig he brushed past, every stone the dead rabbit's legs bumped over. And then I tuned out, exhausted. I must have blacked out.

Lara had been out looking for me by the time I returned to camp. I had been gone longer than I had intended, and I felt so much older.

"Eve! I was worried! You left hours ago, and no one knew in which direction you had headed. You must tell someone. Please." She held my face in her hands and looked at me earnestly. "Please, Eve, please tell someone next time."

"Sorry," I mumbled. I wasn't used to this kind of concern from an adult. I'd only experienced it with Peter, and I thought it had stemmed from a childlike need. I allowed Lara to hold my face a few seconds longer, and then stepped away at the first possible chance I could without being rude, laughing awkwardly. But then I paused. I felt a wave of something coming from Lara; gentle but insistent. I felt her concern, her genuine, adult worry for me, out there alone in the woods. It was different from Peter's response, I saw. This wasn't Lara's need of me, this was her concern for me. I didn't need to do anything for her; she just wanted me to look after myself better. I felt I'd been rude.

"Thank you. Sorry. I'm sorry if I worried you – I hadn't meant to be gone so long. Something happened out there."

"What happened? Are you OK?" Lara asked.

"I think so. Just very confused." I smiled at her. "Nothing new there! I've been pretty confused since I got here! Really; I'm fine. I just need to eat and sit down somewhere."

"Easily achieved," Lara beamed. "Three of the men that went out looking for you came back with boar, so we'll eat well tonight.

And Eve, if you want to talk, you know where to find me." She smiled back at me as she walked off.

Sula walked over to me shyly. I could see that someone had tried to brush her hair and wipe down her face. "Hi there. Had a bit of a bath today!" I said. She dipped her chin down to her chest, a gesture that I was beginning to understand as an acknowledgement that I had guessed correctly. She slipped her hand inside mine, but wouldn't look up at me. We walked together towards the main tents and the fire, and then she darted me a quick smile and hurried away. I looked down at where her hand had been, and saw a tiny piece of paper. It had been folded over and over until the fibres had refused to bend over even once more. I unfolded it carefully. In the centre was a simple drawing of a butterfly, and the words: 'You can save her'. They were the first words she had ever given me.

* * *

Sula's words ate away at me. Save her. She hadn't even been asking for anything for herself. From the little I had managed to find out since I had got here, I realised she must mean Alette. So much seemed to hinge on that little girl, and I needed to understand more. I sought out Raul that evening.

"This is one land – it was always meant to be one, but it was split into two. All I know is that that split has caused us great pain and suffering. Somehow, the Oracle says that if we save Alette – save innocence – the land will be whole again," Raul said.

"But why her? Why Alette?" I asked.

"I'm not entirely sure. Perhaps it is simply because the Shadow Beast has her: it is miraculous that she is still alive and has not become one of the Riven, his personal guard, or the Craven, the creatures of the Shadow Beast. Perhaps it is because the Shadow Beast himself prizes her, and keeps her just out of our touch, taunting us. And perhaps it is simply because she is alive, she is a child, and we have a chance to save her. If you had the chance to save a child, wouldn't you take it? Wouldn't that be enough reason in itself?"

"Yes." I whispered. Oh, I would have died a thousand

deaths to have the chance to save Laila again. I had replayed that moment so many times in my mind, what I could have said, could have tried, should have done differently.

"Yes," I repeated. "But I don't think I am the person to help you. I think I will let her down."

"You're talking of Laila," Raul said, very gently, and it wasn't a question.

I nodded, unable to trust my voice, not even able to ask him how he knew.

"Lara told me. I hope that's OK? She didn't mean to betray a confidence, Eve. She just felt I should know, so you weren't pushed into something you couldn't take on."

I looked up at him then. "And do you think I couldn't take it on?"

"No, I don't think that at all. But you already know that. And you know that it has got to be your decision. None of us can make you. But I can try my best to persuade you," he added, with a smile.

Then his face became serious again. "Yes, I do think you can take this on. I feel that. And this isn't Laila, Eve. This is an entirely different situation.

"You aren't a little girl who found herself in an unwinnable situation. You are grown now, and you have choices in front of you. You can make whichever one feels right for you. No one is going to force you into anything."

I glanced at him rather sharply then, wondering what else he knew, but he seemed surprised by my reaction, so I relaxed.

"If you do go into this, don't go into it thinking you are trying to save Laila, Eve. You might as well throw yourself into a torture chamber. It will feel too painful, too full of guilt and doubt, and you couldn't bear it if we don't succeed. This isn't Laila – do you see that?"

I nodded vigorously. Of course I nodded. And of course, if I did this, I would be doing it for Laila, for reparation, for my own redemption. How else could it possibly be?

Raul sighed. "Oh god, I don't want this to pull you apart, Eve." He ran his fingers through his hair, and looked down at the soil beneath us. "You shouldn't do this if you are doing it for those reasons. I can't let you."

"I think it is about time I decided my own reasons for doing things, even when that makes other people uncomfortable. I'm not saying they are the right reasons, but they are at least mine right now. If they are compelling me to action, then, god, I'm going to follow that feeling, because it is feeling. And I've missed feeling. I've been acting for so long, but this is so different. Same word, entirely different meaning. I am going to stop acting, and start to act.

"And you don't have to 'let' me. That is for me to do. You just have to respect me."

Raul gave the warmest smile, that lit me up from inside, and he subtly inclined his head in concession.

Everyone carries a shadow,
and the less it is embodied in the individual's
conscious life,
the blacker and denser it is.

Carl Gustav Jung

Wings

A week later, Lara pulled the bandages away reverently, unwrapping me slowly. I felt different. Not just better, although the pain had completely gone from my shoulders, but different. I eased my shoulders up and down, expecting some stiffness, but there was none.

"They are here," Lara whispered.

I turned to look at her. "Who is here?"

She smiled at me and stroked my shoulders gently. "These are here."

I turned my head as far as I could, and caught a glimpse of something dark and shining, just under my nose. My adrenaline surged. "What is that on my back?" I asked urgently, frightened.

"Your wings, Eve. They are growing back."

* * *

Later that day, I went into my tent to be alone. My mind was straining under the burden of the last few days, and all that had happened. I had kept my new wings hidden from view all day, uncertain what to do with them, and strangely shy about their being seen. They felt peculiar and astonishing. Every time I thought of them, I felt a thrill go through me, a hunger that I couldn't understand. "You are starting to heal," Lara had said to me that morning.

I had been told on and off through my life that I 'had healed'. But how do you learn to live without those you love? People say that time heals. Not true. Time just allows you to scab over, to find new ways of being in the world, to survive. But that isn't healing. It is stasis. Longing for them back every day, bracing yourself for the future, tortured by the past. Each day takes you further away from them, and more than half of you wants to stay where you are – that bit closer to them than you will be tomorrow.

Never hope to return to the state you were in before. Let go of that dream. It will drive you mad. That state has gone for you. Chasing after it is a fool's hope; a butterfly, always out of reach. The only way is forward, to squeeze through those thin corridors of pain, and hope to emerge on the other side.

I am still not sure which is the greater betrayal: to move ever further away from them, carried along helplessly in the currents of time, struggling to stay but condemned to go, or to move on willingly, embrace what you have left, and let them go. I don't even know how you do that. Both seem sacrilegious. So I drift in no-man's land. I can't go forwards. I can't go back. I am stuck here, and I don't know what here is.

I feel them, every day. I can feel their forms in the shapes they left behind when they disappeared. If only I could recreate them from those shapes, those moulds. But I know it doesn't work like that. Still, I am left with eternal indentations in me, around me, the shapes that they were, the way their fabric was interwoven with mine. The way I had grown around their supporting threads. And now mine looks strange, fabric hanging oddly, missing more than half of its pieces, its warps and wefts, forever bent around shapes that no one else can see. That no one else can make sense of. But that is my shape. That is what I am left with. That is who I am.

* * *

I removed my jacket, and twisted around to see my wings in the mirror in the corner. I gasped. There they were, small and dark on my shoulders.

"They are beautiful," said a voice from the shadows, and Raul stepped into the light. I gasped again; I hadn't known anyone was in here.

"I had to see them for myself. Lara told me a few days ago what she hoped. When I saw her this morning, I asked her how it had gone for you. I had to see." He smiled ruefully. "I am normally patient, but not today."

He stepped closer, reaching out with his hand, and touched my wings lightly.

"They are beautiful, Eve. They are a part of you."

"What is happening Raul? I mean, that's the obvious question, isn't it, but also I mean so much more. Like, they are there, but they are tiny; I can't use them. Why are they there?"

"They are there because they are a part of you. A

164

growing part of you. They were always a part of you. You were born with wings, Eve. Life cut them off from you. Over time you stopped remembering they had been there. They wouldn't be growing back without you being a part of it."

"But what is happening to me?" I asked him, urgently.

"You are simply coming back to life, back to yourself. Nothing strange is happening, Eve. This is how it should be."

"But I can feel so much, hear things I shouldn't be able to. It's as if the whole world is calling out to me."

Raul smiled at that: "It is. It always was, but you chose to turn the volume down. Now you can feel things in their true form again. It is a special gift, Eve; you shouldn't fear it."

"But it feels overwhelming. It feels as if there is too much going on for me to keep up with, keep aware of. If I can't make sense of it all, then what sort of gift is that?"

"It is one that you will learn to handle, learn to tune into. Your instincts are right; you just need to trust them. All this stuff that you are pulling in, even if you don't feel you can make sense of it, you will be forming an instinctive response to it inside. Trust that, Eve. That is the gift."

"What do I do with it all in the meantime? How can I switch it off when I need to?" I asked.

"You'll find that you will learn to control it better, be able to amp it up when you need to. But even on quiet, you won't miss a thing; the volume will just be easier for you. And when it is all crashing through you, you'll know what to do with all that."

Raul paused, and then looked at me directly. The lantern light caught his furs, like paint roughly brushed over a surface, catching just the tips. "You have a place in you that can absorb everything. It is your well, like an inner pool or sea. You've always pulled everything into that place for many years, without even realising it. If you hadn't, you would not have survived. You've pulled it all in, good and bad, absorbed it all and held it. It is down there, below the surface of that inner sea, and you can go there and visit it whenever you need. Until then, it holds it all for you, and allows you to function."

He paused, and then: "And your wings will get big enough to use, if you let them. You need to rest, eat well, and just let them grow.

Good night, Eve." And he turned and left.

Trying to fly

A few miles' hike towards the east, the trees of the immense forest petered out, making way for grasses which led down to dramatic cliffs. This was the eastern edge of Enanti, where the land plunged downwards into the sea.

I stared out from the cliff tops, over the sea. It roiled and sucked below me. Such intense dynamism close up, and yet such aching calm at the flat horizon. I needed both right now. I needed the complexity of right here. Here, where two worlds, two elements meet. I felt so much, and I needed to be where I could give voice to those feelings.

I slipped my hand into the little pouch I had tied to my belt, and closed my eyes as my fingers slipped around the piece of sea glass. I rubbed it with my thumb, and then lifted it out. I held it in my hand as I looked at the cliff line stretching away from me on both sides. The sea waves kept up their assault. I let my mind drift. Here, the sea is gradually abrading and corroding the land, wearing it down. Cutting it and carving it. It throws weaponry that it has stolen from the land, and uses it to take more. It shapes the land, scouring it raw, but creates things of such beauty. Destructive yet creative. Damaging but healing.

The carved out legacies of erosion – arches, caves, stacks – have an eerie beauty in their transitory form. They can still be beautiful, still hold a magnetic power, while being worn away, bit by bit, changed eternally in a huge cycle, ultimately returning to dress the beach in powder sand.

The clash of two worlds is a powerful place. One, perpetually doomed to be worn down by the other, yet retaining its own ability, too, to build itself anew. And the watery embrace that erodes it, clasps the land from around the entire globe. Little pieces of rock, broken off and swallowed by the sea, become limitless travellers. Once broken off from home, they journey out into the infinite, and take on new forms, find new homes. Perhaps only when we are broken off from everything, are we truly free. They are free.

And then there is the sky. Where two such seemingly limitless entities meet – sea and sky – there is a special sense of the infinite. Definites seem to dissolve away. Things seem more possible: special things could happen. There is the feeling of a portal here, to all the secrets of the universe, to all the people we have loved, to all the enormity of loss. Here it feels relevant, not out of step. I stand in the wind and it understands me.

I had a visceral sense of touching the truth – the essence of life. Being separated by just a breath. I reached out with my fingers into the wind and gently touched the veil between here and other, feeling the fabric brush across my fingertips, yielding and soft.

From here, we could step off this cliff and take off in flight, know something beyond this world, this life. Break free, break these limits, 'shaking off this mortal coil' in a very different sense.

I watched as a seagull flew over my head, to the edge of the cliff. I felt a rush of pleasure. I watched as the gull took the shift of worlds in his stride, an effortless transition as the cliffs fell away, and he soared onwards, over the sea. If anything, the shift from land to sea actually boosted his flight − the uplift taking him higher as he left the safety of the land. I wanted to step off too; make that transition; live higher.

I felt exhilaration, pure joy and a promise of freedom. I felt as if I could just step off this cliff top into a bigger life, a greater consciousness, a new way of being. It all felt so tantalisingly close. There is something here, at this junction of worlds − land, sea and sky − that is waiting to be discovered, pulling me back here until I find it.

I suddenly realised that part of me already lived in this precious space, inhabited the infinite, and was simply waiting for the rest of me to join it. Otherwise I would never have recognised it; would not have heard the call. There was a sense of coming home − if I could find the way.

At the very edge of the world, we find the limits change. We find ourselves. We get a sense of the eternal. We find we are just at the start of something, not the end. I could feel the whole world calling out to me.

***

Sensing someone approaching me from behind, I turned,

as Raul walked up next to me. I could feel his anticipation.

"Why are you here?" I asked.

He smiled, "One day, you will stop asking that question." He paused for a long while, and then, gently: "This place is special to you, isn't it? It speaks to you."

"Yes," I replied, simply, unsure of how much he already knew, but knowing that somehow he didn't need an explanation.

"And it is here that you will try to fly."

"I'm not ready!" I burst out, shocked.

"You are, Eve, you were born able to fly; you've just forgotten. And I know you've dreamed of stepping off right here – stepping off into another element. And you can.

"And you must be able to fly soon. We need you up in the air. It just can't work without that."

I didn't know what to say. My mind was racing, and I could feel the panic pumping through my body. I wasn't ready. My wings were not big enough, and they couldn't possibly support me. I was able to move them now, and have some control over them, but I was far off having the confidence to control them up in the air. The most I had done was beat them, extend them, feel a little lift from the ground. I didn't know what to say to Raul. I knew he was right about the battle that was coming. I knew they needed me to be up in the air but I hadn't known it was coming so soon. I didn't want to let him down, but I couldn't fly yet.

"You can," he said simply, "and it is not to do with letting me down. It is never to do with letting me down, Eve. This is about you, and yourself. It is not about me. As long as you are true to yourself, you couldn't let me down. Even if that means doing something that harmed me, you wouldn't be letting me down."

"I would never harm you!" I was shocked that he had said it; thought it, even.

He took my hand, and enclosed it in his.

"You would never intend to harm me; I know that. But there may come a time when for you to do the right thing means that I must be expendable. And you must do the right thing then, Eve. And do it well."

I didn't like hearing this, so I turned away and continued to the edge of the cliff. Raul came to stand with me, and we looked out over the sea together.

"I can't do it," I whispered.

"You may not do it this time, but you can," came his reply. I could hear the resolve in him. He fully believed I could. "You need to trust the wind, Eve. The wind will take you under your wings, and you will fly. If you don't trust the wind, it won't work. Eventually you'll learn to trust yourself. And if you can't, you won't fall far. You are completely safe; I will catch you."

"OK. I'll try." I think we both knew my tentative response wasn't the attitude I was hoping for on my first flight, but I was full of doubt as I walked up to the edge.

I closed my eyes, and breathed in the salty tang. It sharpened my mind, and when I opened my eyes again, I felt there was a chance.

"When you are ready, Eve, you need to open your wings, and step off."

I unfurled my wings, their presence still felt strange, but I also experienced the shard of exhilaration and hunger I felt every time I moved them. I had not yet learned to stow them away completely out of sight when I wasn't using them. I opened them out, and turned my head to see them extend. I was still mesmerised by the sight of them, the feel of them. I felt like a toddler staring transfixed at her own hands, unable to comprehend that she could control these wriggling appendages. I beat them up and down slowly, once, twice, stirring the air. The light caught on their feathers, and I saw the flashes of indigo, teal, turquoise, cobalt. My colours, the colours of the sea and sky. I wanted Raul to be proud of me.

I clutched his arm as I stood there at the edge of the earth.

"Eve," he said softly.

"What?" I asked, face tight.

He caught my gaze and drew it down to the sight of my hand on his arm. My fingers were clenched, clawing into him in such a way that my knuckles had turned almost blue.

"You're holding on so tight that you are cutting off your blood supply," he said softly, looking straight at me now.

I turned to face outwards. Releasing his arm carefully, I flexed my fingers back to life. I let myself feel the wind rushing up the cliff face, and under my extending wings, giving me lift. The wind that knew me so well. I hesitated, and then stepped off into the sky.

With my wings fully extended, I glided out over the sea, dipping a little. I tried to correct the dip, but it made things worse. I felt the wind start to lift me under my shoulders, but it felt strange, and I panicked. The sensation under my wings was so foreign to me that I jerked away from it. I pulled them in sharply, which sent me tumbling downwards. The sea rushed up towards me at terrifying speed. I screamed as I plummeted down. Then my trajectory abruptly shifted as I was hauled upwards. Raul's arms were around me, and I clung to him as he landed us on the beach below.

"It doesn't matter," he said, as I sat heavily on the sand. "You tried, and you will keep on trying."

"But I couldn't do it; I wasn't ready."

"You are physically ready. Your wings are big enough, strong enough. But this isn't about the physics of it. It is about the feel of it.

"And you tried to do it to make me proud of you, not for yourself. That's not the right reason. Next time, do it for you. By doing that, you'll be doing it for me, anyway." He smiled then, trying to lighten the mood.

"Time to go. We have a lot to do, and a lot to prepare."

* * *

Later, as we gathered around the fire, I had a chance to reflect on the deluge of new information that had swamped me over the past few days. Bits were starting to slot together, but my awareness still felt tentative, sketchy.

"What is this?" I asked Raul, as I turned the strange object he had given me over in my hands. Its cylindrical form fitted comfortably into a hand's grip and was about as long as the distance from my hip to my knee. One end of the cylinder swelled to an almost spherical shape, like a giant version of the flask from a Bunsen burner. The other end was flat, and the whole was covered in a snakeskin-like tessellation of tiny glass pieces.

"It's a caught-beam. It's what passes for a torch here."

"How? Do you light it? Does it burn slowly?"

"No, it doesn't burn at all. It captures light from the sun during the day, storing it here." He took it from my hand and touched the curved bulb at the end, "and giving the light back out at night, when we need it."

"Like a torch?"

"Yeah – just like a torch. Except that there aren't many places to pop out and get batteries here, so this works better for us." He smiled at me.

"We don't have as many left as we'd like," he continued. "We lost a lot when our towns and villages fell. But we have enough to spread around our group, and each band of us Free has at least a few to go around. The skin on them – look; this stuff – is sometimes all we've found when we've gone back into abandoned towns. We've got a few techno-wizards here who have managed to harness these patches of cells on the tops of our tents to provide some interior lighting. But it is these intact hand pieces that are so valuable, as we can take them out with us. And this one is for you. You need to carry it at all times, just as we do."

He handed it back to me, and I took it willingly. "Thank you."

"How many bands of The Free are there?" I asked

"In the furthest, southern reaches of Enanti – the sides furthest away from the Shadow Realm – you can still find some villages and small towns that exist pretty undisturbed. But it is only a matter of time. The black hand of the

Shadow Beast stretches over our land, and he reaches further with each passing day now. Soon that hand will close over the remotest parts of our shores, and he will drag it back towards the Shadow Realm, pulling all inside with him," Raul answered.

"But there are also many gatherings such as ours," Silas continued. Groups that live out in the woods and open land, moving on occasionally to keep themselves safe. It is a nomadic life for these people now."

"Aren't you one of these people?" I asked.

"Well, we've always lived this way." He glanced around at his brethren. "Some of us have always been nomadic, and have lived from the land around us, wherever that may be. Our lines have always relied on the forests. And now, those skills have proved invaluable for helping the villagers adapt to this life. For the past few years, we have been covering the land, looking for survivors from attacked villages, trying to persuade people to leave villages that were not yet destroyed. Our numbers have swollen. And then, more recently, we have been trying to form some kind of response; trying to find ways to fight back. Since the Beast took Alette around the time of the Fall of Albedo, we knew we had to get her back, but we were not organised enough to know what we could do. We hadn't learned yet how to defeat the Shadow Beast's forces. We were just hiding out, waiting for a turn in events. And then we gradually started to learn. We learned how to exploit weaknesses in his armies, however small those weaknesses may be. We started to feel we had a chance."

"And now?" I asked.

"Now you are here," Raul said quietly. "And that has the potential to change much. We learned from the main oracle that to save Alette, all we need to do is touch her. She is so rarely within reach; she is kept mainly in the Shadow Realms. But she has been seen here on these shores – I think, to taunt us. One of us, in a battle last year – oh damn – it was the closest we'd ever come [Raul kicked the earth with his heel], one of us got close enough to touch her. His name was Elan. He was young and brave, and he had rushed in without us close enough to protect him. He reached for her. He managed to touch her – it was extraordinary. But nothing – it didn't work. He was cut down by the Riven." Raul closed his eyes, tormented by the memory.

"So it doesn't work!" I exclaimed.

"No – we feel sure it does. We just don't understand exactly how we should do it: where might make a difference; who; when? We don't know. But we feel certain that you have a role to play here, though, again, we don't know exactly what it might be."

I felt as if I was walking into a giant puzzle to which no one had a solution – if indeed it had one at all – or by whom it had been created, or for what purpose.

"Can you all fly?" I asked.

"Only those of us who are truly ourselves. Which is all my close band, and many of the others at camp. Many people and creatures lose their ability to fly, but it can always be found again; you've proven that to yourself. But we fly rarely now – the cover of the forest helps to keep us safe, undetected. Flying above the canopy is risky with the forces of the Shadow Beast so close at hand. And we don't all specialise in flying. I am competent, but it is not my forte." He grinned at me, enjoying the shock on my face. He laughed. "Well enough to stop you crashing into the sea! But I am not like you. You are predominantly of the water and the air; you are from different elements to the ones I am from."

"But you said that we are all of the elements – so aren't we all the same?"

"No, each is unique. Yes, we are all of the elements, but those elements find a different balance in each of us. Some people just display one very strongly, others have a complete balance of all.

"I am of the earth. And you are of the sky and sea. You weren't just born to fly, Eve; you were born to really soar."

He grinned at me again, his eyes dancing. "Although it would have been tough for someone to believe that up at the cliffs this morning…"

I smiled wryly, savouring this new ease I felt when I was gently teased. "Mmm, it was quite a glorious display. It's a shame it was recorded for posterity."

"Oh, don't you worry. I have it playing on loop in my mind; I've been enjoying it all day," Raul said, nudging me gently.

I smiled, transfixed by the flames of the fire, drawing in its warmth.

"What does being from the water and air elements mean?" I asked.

"It is just a way of seeing what you already are – understanding it better, being in tune.

177

"Water is all the fluid, flowing things in the world. Even the plants are part of it, as they adapt to their environment, nudging towards the light as it changes direction down the seasons.

"Your nature allows you to quickly adapt to any situation. If you encounter force, you do not resist. You rather absorb the energy and redirect it – just like the sea. This is how you can fight best, Eve: by taking on and absorbing the energy from your enemy.

"But this energy needs to flow. You've absorbed, but not redirected. Behind the walls you'd constructed, it has built up, filling your well with unimaginable power. But that needs to find release now; it needs to inform your daily life."

"And the air part?" I asked.

"That is the most observant, creative and forward-looking of the elements. You will constantly be on the search for truth."

His words brought to mind the feelings I had experienced standing on the cliffs – wanting to leap off, take that step. I had felt an inexplicable closeness to something important there. Eternity seemed within touching distance. Some immortal truth just hanging in the air, waiting to be grasped. I hadn't grasped it then, though; I hadn't known how. I was beginning to see little cracks of light that, without showing me yet how I could, made me feel that it was at least possible. I held that thought in my mind for a while, enjoying the feel of it, the potential of it. It soothed and excited simultaneously.

I nudged him back now, still tentative in our new intimacy.

"What about you then – if you say you are mainly of the Earth?"

"I live by my instincts. I can read the signals of the birds and the animals. I listen to what the earth is telling me. I can run faster than you can imagine, and I never lose sight of what I want. Yep – that pretty much sums it up. I am part of the Earth, Eve, I come from it – and I understand it."

His words reminded me of how I felt when standing in the wind. I told him.

"That is exactly it. You feel the wind understands you, because you are part of it. You always have been. Everything you are doing here, Eve; it is helping you get back to yourself; helping you to get home."

His choice of words cut through to the centre of me. The tears blurred my vision before I even had a chance to control that emotion and bury it down. "I want to go home," I whispered.

"I know," he replied. And I knew he knew I didn't mean London. I knew he understood so much more than that.

"How did I get here?" I whispered to him.

"Through the Shifting Pools. They can take us anywhere – and you came through one when you went underwater at the swimming pool."

"So, I can change worlds when I enter these pools?" I asked Raul.

"Not just other worlds or realities, but also different parts of the world that you are already in. They are all connected, anyway - these pools simply offer a convenient fast-track."

"How do you know where you'll end up?" I asked.

"It's like everything you are learning here; you are able to control where you go, but you have to learn how to control it. That will come."

"So I can just command it?"

"No; it is much simpler than that. You just have to feel it – feel where you need to be. And if you don't know where that is, you just need to think about what you might need, and you'll be taken somewhere that you can find it."

"What if I don't know?"

"It doesn't really matter. Whether you know consciously or subconsciously, you will always be aware on some level of something that you need – and the Pool will read that.

But this is only one way to do it; there are other ways to get to where you need to go, and sometimes using these Shifting Pools is not the best way. Some things are best done slowly, best done with more conscious choice."

"What do you mean?"

"Well, if I fought my way through forests and grasslands, meeting friends and brothers along the way, listening to the tales of that land, and letting my heart become gradually clearer on what I should be doing next, I would have been on a very different journey from one in which I was suddenly dumped down into a forest where a great final battle was about to take place. Sometimes, it is that journey that is the greatest gift. It reveals more to us about our place in the world, ourselves, our motives and our values. If you fast-track things too much, you can feel disconnected from what is around you, from why you are there. As if you are in a sort of shock."

He smiled down at me then, squeezing my hand. "Sorry, Eve, I didn't mean to make this too personal."

"All of it is personal, and I'm beginning to think that's a good thing. I'm beginning to think that that is why I am here," I replied simply. "Please, don't stop."

"Ok. All I was going to say was that these sudden shifts between worlds can be unhelpful. We Free don't use the Pools too often; we always see if there is a better way to proceed first. Sometimes, the best work is done slowly. It can be the only way on occasion for us to know our true minds, to find what we really need. There is so much to treasure in the space between events and actions."

I thought of my mother's words about her beloved Enigma Variations – on how the gift and the magic is in the journey itself.

"And the Pools can be risky," Raul continued.

"I've sometimes been sent to places that really tested me. I knew there was something in those places that I needed, something I needed to learn, but they were painful experiences. We've known some who have never reappeared here. Whether they are fine and happy living elsewhere, or trapped in an endless test, we can't know for sure."

"But surely, if you are stuck or in a trap, you can just use the Pool again to get away, to go to another place you want to be?"

"Yes, you can, but it is not as simple as that. When you are in such a place, facing something that intimidates you, it can be hard to remember how you got there – and how you can get away – you are just consumed by the feat in front of you. The Pool can become so well hidden in your new reality that you can't see it, can't remember where it is. You need to find a new way to move on, get out. Or you just stay."

"But you can remind each other! Even if one of you forgets, surely the others won't!"

"Ah, but you can only go into them alone. Such is the nature of the Shifting Pools that even if you wanted to go in with another, you'd probably both be taken to slightly different places; one person's need is never exactly the same as another's. You might meet people in there who can help you, but you arrive in each place alone."

"But – there's got to be a but, surely? You do use them, don't you?" I was beginning to doubt that there was any point in using them at all – and I didn't want to think that, as I needed to know I could get back.

"Yes, but sparingly. Occasionally, just as with your coming here, we benefit from that shock of a suddenly shifted reality. It is especially helpful if we find ourselves stuck somewhere, and need a jolt to see it. From what you've told me, perhaps that is what you needed…"

I thought back to my life in London. Was my entire life there, the life I had consciously created, an endless trap? Had it happened by such slow degrees that I hadn't seen myself ossifying?

Perhaps he was right that the only real solution for a situation brought about by such shock was to treat it with another shock – another shift. Was that the only way to find a fissure into the fossilised pain, to crack that shell open again?

I leaned into Raul, his bulk and his warmth. The hairs from his cloak irritated my cheek, so I burrowed in further, pressing harder into the furs. It's funny how the same thing can affect you differently, I thought, if you only press harder. Like grasping a nettle rather than just letting it brush past your fingertips.

His arm came around me. The kiss he placed on my forehead flooded me with a sense of return. To what, I don't know, but I felt it all the same.

Shifting worlds

"How can I be sure that I can get back to London?" I asked Lara. "Raul explained the Shifting Pools to me, but how do I know I can really use them to get back, that I can control it?"

"You can consciously hold that place in your mind, and that usually does the trick. But, if your subconscious is thinking of a different place, a different need you have, then it may be holding that more powerfully. But you can start to control it more with time. And as you get to know more of your subconscious, there will be fewer surprises."

"Can I try? Just so I know I can get back?" I asked.

"It's risky, Eve. Without the proper control, you don't know where you'll end up," Lara said.

"But then how will I ever learn?"

"Touché. I'll speak to Raul."

"This isn't Raul's decision! It's mine!" I was feeling ruffled now. I didn't like feeling that my life was yet again under someone else's control. I understood that Raul was in charge here – albeit in an unspoken way. I was surprising myself. Usually I would have surveyed the terrain, and then done my best to blend in, adapt into virtual camouflage.

But I felt change coming: a restlessness in these old ways and observances. A new sap was rising in my veins, making me want to kick against anyone trying to determine my path for me.

Lara must have seen the look in my eyes. She put her hands up and smiled. "Woah – OK! Yes, I agree it is your decision, but you had best know that Raul won't like it, and we do need to speak to him about the best way to make it as safe as possible, if you are going to insist we go ahead." Then she added, "I, for one, am glad to see the fire in you, Eve. I recognised the embers of a fire that had once been burning brightly in you, as soon as I saw you. I like the fact that you have nursed them back to a little flame. They never go out entirely.

"Come – let's go and see what our Lord and Master has to say!"

We both ducked out of Lara's tent, and braced ourselves as the night air stole our breath. We found Silas and Esker sitting talking around the fire. We could ask them, I thought. That way we could avoid the Raul issue entirely.

Lara wasn't keen to circumvent Raul – I could see that in the way she sat reluctantly, casting around in the hope of finding Raul before this all went too far. I pulled on her arm encouragingly, and started to explain to Silas and Esker what I wanted to do.

"It's not your greatest idea, Eve," said Esker, bluntly.

"It's bloody stupid," added Silas. "I'm sure Lara has already explained the risks to you, and you are way off being able to have a degree of control over where you'll end up."

"I have to start somewhere," I said, feeling frustrated by this stonewalling.

"You start by learning to crawl, before you even think of running," Silas snapped back.

"If you think I don't know how to crawl – don't know a whole lot more than that – then you know nothing about me," I said directly to Silas, furious at his dismissal.

"OK, let's cool this down," Lara said. "This isn't getting us anywhere. I don't think it's a brilliant idea, either, but Eve does have the right to choose. If she wants to try getting back to London – to know she can – then we can't stop her. If she wants to go, we have to let her."

"Over my dead body," Raul's deep voice spoke quietly over my shoulder, and I twisted around to see him standing there, having heard every word.

"What right do you have to hold me here?" I shot at him, my fire up. "Am I a prisoner?"

"No – you know you're not. Have we been treating you like a prisoner?"

"Well, keeping someone in one place against their will...that smacks of prisoner to me." I felt surprised at my own words, even as they came out. I was never this confrontational. But it felt important to me, to draw my own lines in the sand.

"You are free to go anywhere," Raul gestured with his arm out towards the black night, "the forest, the grasslands, all around here. But you don't want to go anywhere; you are too scared. You are making yourself a prisoner here."

"I don't want to go out into the forest. That place is as alien to me as London is to you. You've lived here all your life; you know it; it is familiar. Right now, London is my sense of the familiar. I want to know I can get back."

"You can. That is enough to know. You will be able to. Trust me on that," Raul answered.

"Why? Why should I trust you on that? Because you think you are in charge of everything, because you have the power to make it happen, or is it because you believe you need me here for something, so my choices go out of the window because yours are more important? In my view it is a bit of the first reason, and a lot of the last. So, yes, that makes me a prisoner."

Raul looked me hard in the eye. He still hadn't come around to stand in front of us, so I was sat there, craning my neck around to argue with him. I stood up, turned my back to the fire, and faced him, waiting.

It was Lara who spoke next, gently. "Raul, you know you can't refuse to let her, if that's what she chooses. We are not about forcing people to do what we want them to do – that isn't you. That's never been you. I know how long you've anticipated her arrival here, but don't let that blind you to what is right. Please."

Raul sighed, then turned back to me and said, "I do have the power to help you get back, and I don't want to force you into something you don't want to do. I know you haven't decided if you want to help us yet. And I know that's your choice. But yes, I don't want to lose you before you've had a chance to properly see what is going on here, and what you could bring. Everything we do is to protect our land, to face the Shadow Beast, to save Alette. I'm sorry if that made me too forceful. Yes, I want you to stay,

187

and I can't make you. But I am asking you to."

I was wrong-footed. I was all prepared for a fight now, and Raul had gone and pricked the bubble of my indignation. It sagged slowly to the ground as I felt my hands unclench.

"I'm not trying to leave. I just want to know I can get back. Know for myself," I said quietly.

"Can't you just trust me on that?" Raul asked.

I thought about that. I didn't just answer automatically. "No," I said. It was honest, and I knew he would feel that.

He nodded his head slowly, sadly I thought.

"I don't want you just walking out into danger, Eve – that makes no sense. And I believe you are potentially too important to events here to allow that to happen." He raised his hands as I started to object, and continued, "I know you haven't decided to be part of this yet; I said, potentially. You still have a choice – I know that. But it makes no sense to have you step into a Shifting Pool and end up god knows where. That said, I know I shouldn't stop you." He glanced at Lara here, who nodded back. "I could, though," I think he muttered under his breath.

"What then? Will you tell me what to do? How to do it safely?" I asked, suddenly elated.

"Yes. But there is only one way we are going to do this. My way."

"What is that?" I asked.

"You're going to be linked, so you can't get lost – so you can't arrive somewhere strange and be unable to find your way back," Raul said.

Esker, Silas, Sorcha and Lara all started speaking at once, but Lara's voice cut in above the others: "No, Raul! I know what you are thinking now. No!"

"That's the only way it's going to happen," Raul said softly. "Take it or leave it."

"What? What is being linked?" I felt confused now, as if they were speaking in a code.

"I am going to link you to this place by holding on to your hand as you enter the Pool." Raul carried on, despite the others all clamouring at once, vehemently disagreeing with his plan." He silenced them with a glare, and then asked them just to trust him. Unlike me, they did.

He continued: "If you go into the Pool holding onto me, it means I can pull you back if you panic, if you end up somewhere you weren't expecting, or if you just change your mind. You just need to pull on my hand, and we can get you out of there."

"Right, that sounds like a good idea – but then why is everyone so against you doing that?"

Raul silenced them all again with one look, and then answered. "The Pools don't really like the linking. Although only a tiny part of me will be in the water with you – just my hand – it sometimes makes it less clear where you are going to go, as the Pool is reading part of me, too. That's all, but if I try to think hard of your home, too, then it should get you there."

I looked around at the stony faces of the others around me. "Is that all true?" I asked. Silas, looking thunderous at this blatant lack of trust in his brother, snapped to his feet, and strode off into the darkness, muttering under his breath.

Lara answered my question, but she, too, looked rattled.

"Well, yes, it is all true. It can be done that way." I noticed how her eyes shifted between mine and Raul's as she spoke, and she looked uncomfortable, but I felt the truth in what she said.

'When?" I asked Raul.

"Tonight," he said simply.

I beamed at him, and then at Lara, who managed to return a weak smile.

The Shifting Pool

It was only an hour or so later that we were walking quietly through the night forest. Esker, Arno, Sorcha and Lara walked with me, while Silas brooded behind us. Raul led the way. He had disappeared by himself for some time after our confrontation around the fire. When he had reappeared, he had simply told me that we were ready to set off. I was so thrilled to have achieved what I'd set out to do, that I didn't question the sombre mood of our party. We travelled with no caught-beams. The moon was nearly full that night, and Raul said we needed to retain our night vision.

The wood was alive; I felt it all around me. Not just in the haunting cry of owls that carried to us, but in the tiny rustles in the leaves to the sides of us, the calling of frogs and crickets, the scream of foxes.

At the heart of every forest is a darkness that is just waiting. You can feel it creep back in as the golden shafts of late afternoon angle lower and lower with the dying day. As the light retreats, the black crawls back, coating everything, reclaiming it for a few more hours, like the tide of the sea. Providing an utterly different world for the night creatures. When the light returns, the forest will be subtly altered: some creatures won't have made it through the night; some will have mated – new life may be on the way.

After about an hour of walking, we reached an open glade, with an inky pool glistening in its centre. Moonbeams danced on its glossy surface, and you could have mistaken it for a huge mirror laid out on the forest floor, so smooth was its glaze.

"I thought we'd be going back to the Pool in the cave – the one I came in on… I thought that would be closer," I said.

"It is. But this one is clearer. Some have more crystal water. Less sediment muddying them – they are more able to read the conscious mind. The one in the cave has cloudier water. I don't trust that one to hear your conscious thoughts so strongly," replied Raul.

"OK. What do I do now?"

"You hold onto my hand, and you get in. You jump in this time."

"Jump?"

"Yes. If you jump in quickly, they tend to listen more strongly to your main conscious thought. If you get in slowly, they have more time to read all of you – conscious or not. That can be useful sometimes, but not this time."

"Why not? Why do you think my subconscious wouldn't want me to go to London?"

"Because whether you believe it or not, your subconscious brought you here." Raul said tightly. "Now – do you want to do this or not?"

I walked up to the edge of the Pool. It was hard to believe I wouldn't shatter the surface, it looked so solid, glinting there. Raul knelt by the edge of the Pool and held up his hand to me. I looked at it, then took it tentatively.

"You need to hold it tightly, Eve. I'm trying to help you." He sounded weary, and he kept his head down. But his hand held mine tightly. "Remember, if you find yourself somewhere unexpected, just pull on my hand; I can bring you out. Just don't take too long, OK?"

I nodded, even as I wondered about his last comment.

He continued. "And this is just to prove to yourself that you can, OK? As soon as you see yourself in London, as soon as you've satisfied that need, then again, just tug on my hand and I'll bring you out. Don't let go, under any circumstances. OK? Just see what you need to see, then come back. And please, don't take too long."

"Don't let go; don't take too long. I've got it." I stepped right up to the Pool's lip, where grass became liquid glass. I paused for a moment, and then I leapt in.

Icy water chilled through my body, and electricity seemed to flow up and down my length, as if something was assessing every part of me, drinking me in. I felt Raul's hand tighten its grip as I started being sucked down. Water roared in my ears. So many images flooded past my eyes – it was like seeing some of my own thoughts put up on the big screen and played out for me. Was this the Pool reading what I wanted? I tried to keep the image of the swimming pool in my mind, to hold onto it, as I also fought to hold on to Raul's grasp.

Slowly the curtains of water looked as though they were

receding – I could start to see through them, start to see the shadowy outlines of my local leisure centre. But then the scene changed suddenly. As the waters parted and their noise receded, I saw the forest around me, and the silhouette of a man in moonlight standing in front of me, completely naked, and holding out his arms to me. I stepped towards him, as the moonlight caught his face and revealed Raul. I looked down and I was holding his hand.

I gasped, shuddering inwardly from this reality, stepping back hastily into the clamour of the water, and pulling on the hand that held me. I didn't know which version of Raul was holding my hand; I was completely confused. I just knew I wanted to get away. And as I felt that hand start pulling me out, I caught a glimpse of the swimming pool through the watery curtains to the side of me as I was being hauled up. I tugged back, incoherently angry that the hand pulling me back belonged to the scene that I was trying to get away from. I pulled suddenly with all my might to step through the skeins of water separating me from the tiled whiteness of the pool, and I succeeded in stepping through. Raul's grip was insistent on my hand - I could tell he was concerned, but I didn't care. I was thrown by the reality I had been taken to. I didn't want it.

Although I could feel Raul's drive pulling me back, I could also feel his strength failing. That surprised me, but I felt angry, and scornful – and I wanted his hold over me to diminish. So I pulled hard on my hand, deliberately twisting my arm to release myself from his anchor-point. My hand jerked free, and I thought I heard a cry high above me, as the swirl of waters rushed and receded behind me and I was left suddenly silent, floating on my back in the swimming pool, my ears just under water, staring up at the ceiling.

It took many minutes for me to settle my breathing. I was deeply shaken. I couldn't accept that any part of me would have taken me to that first place I had glimpsed. And when I reasoned that perhaps it wasn't my subconscious that had done it, but Raul's – then that didn't help settle me, either.

I suddenly hoisted my body upright, treading water, for all the world like I had done after a thousand reveries in the past. My hand whipped around to my back, feeling for something there. Nothing. No budding wings, no rupturing growth – just my scar, familiar and knotted.

Doubt

Sometimes, when I look in the mirror, I get the strangest sense; it's as if I don't know which one is me.

She does what I do, but she isn't real. I feel like her sometimes; just mirroring the actions of those in front of me.

Does she have nightmares, there inside the glass? There is something in her eyes. And then I'm not sure whether the glass between us is trapping her in, or keeping me out.

I feel encased in glass, as if I were dipped in liquid glass a long time ago. It muffles everything, but I can still see it all happening. I think sometimes, that if I hit myself hard enough against a surface, if I fall from somewhere really high, perhaps that glass will break, the mirror will crack and the pieces fall away. And I can get out.

* * *

I couldn't stop thinking about my dream. I couldn't help wondering if it had been a dream at all. It felt so real. I looked around at the poolside, half-expecting to see a caught-beam lying on the tiled floor. Of course there wouldn't be – we hadn't taken any to the Shifting Pool. What am I even thinking? I thought to myself; there is no Shifting Pool; there are no caught-beams!

I resolved simply to get back into normal life as if nothing had happened. Nothing had happened, I reminded myself! I felt confused, though, as I climbed from the pool, motioning to Marni that I was heading for the changing rooms. My mind was literally in another place. It was a Sunday morning, I told myself, and I just had to let it go.

Once we had headed home to Marni's, and Peter was engrossed in a game, I told her about my dream, and she listened intently.

"Woah, Evie, it sounds pretty complex – like a whole world. Although I'm not surprised with the amount of reading you've done recently on all this stuff. It's bound to play out in your mind somehow."

"You're right – I hadn't thought about it like that. That's probably exactly what Claire will say, too."

"What else did you think she would say?"

"Nothing. Well, it just…no…it's just…it felt so different from my normal dreams. God, it felt real!"

"Well that's a good thing! Maybe it's showing how much has changed for you; showing you that everything you've been trying is bearing fruit...?"

"Yes, you're right. That must be it." I reached across the table and found Marni's hand for myself. She seemed surprised, but so pleased. "Marni, if there is anyone in this world I want to be linked with, it's you. I want you to know that. Every time I've felt like I was lost, it was being linked to you that kept me here, kept me safe. Thank you.

197

Thank you for holding on to me." My voice was almost fierce from the passion I felt at that moment. I had never really appreciated the way that Marni had always held my hand. I'd never really thought about how that might have cost her, what effort it would have taken. "Thank you," I said, quietly now.

Tears were rolling down Marni's cheeks, and she quickly brushed them away and smiled at me, embarrassed. "What are you talking about sweetie? I will always be there for you. I love you – you know that."

"Yes, yes I do. And it means the world. I love you too."

Marni was right. Claire did read the dream the same way. A quest was typical, she said, a perfect symbol of our need to find something precious. And saving Alette was deeply linked to my guilt over Laila. Even I had known that, as I was dreaming.

"That might be the key to unlocking all of this," she had said to me. "That need you feel for redemption."

I left feeling strangely unsatisfied, though. As if I had known something that was now covered over. The shape of it was still there in my mind, but I couldn't make out what was under the cloth. Something flickered just out of reach of my conscious thought. Every time I looked towards it, I saw it less, like looking at the stars at night. You need to look to the side of a bright object in the dark, to see it more clearly.

I lay back in the bath the following weekend, facing the long French window. It was elegant and soaring, from floor to ceiling. The thin blind was pulled down halfway, to meet the frosted bottom panel of glass in the door. It was discreet, private and liberating. The day was full of dancing sunlight. Light oozed through the thin blind, filling the bathroom, and creating a gentle, pulsating ambience that bathed me. It was alive and nourishing.

As I lay in the warm water, it was this light that washed me. With the thin blind acting as a form of barrier, the scene acquired some anonymity. I felt transported – transposed? The rumble of traffic outside became a stabbingly familiar part of my childhood – alive and part of me. The sound of chatter and laughter, cars droning past, horns tooting, all connected me suddenly to another place. I closed my eyes and let the long-lost familiarity flow through me.

My eyelids were another blind, but also a passage down to a shuttered part of me. The sounds from outside were soothing, comforting, like a homecoming. How could I have stayed away so long? How can I ever get back? With my eyes closed, I felt the sensual touch of the sun, bright on my skin, bleaching out the façade – claiming me back. The sun spoke to me: "I know who you are. I've always known you. It is all OK. You are known.

"I've been waiting for you to come back and embrace me again. I am always here. And you have always been here."

It was a kindness, a warmth, an acceptance, a welcome home. A sense of something infinite and permanent, just waiting for me to be ready. I felt choked with emotion – it was so incredibly intimate. As the sun stroked my skin, I was a little girl in the stark heat of the desert again. The little girl was still there, always there, being carried onwards in the vessel of my changed body. Still innocent, still unviolated, still completely accepted and loved. And the sun understood why I had hidden away. Its gentle stroking fingers carried no blame, just a blissful recognition of ME, me inside me – the most perfect recognition. It would always know me, however I hid, and would silently watch me through my journey from childhood to old age. Letting me know that, decades on, I was still there. I was in the world.

The emotional impact was overwhelming. It had a sense of the sacred to it. I felt so deeply grateful for that moment, that gift, that sense of understanding – given and received.

I also had the strangest, urgent sense that this wasn't where I needed to be. As I lay in the bath, my eyes caught the little pouch on the chair next to me, along with my discarded clothes. My sea glass. I loved the little pouch that Marni had made for me; stitched lovingly in the softest leather, it felt creamy to the touch. I usually wore it around my neck, but tried to take it off for baths.

I reached out my arm and quickly dried my hands on the towel, before I picked it up. As I slipped the sea glass out into my waiting palm, something followed it out. A little piece of paper, folded over and over. A tiny scrap that made my heart race. My fingers shook as I unfolded the scrap, knowing even as I did it what I would find in the centre. I hadn't dreamed it. I hadn't been going mad.

I sat there in the water for a long while, staring at Sula's precious note. So much flooded through me, and I let it come. My mind was full; I wanted to go back. I felt no fear – I knew now that I could come back here at any time. But somehow, by being here, I had forgotten about Enanti, and I was suddenly aware that I needed to see that through. I thought of Raul's hand, trying to hold me safe.

I had pulled away from him, had thought he was trying to control me, but I realised now that I could have let go at any time – as indeed I had – and that he had simply been doing what he had said he would: giving me a safe way back if I had wanted it. I hadn't at the time; I had wanted to run away, and now I didn't really know how to get back. I knew that there must be a way, and I knew that it would have something to do with water.

I still didn't know how I would face Raul – not just because I hadn't trusted him, but mainly because I would find it hard to look him in the eye. Whether that first world I had nearly entered in the Shifting Pool had been my own subconscious or his, I didn't want to examine too closely. I just wanted to throw myself into saving Alette. Raul and I could just get along; we didn't need anything more. I had Lara there, and others to help me. I didn't need Raul.

I wondered whether anything could be used as a Shifting Pool? I remembered back to all the times I had felt an odd tingling when I had been in the water. What was the variable, though? What had caused me to Shift those times and not others? I had a thought, and I wanted to try it out. But I also wanted to be prepared, just in case it actually worked. So I quickly leaped out of the bath, pulled on some clothes, and grabbed my pouch with its precious contents. Then I climbed back into the water, took a deep breath, and slowly lowered myself full-length under the water. I knew the second the water closed over my head that I was right; I felt the grasping pull from beneath me, and I was sucked down.

Connection

I was slammed back into another reality; I was back in Enanti. All the breath had been pushed from my body as the swirl of water had spat me out. And I knew something important then: I wanted to be here. All parts of me had conspired to bring me here this time – I hadn't even seen any other worlds through the water; this was all I could think of.

I was face down, sodden, by the edge of the same Shifting Pool I had stepped into just a few days ago. God! Was it a few days ago here, though? I hadn't even thought about that in my desire to get back here. I didn't fully understand how time worked between these places. Time had become a far more elastic concept to me. I pushed myself up on my hands and knees, exhausted by the shift of worlds. I watched as drips from the Pool travelled down my hair, which hung in front of me like a patchy curtain. The drips bulged at the tips of my hair, desperately trying to hang on, but being pushed from behind. And then they fell, so suddenly, and sank back into the earth.

I knew the way. I wasn't sure how, but I was aware that I knew. After less than an hour I walked straight back into camp. It was just the same. I felt a wave of relief that I had been holding at bay until now. Familiar faces were walking past. Most of them smiled and seemed pleased to see me, but a few looked concerned, and hurried on their way. It was unsettling; I wasn't sure what had been going on while I'd been gone. I couldn't have been gone for long; everything looked so familiar, and I knew that Raul would have ordered the camp to move on as normal if I'd been gone more than a week or so.

I looked around for him, his friends, Lara, Sula, but I couldn't see them anywhere.

"I'm amazed you decided to show your face again," someone ground out behind me. I didn't need to turn around to know it was Silas.

"Why wouldn't I?" I countered, already weary that we were falling back into the same patterns.

"After what you did? You really need to ask?"

I felt an unease creep over me. What had I done? I sensed that Silas really meant it; something was seriously wrong.

"What is it? What's happened?"

"You really don't know! He asked you to do one simple thing. He even asked for your word on it, which you gave. Which you broke. Which he is paying for. I for one am not glad to see you back here."

"Where is Raul?" I managed to say through a mouth that had seized up on me. Something was very very wrong here. "What do you mean about him paying for something?"

I hardly dared ask. My mind was working furiously as my body shut down, trying to think what all this meant. And then I got it. Raul had asked me not only to be quick,

203

but to promise not to let go. Was that it? I thought that had just been his way of exerting control over me, and I hadn't given it much thought. And anyway, if he was just single-mindedly obsessed about having me here to help save Alette, then I was back; no harm done.

"I came back, didn't I? That's all Raul wanted; and here I am." I spoke more confidently now, annoyed that I was somehow in trouble for something that just seemed like a bit of lost pride.

"You have no idea. Do you think that is all? Do you think it was just about keeping you here? That he linked to you just for his benefit?" Silas was really angry now. I could see the colour rising in his face, and the vein on his right temple starting to protrude as he glared at me.

"What, then? No – I don't really understand. But that's not surprising given that none of you really tells me anything. I'm apparently meant to work it all out for myself. So, no, I don't know what's going on, or really what I've done. Where is he? Where is Raul? I need to talk to him."

I hadn't planned to talk to Raul, in fact I had a sketchy plan before coming here that I would keep some distance between us. I felt awkward and embarrassed, and wondered how much he had seen of the world I had seen. But now my senses were on alert. Something was wrong, and I needed to see him. I repeated myself: "I need to talk to him."

"You're not going anywhere near him. I think you've done enough damage."

"What! What is going on? Where is he?"

"He is in there with Lara, in her bed. Where else would he be?"

"Oh." It made perfect sense, but I still felt like a blade had been pushed into me. Why? I tried to shake the feeling off. They were both my friends; why should this bother me in any way?

"Well, I'll talk to him when they've, well...you know... after...when they've finished – not busy, I mean," I said in a rush, and turned sharply and walked off, leaving Silas looking after me, shaking his head.

I sat alone on the very edge of the camp, resting on a low branch. My elation from the morning, from finding my way back, had dissipated. I felt resentful at Silas's welcome, confused about what I had done wrong, but more than anything, thrown off balance completely about the idea of Raul and Lara being together. I was bewildered by the storm of dark feelings that it had unleashed inside me. I didn't feel as if any of them belonged to me. I didn't want anything to happen between me and Raul – I knew that even the possibility of that, seen in the Shifting Pool, had sent me running for cover; literally tearing our hands apart. So what was it, then? Was I jealous? Of whom? Was I jealous because Raul was my friend, or because Lara was? I really didn't know, and the more I tried to untangle the knots swirling inside me, the more distracted I felt.

Raul was not someone I would ever get involved with. I had very strict rules surrounding relationships and sex, and he didn't fit any of them. The rules were there to protect me, and they worked. I had never wanted real intimacy with a man – on some level, I suppose I feared them all, where they could put me. I would never be put on my knees by a man again.

I hated the idea of a man protecting me, controlling me, feeling I was his. So I made sure it never happened. Sex was empty – a quick fix – meaningless. The few brief relationships I had had were just more of the same, each of us finding a use in the other temporarily: a date for a big function, a trophy for an important work do, or simply a body to fulfil sexual needs as and when. It wasn't the healthiest approach, but it worked for me.

And Raul didn't fit this type. He was too aware, too observant of me for me ever to feel comfortable with him in that realm. Silas, possibly – he didn't care one bit about me; had no curiosity beyond the needs of one night. (Silas! Where had that thought come from! But I could see it. He had such a low opinion of me that I knew sex would work with him. It would be so easy to hate him.) But not Raul. I wanted him firmly in the friend box, the androgynous box, and I couldn't understand why the lid wouldn't close properly.

Or was it Lara? Did I feel less safe, knowing that my confidences with her may be shared with another, someone closer to her?

I was pulled from my thoughts by the sight of Lara hurrying off into the forest, a basket under her arm. She startled when she caught sight of me, then rushed over to give me a hug.

"Oh Eve, thank goodness. I was so worried about you. I'm so glad you are back!"

'You seem to be the only one!" I replied.

"Oh, I'm sorry! Have you seen some of the others already? I didn't know you were back; I've been so busy. Silas is in a particularly black mood."

"Yes. But I don't understand why. Umm…um…well, he told me about you and Raul. Is that why?"

"What did he tell you?" Lara asked, surprised. "I'm surprised that Silas was forthcoming; I thought he'd just enjoy torturing you."

"He um, he just told me that you and Raul were… er…busy…you know, together in your tent. That's why I didn't come looking for you. I didn't want to walk in on anything!" I tried to sound lighthearted and jokey, but failed abysmally.

Lara shook her head, took a deep breath and sighed. "How about you come with me, and we can talk as we go?"

I nodded, and slipped down from my branch, which bobbed up and down a few times, pleased to be free of my weight once more.

"Where are you off to?" I asked.

"I need certain plants – medicine."

"Is someone ill?"

"Oh Eve, it's probably best coming from me, but yes: Raul."

I felt the blood in my veins run icy cold.

"He's not doing too well." Lara spoke gently, looking at my face carefully the whole time. "That's why he is in my tent. The only reason," she said carefully. "So I see that Silas was actually torturing you after all," she added, under her breath.

"What happened?" I whispered.

"Oh damn. You're going to feel worse once I've told you, but you should know. You could probably see that the rest of us weren't thrilled by Raul's idea to link with you in the Shifting Pool."

'I just thought you all wanted him to let me be free to come and go as I wished – to respect my choices. wasn't that it?"

"No, Eve. He did that for you, not himself. He was worried that you would end up somewhere you weren't ready for, that could do you harm. Yes, he wants to keep you here – but he would never have forced it.

"He did it to keep you safe - so he could get you out. But any form of linking in the Pools has a cost. That's why we didn't like the plan. The longer you stayed in there, linked to him here, the higher the cost. It literally sucks away your strength. It can only be done for a short time. The energy needed to keep him rooted here, while you Shifted, is enormous. Part of him was between worlds, fighting to remain in this one. We knew it would wipe him out."

I could feel the blood leaving my face, awareness circling close by, ready to land.

"He knew that would happen...? And he did it..?" I wasn't really asking. Lara nodded.

"We thought he had judged it right. We weren't happy with the idea, but it was his choice. And we knew he'd be careful. Get the parameters somewhere he knew he could handle. That's why he made you promise to keep linked to him at all costs..."

"No!" My mind shot back to the moment that I had tried to get my hand loose from his. I had felt it then, the strength leaving his grip, and I had revelled in it, as I had twisted my way free of his hold. I hadn't known. I hadn't known!

"What have I done to him?" My voice was thin, reedy, someone else's.

"He is really weak, Eve." Lara placed her hand on my arm as she spoke. "But we are doing everything we can."

"Tell me." I whispered, desperate to know.

"He collapsed by the Shifting Pool when you broke your hand free from his. He could feel you trying to, and he fought hard to keep hold, but he was already weak by then, and he couldn't contend with both you and the Pool trying to separate you. We carried him back here – it was about a week ago. He wasn't conscious, but he is now coming to the surface every so often, and I am hopeful. He keeps asking for you, and every time we've had to tell him that you haven't come back, he has retreated again, back into darkness. He blames himself. He thought you were stranded somewhere, suffering."

I felt sick. I couldn't comprehend what this man had done for me, and what I had done to him. I felt as if I had stabbed him in the back.

"I'm afraid that that's how Silas sees it," Lara said quietly. She had the same unnerving way as Raul of reading the direction of my thoughts.

"Will he be OK? He's got to be OK...I..."

"I'm doing everything I can, Eve. And it may help him to know that you are back. I'm so glad that you are back!" She threw her arms around me, half crying now. "It's not your fault. You weren't to know; someone should have told you."

"But I promised him, and then I broke it."

"Yes. But you did that without knowing the cost. And that makes a difference."

She pulled me along with her now, keen to find the plants she needed from the forest. She explaining the purpose of each, as we filled her basket with white willow, meadowsweet, black elder and yarrow.

The light was starting to fail now, and we had no caught-beams on us. The animals of the twilight were starting to stir, making the forest come alive with different sounds.

We headed straight for Lara's tent as we entered camp. I saw immediately that Esker, Koni and Silas were standing guard outside, and I assumed that Arno and the others would be inside, or nearby. They moved out of the way automatically to allow Lara to enter, but as I tried to follow, Silas put his body between the tent and me, forcing me to smack into him.

"You are going nowhere near him!" he growled, looking down at me.

"This is ridiculous!" Lara exclaimed as she came back out of the tent. "She is coming in with me. This is my tent."

"And you have our man in there, vulnerable. She's not going in," Silas countered.

Lara turned in appeal to the others.

"This is crazy! Eve isn't the one to blame here! She had no idea what the linking would do!

"Wait!... Or any idea what breaking her promise would lead to," she said directly to Silas, to halt his interruption.

"She still broke it though," Silas said, refusing to remove his bulk from my path.

"Yes, I did." I said. "I broke it, and I'm so sorry. If I could go back and undo that, I would. But I can't. I had no idea what could happen. I thought he was just trying to keep me here, by making me promise."

"Then you don't know Raul at all." Silas shot back. "Were you always planning to break free of his grip then, as soon as you were in the Pool? Were you lying as soon as the promise crossed your lips?"

"No! Really, I wasn't. I was going to hold on, but…I saw…No. Look – I just panicked. OK?"

Lara gave me a thoughtful look, and I hoped fervently that she couldn't read this one from me right now. I didn't want her knowing what reality I had been taken to first. I didn't even want to think about it myself. If it had been a nameless man in that reality, I would have used Raul's hand to pull me back. But how could I have used this hand as an anchor, when it was the same man I was running from? Lara was still looking at me curiously, so I forced my mind to stop the run of images through my head.

"Please." Lara spoke directly to Silas. "She didn't want any of this, any more than we did. And you know if you are being honest, that it will help Raul to know she has come back. Otherwise it was all for nothing, in his mind."

"Best that she had never come back, and just let him get over this, over her…" Silas muttered, almost to himself, but his hulking frame started to move to the side. Before he moved fully though, he shot his arm hand out and gripped my upper arm – painfully hard.

"You ever betray him again, no fucking world will be safe enough for you to run from me."

He meant it. His eyes burned down into mine, and his words were branded on to me. Then, just as abruptly, he released my arm and stepped off to the side, causing me to stumble forward and clutch at the tent.

I walked in slowly, dreading what I was about to see, needing to see it. Raul lay on a bed in the middle of the dimly lit room, piled with furs and quilts from his chest down. His eyes were closed, and his lashes rested on hollowed cheeks, that looked as if they had had their life sucked out of them. He was so pale, his skin, usually so coloured from his outdoor life, was almost translucent. He looked waxy and unreal. I stepped closer, reaching out my hand to his face, as if to convince myself.

He looked like a ghost of the man he'd been. I had a sudden shocking image of myself as I had appeared arriving in England all those years ago – a little ghost. Was that what had happened to me when I had finally crawled out of my brother's arms? Had I been using every ounce of strength I had to keep him rooted into my reality, with me? I know we had been linked in such a primitive way, beyond choice, beyond understanding – and the need to keep that link had been agonising. Once I had realised that he was gone, that he no longer walked the same world as I did, I had admitted defeat, my strength gone, and I had climbed out of his embrace. He wasn't there any more. He had left his beautiful face, his gentle hands. His body was just a shell.

Had I been like this ever since that day? Utterly spent, on

the brink of life? Is this what I would have looked like to anyone who had really seen me? My eyes closed, my lashes fanned out on my pale cheeks, my body barely breathing? A 20-year coma?

Lara went around to the other side of the bed. She busied herself by laying out all the plants we had gathered on her table at the back of the tent, working quickly to chop, knead and crush the ingredients. The tent was suffused with fragrance, so thick you could almost see it hanging there in the beams of dusty light from the dim lamps.

As she worked I simply stood there by his bed, my fingers gently touching his shoulder. It felt so wrong, wrong in every way. Even the power dynamic of me standing over him like this felt wrong – reinforcing my betrayal. So I knelt by the bed, relieved to find some small way to retreat from the imbalance between us. His current fragility was palpable. It was there in the weakness of his breath, the effort needed for the rise and fall of his chest as he slept, and it broke my heart. I had done this.

A whole host of emotions crowded in on me, and the air turned sticky. I had been trying to do what Raul had kept encouraging me to do – choose for myself, understand what was going on inside me, act on it more – but somehow I had got it all horribly wrong. I wanted to shrink back into doing what was expected, what was safe, what always worked.

Lara then moved quietly to the other side of Raul's bed. She held a carved-out wooden drinking bowl, cupped in her hand. With her medicine ready, she started gently trying to rouse Raul from his sleep. His head turned reluctantly towards the gentle pressure she was exerting on his other shoulder, and his eyes flickered open, away from me. Lara smiled down at him.

"You've got a visitor," she said.

He looked confused for a second, and then slowly turned his head back in my direction. He blinked a couple of times, and then a slow smile spread on his face. His lips looked cracked and dry, but he moistened them before he tried to speak.

"You are OK! And you are here. You came back!" His voice was barely more than an exhalation, but it was beautiful to hear. I could only nod dumbly, over and over.

"Did you get to London? Is that where you went?" he whispered huskily.

I nodded again, and was rewarded with a smile.

"Thank goodness," he said, as he closed his eyes and settled his head straight on the pillow.

I touched his shoulder again so lightly, needing the contact. "Thank you," I said. "I'm so sorry, but thank you."

He opened his eyes again and smiled at me. "I can't say it was a pleasure. But I would do it again. It's OK, Eve."

I tried to smile back, but it felt very skewed and I couldn't control it properly.

"You don't know how good it is to see you. That you came back. So good. Worth it." He winced as he bit the words out, and Lara moved back in to end the conversation, and get the medicine into him. As I watched her cradle his head to help him sit more upright to drink, I suddenly felt as if I was intruding, so I slipped away.

He made steady progress from then on, gaining strength

every day, looked after unstintingly by Lara and his friends. They truly were his family, I thought, as I watched them tend to him. I went in to see him on a few occasions, and he always seemed pleased to see me, though I had the uneasy sense that I was infringing on some family intimacy. Yet, he did nothing to lend any weight to that feeling, always asking me to sit with him and talk for a while. He seemed lighter in spirit as the days went past – almost strangely so – and I noticed that he smiled and laughed often, with his eyes as well.

Lara caught me looking at him as he chatted casually to his friends, who had crowded into the too-small tent to see him en masse, as they tended to do in the evenings. She came up just behind me, and whispered in my ear: "I told you that it would do him good to see you..." and I felt a little nudge from her elbow as she smiled behind me.

I didn't know what to make of it, but I delighted in his recovery. I had started to realise just what a friend I had in him. I was humbled by what he had done for me, still eaten up with remorse at what I had done to him, but the wonder of the care he had shown to me was the main feeling to which I kept returning. Only Marni, I knew, and perhaps Lara, now, would have done something of that magnitude for me. All my frames of reference were having to be reassessed and drawn up anew.

Finding a place

For 20 years I had known the shape of the socket I should fit into. I just couldn't get myself into the correct shape. I could shave off bits here and there – enough to allow me to slip in – but it was never a good fit, and staying there was grinding work. The grating feel of bone scraping on bone.

Here, I had a place. A place that I moved in perfectly. I hadn't felt it to start with, but now, slipping in without pain or effort, it felt amazing. A bit like how I would imagine being at home. I had no idea what this place was, or where it would take me, but a place is a place. I'd take that for now.

It was weeks later that Raul was well enough to be out of bed, walking carefully around the camp, trying to get back into the rhythm of normal life. It felt like a gift to have him back around the campfire in the evenings, watching him smile at the stories told, and laugh at the jokes made. He had a stillness about him that I had missed so much. Although his whole body quivered with life again, and I had seen how decisive and physical he could be when out hunting, this was the core of the man – this immensely powerful stillness. He always watched, assessed and then

216

acted. He never rushed in.

I could almost see him tasting the air, listening to his gut, cocking his head to hear.

One evening, I found myself sitting next to him around the fire. It was one of the first times we had had to speak in relative privacy. I needed to thank him; I wanted him to see how much it had all meant to me. I wanted to give him something of mine.

"I wanted to tell you that I've decided to stay," I said to him quietly. "I don't know if your faith in me is wildly misplaced, but I am willing to stay and see. I'm sorry if it is; sorry if I let you down."

"Are you sure?" Raul asked.

"Yes," I said, directly into his eyes. The flames crackled and popped a small distance from us, throwing up golden flecks in his eyes as he looked at me.

"You need to stop worrying about letting me down. It can't be about that."

"I know. I want to stay for my own reasons, and there are many, but that is part of it, I suppose."

Raul nodded slowly, seeming happy with my answer. It was honest at least. Then he turned and caught me in his gaze again.

"Why did you pull away from me in the Shifting Pool?" he asked quietly.

I sucked in my breath. I wasn't ready for this conversation. Back in London, I had prepared a few stock answers that I could throw him off with, but with what had happened since my return, all of them seemed too trite, too dishonest. Yet I couldn't tell him the truth, either. I wasn't ready for that sort of exchange. I never would be. I pulled my eyes away from his, and stared at the ground, feeling his assessing gaze on me the whole time. I had no idea what he had seen, no idea whether what I had seen came from me or…or both of us? I was utterly wrong-footed.

"I…I just didn't want to feel controlled by you. I wanted to choose to be here on my own terms; that's all – just like you'd told me," I managed to get out. "I didn't understand why you were holding onto me. I thought it was just so I wouldn't be able to get away. I knew that you badly wanted me to stay here to help you, and I thought that was why you did it. It was just a childish reaction to being told what to do. I'm sorry."

Raul kept looking at me. I could feel his eyes resting on my profile, but I couldn't look up and meet them.

After what seemed like minutes, he just said, "OK."

I couldn't tell whether he believed me, or whether he was simply aware that I couldn't say any more on the subject – that I wanted to run from it and never have it mentioned again. I was good at that. It actually worked. If you tried hard enough to bury something, the rubble only slipped every so often. Most of the time, you could even be surprised to find it there.

The next few weeks were a happy time. I had chosen to be here, and that in itself made everything feel different: more poignant, more personal. I started to feel more useful around the camp, even welcomed on some short trips out into the forest to collect necessities. My conversations with Raul were factual, friendly, but had a certain distance to them that I found helpful, familiar. I wondered whether

218

he was doing it deliberately – not pushing me further than I could go at any given time. I asked him more about what it was he believed I could do. It seemed to revolve around some belief in my senses, which apparently had the potential to be more acute than anyone's in the camp. It was this more than anything that made me think that someone had made a big mistake, and I worried about it. I had deliberately blunted my senses over many years. There was a thick layer of glass between me and the rest of the world.

He also thought that my potential for flight, sensory input and swimming outstripped anyone in the camp. But beyond all that, he believed, without any clear guidance or evidence, that somehow I was pivotal to saving Alette – that I had some particular ability to save her, although he didn't understand that himself.

My wings were large now, which I found exhilarating. I hadn't attempted to fly since my failed flight up on the cliffs with Raul, but I somehow knew that things would be different next time. I needed to try. If I was resolved to be here, to see this through, I needed to see what I could do. I needed to try to reach some of these potentials. I started to think I could.

The colours of people's wings seemed to be based around family lines. Raul's were the colours of a hawk – hues of ochres, sepias and burnt umbers – all mottled through. Those of his close band were similar, ranging in their depth of colour, but sharing the same palette. I didn't actually often get the chance to see them, as they rarely showed their wings, rarely took flight at all.

It was easier with Lara and some of the other villagers in the camp. Her wings were very pale – almost white – a trait she had shared with her family. Most of the other people had wings in hues of grey and silver, again, all differing slightly between the individuals of various nuclear families. One family, however, had purple feathers mixed in through the grey – their wings were magnificent. Children differed slightly from their parents, showing a mix between the prominent colours of both sides, but ending up with a pattern and hue entirely their own. As individual as fingerprints.

My own burgeoning wings fascinated me. Their colours were like nothing I had seen here. They were dark, glossy. It was only when the sunlight caught them, that their true nature was revealed. They shone with iridescent indigo, teal, turquoise and cobalt. A couple of times it had seemed as if some violet hues were also in there, as when the light hits a drop of petrol in a puddle, or the hidden majesty of a starling's feathers is exposed by the sun.

I loved them, loved the impending sense of freedom they gave me, loved the act of growing them. And I loved their rich colour, although it also made me acutely aware of my lack of any family. They functioned as a very obvious signal to all who saw me that I had no family here.

"Can you change the colour of your wings?" I wondered aloud. "Does the colour signify anything? Do they change as you change?"

"No," Raul replied. "The colour is yours forever. It makes no distinction between good and evil, right and wrong, light or shade. It is the colour you were born with,

220

it doesn't make you who you are. It simply signals where you came from. The rest is up to you."

That answer satisfied me. I'd been struggling with the idea of destiny – everything being pre-ordained. I had worried that the colour of your wings, in some strange way, controlled your path in life, highlighting your inner self, your deepest intentions. But it was simply a way to show kinship – nothing more important than sharing your mother's hair colour; nothing less important than bringing something of the past into the future.

"But what about the Craven? You've mentioned that they all have red wings. Why? I don't get that. Surely, if they are the lost, as you say they are, they would all have different colours, have come from different places."

"That is true," Raul said. "They did all come from different places, for different reasons. They are the lost souls, those who have donned the mask permanently, and fight for the Shadow Beast. He is their master now; they have no will of their own. When they give themselves over to him, they have already lost their wings. The sadness is that there will be a million different stories about how that came to be – each one intimate and personal to that one. But once they have reached this stage, Eve, they have chosen a different path. Their wings are gone, and they chose to find wings again under the Shadow Beast."

"What do you mean? They all get the chance to regrow them again, as I've done? That's a good thing, surely?"

"No, their wings are not real; they haven't regrown. The Shadow Beast takes them and he grafts these wings on to their backs. They are made from the blood of others who

221

have lost their wings. They shine bright with that blood. And they are grafted onto these soldiers; theirs but not theirs. They can fly, but it is very mechanical, awkward, unnatural. They only ever fly as a last resort. And they all know that these wings are not their own; they belong to the Shadow Beast, and he can take them back at any time, offer them to another who pleases him more. He hacks them off, and they are once again wingless, flightless.

"Most Craven are not people any more, Eve. They are the parts of people that remain after all is lost. The shadows that remain when a person has not only given up trying to save him or herself, but has now died. The darkness created by such things coalesce into these shapes, forever trying to find their way back, searching for some form of peace. If they were still people, they could still be saved, they could still find a way. There is always a way back, however far down the road you have gone. But these are the shades of people; the ghosts that remain. Yet they retain a power in their darkness, in the pathos you will feel. Unmasking them allows the truth of them to be seen, and there is a peace in that for them. They cease to be. They are discontent, yearning, loss and void. When that is exposed, they find their rest.

"Just occasionally, you will see one of them wearing his or her own wings still. They are those who have come to the Shadow Beast for a multitude of reasons, and have offered themselves to him, with their own wings. They usually have damaged flight – their wings are dying. Some don't lose the ability to fly abruptly, they go into a long decline. And some people then choose to follow the Shadow Beast

– to gift him what remains of their flight in return for his power, his ability to lend some strength to their wings once more. But they are also the most complex. Rather than being ghosts, they still have the person within them – they can still choose another way. They are a hope, even though they feel hopeless. Once unmasked, they can go either way. Be wary of them, but be compassionate, too. That's all they know now. But they weren't always that way. Life has brought them to such a pass. Any one of us could be in their position. Don't make the mistake of thinking you are above it. None of us is."

* * *

A few nights after this exchange, Raul found me standing alone beneath the trees, staring out into the dark of the forest.

"What is it?" he asked.

"I don't know, really. Just a strange feeling of being hemmed in. I love to retreat to the safety of these woods; it feels as if they hold me. But I am feeling restless, like I need to be in a wide open space."

"That is completely normal. You are from elements more open than this. You can rest here, but to feel truly alive you need to feel the sky or the sea – and it's been a while since we've done that. We camped here longer than we normally do, because I needed the time to recover, but we will be back to moving on every few days from now on. With the forces of the Shadow Beast at large in the land now, It is too risky to stay in one place for too long."

"But I do feel at home in these woods, so I don't know why I'm feeling like this."

"You can feel at home anywhere. One day I hope you really feel that – not know it, but feel it. Not like you are masquerading somewhere, but that you are fully alive, in each place. And that will happen if you let it. As long as you have a balance; do enough of what you need to feel alive."

The Sea Holds Dreams

I watched as the sea stroked the wet shore, over and over. As I looked more closely, I saw things that had been washed up in the strandline, left in that place between sea and land. Strange things: an old photograph, a doll, sheet music, a ring. I couldn't understand. From a distance I hadn't seen them – but here, up close, there were items all along the beach. Things I knew, from somewhere far off.

The sea holds our dreams, and washes our shoreline with them.

I came like Water, and like Wind I go.

Omar Khayyam

Meeting the wind and taking flight

It was only two days later that we moved on, reaching another stretch of coast, and set up camp in the forest nearby. I dragged in great breaths of salty air, and something in the dancing of the wind here made me feel more vital and alive. My walks out to the clifftops each morning became something of a ritual.

Raul found me lying in the long grasses up on the cliffs one morning, watching the field buntings flitting and darting through the stems.

"I love watching them," I smiled up to him as he came to sit beside me, and I pulled myself up to sit in tandem.

"You're no songbird you know, Eve. You've got far more of the predator in you than that."

I was surprised at his words. Did he know? Did he know that I wanted to identify more with these tiny little delicate birds that hummed with life and business – wanted to believe that my song, one day, could rival theirs? I didn't want to give voice to the growing feeling within me that I had far more in common with the predatory raptors that swept down on these little creatures. I had always felt it, had always been drawn to the look of otherness in their alien gaze, but I hadn't wanted it. Now, I was beginning to feel more of the savagery within me every day; the songbird was morphing into the hunter.

"Not morphing; it was what you always were." Raul spoke quietly.

I looked at him fiercely, not needing to say anything, not having anything to say in rebuke this time. Instead I turned and watched the seagulls dipping up above the cliff-line, then diving back down out of sight. That was the sort of bird I felt I was – alive and free in the wind, not in a pretty hedgerow.

"We are all predatory in our own ways – some of us more than others. That doesn't make us evil, Eve; it just makes us more aware of our true natures. You are starting to see yours. Come with me." Raul extended his hand, and I took it.

He led me down to where the rough grass and scrub gave way to boulders and smooth pebbles on the beach. We crunched over them together, right to the water's edge. It felt wonderful, fresh and invigorating. I beamed up at him, elated.

"I want you to meet someone – if I can call it that," he said.

"Who?"

'You'll see. I'm going to head back now. Take as long as you need. You'll be safe here."

I watched, puzzled, as Raul strode back up the rocks towards the tree line. Then I turned to face the view.

The sea was mesmerising – glowing in the low sun's light, luminous and alive. I drank in the sight of the surface, and then I allowed my eyes to focus down into the water, to see fish in vast numbers move as one, their metallic sides flashing as they moved, to forests of seaweed rocking ceaselessly in the unseen currents of the deep. I wanted to dive down into the depths there and immerse myself in the dark water.

"You can do that whenever you fancy. That is your world, too – down there in the depths. But for a moment, stay with me."

I glanced urgently about, having seen no one else on this desolate stretch. The voice had seemed to reverberate around me, coming from every direction at once. A voice carried in on the wind.

"Almost," laughed the voice, pure as a breeze. "I am the Wind. I know you Eve. And you know me."

'Yes," was all that I could manage.

I knew it was true. I felt it deep inside – absurd as that seemed. And so many things were not as I had thought them to be, now that I was less closed off to these possibilities.

"You did it, Eve – you flew, for a moment. I was there as you did it; I cradled you. You may not have felt me, but I am a part of the air, and so I am everywhere."

"I felt you," I whispered, remembering the slight push I had felt under my shoulders as I had stepped off the cliffs to try to fly. Just a nudge, but enough to help me to half believe I could leave the ground.

"You always will. You are also part of me, part of everything. Whenever you step into me as yourself, you can be the one that enables yourself to leave the ground and start to fly. You will be within me, I will be within you, because there is no separation.

"You can inhabit all these parts, because you are of the elements – as are all things. You are life. Do not be encumbered by what you think. Learn how to live free by what you feel. You can soar to the highest clouds, you can dive down to the unimagined depths of the ocean, you can flow down the mountainside in the river, you can tremble with budding life within the soil and you can blaze within the fire. And you will feel it all. Don't shy away from that feeling; it is what gives you life.

"You are not them, they are not you, you are parts of them all, and you live among them."

I quivered with the power that the words evoked in me. They landed in the core of me.

My wings, which I had not yet learned to stow away, arched into life on my back. I stretched them and flexed my shoulder muscles. So dark and quiet on my back, they blazed as the refracted light from the sea bounced off them. They shone with colour, dark cyan, cerulean, aquamarine, indigo, teal and turquoise – all tipped with deep eagle green. They beat the air, and I rose without any effort at all, feeling the power flood through me. It was an incredible rush. I could feel what the Wind had been saying, living out the truth of it as I took to the air, feeling it lift me from the ground. I felt no separation, no disconnect from the element around me, as I rose higher and higher. And as I looked down at the sea glittering far below me, I knew just as clearly that if I dived into those depths, I would also be at one there – I wouldn't need air to sustain me. I was already of the air; I would be taking in what I needed with me. The giddying rush of flight would never leave me, I knew. I belonged here, savouring the feeling of the air around me, under me, giving me lift.

I flew all the way back to the temporary camp that had taken shape while I was gone. I saw Raul to one edge of the camp, standing with several of his men as they chopped some wood for the fire. I glided in and landed near them. As I landed I smiled over at Raul, and he smiled back, a satisfied glow lighting up his beautiful face. He didn't say a word.

***

I didn't look back from that point. I went often with Lara up to the hills nearby, where the forest cover gave way to the higher ground. A few trees clung on up the slopes, but fell away to reveal rough grassy uplands dotted with dog violets, buttercups and eyebright. The wind here was uncontained, rushing with delight over the open spaces. It was here we came to practise my flying.

Now that I had decided that I wanted to be here, be a part of it, I didn't want to let anyone down. I knew that some of my new friends had big hopes for my potential. With the gifts they felt I had, locked down somewhere inside me, I started to believe I could make a difference here. Raul wanted me up in the air, scouting, and collecting information well in advance of any risk to our group.

The wind was so untrammelled here, so free, that I

couldn't really fail to fly. I was picked up bodily and held in the air currents. I'm not sure that I really had anything to do with it at first. I whooped with delight and Lara grinned back. As my confidence grew, I started to experiment more, exploring this new element that I could move in. I knew I was only able to do it because of the wind lifting me, but I delighted in it all the same. I felt the enormous shift that a tiny angle change on a wing tip could produce, the heady uplift that could be ridden with wings stretched frank and wide. It was unfettered here, and I gloried in the sensation.

And I got it then; I understood that sense of unbounded joy that could come from being in the right place – feeling a synergy with everything around you. To revel in this freedom while you could. I knew why we flew, we ran, we swam – because summer doesn't last forever. What beautiful joy in drinking in those moments when we know we only have a moment in the sun – what ecstasy in that impending loss. You are snatching something from the void. I think for many years I had been yearning to fly, but never doing it. And one day I would have wanted to try, and realised that that time had gone.

Dream

Breathing in the sea

I fell into the water — it was deep and cold. My legs would not kick hard enough to keep me at the surface and I gradually sank lower and lower, the water closing over my head. My body was alive with panic. I struggled strongly, kicking wildly in the water; still I sank lower. With my lungs burning, I eventually opened my mouth to instinctively drag in a breath, but in rushed the water, being sucked down to the depths of me, racing inside me to fill every void. I gagged and choked, and still the water came in, filling me until there was no space left. I could feel it reaching every single point of my body as I slowly drowned. But then I felt a tingle — something like a distant memory on the edges of my consciousness — a little ripple through my limbs. Like a tiny electrical pulse, I could suddenly feel the very extremities of myself, alive and buzzing. I looked around under the water. I was still alive. How was that even possible? And I wasn't choking anymore; the liquid was pulsing in and out of my mouth as I breathed easily. The crisis had passed. I was back in the sea.

This sensory world

The next days were like entering another world. Having accepted that I could do things I hadn't believed before, I gloried in sampling them over and over, honing my senses and feeling the full force of sensory life.

I remembered back to the dread I had felt when I first came, to being out in the open like this. It had been so alien to me, living outside, being under the stars, having no walls between me and the night. Now, I often chose to lie out at night for a while and look up at the stars. I enjoyed hearing the sounds in the darkness around me, as the nocturnal creatures took their place in the great play. I loved hearing the growing crescendo of the birds in the morning, shouting out their defiance to the dawn; their vitality, their reason for being. I felt more tuned in to what was going on around me in the forest; I had learned the signs of warning that the forest could give, I could read the goings on with a degree more accuracy than I could a few weeks before – not yet in the same way as Raul and the others, but then that wasn't surprising; they had breathed this forest from birth.

Some nights we did sleep out in the open; we would ring

ourselves around the campfire for warmth, and drift off. The pressure of all that darkness at my back had lessened, and I often now slept with my back to the fire, facing out into the blanket of night.

When I thought back to my flat in London, I actually wondered whether I could go back into that box. It felt airless to me now; hemmed in. I had liked the height of it, the wonderful view over the city. But now it felt aloof somehow, looking down on everything from a safe distance. Here, in the forest, you had to be right in it, and I liked the simplicity of that. Something profound had changed for me here.

In my explorations, with the wind giving me lift, I flew down one morning from the cliffs to the sea, seeking an affinity with all my elements. The sea that holds our dreams and washes the shore with them. Every so often it nudges you, there on the shore, leaving you little clues in the strand line.

I waded in, up to my thighs. It was deliciously cool; my legs tingled with the sensation. My fingertips stroked the surface, pushing through the almost imperceptible layer of pressure that was there to test their resolve. This meniscus was the only barrier marking the transition from one element to another. Once one part of my body had gone through, the rest was almost sucked in.

I continued to walk out, pushing through the water with my legs, until only my upper chest and head were dry. Closing my eyes, I took a deep breath and slowly sank in. After a hanging moment, I kicked forward, seeking the deeper spaces. I felt my hair being tugged gently by invisible hands, strands being splayed out and brought to life. There was an energy here – an element totally different to the one in which I lived. Everything moved differently; I moved differently. Different parts of my body were animated, brought to life.

When my breath ran out, I didn't panic. I knew I would have to breathe in – breathe in the water – and that it would sustain me. Even so, opening my mouth to suck in liquid felt profoundly bizarre, against everything I knew. As I sucked the water in, I gagged and choked for a few seconds, feeling the flame of my resolve flicker and dip. But I kept swallowing it down, and then it was over. I could breathe again.

I opened my eyes.

It was dark here, and nebulous shapes moved around me, flashing momentarily into view, and then ducking back into the murk. Some fish skittered closer, curious. They hung in a constellation of tiny stars around me, suspended in space. A larger fish appeared and orbited me lazily. I seemed to be of little interest to him, and he soon peeled off from my atmosphere and bounced back into vastness.

I hung there, and watched this secret world. I saw the kelp fronds beneath me, waving gently back and forth in the watery wind. As I watched their graceful dance, I knew that their movement would be gone as soon as they were dragged from this life. On the beach they would be sad, bedraggled heaps, with no suggestion of the beauty of their dancing. People would walk over them, oblivious to them, oblivious to what they could truly be.

My hair would respond in the same way if I was dragged

from this place, I knew. Plastered down against my cheeks, the vitality snatched away. And what of me? I knew the same had been happening to me for years.

***

The next day, I stood alone in the forest, as it hummed with life all around me. I dragged in a deep breath, pulling in the earthiness of the damp soil, the freshness on the wind, the slight salty tang just discernible on my tongue. I quickened, instinctively feeling that animal rush of response to the senses. The wet ground allowed all the flavours and richness there to infuse into the air, percolating back down in to me. So many messages – I could almost feel the growth of the plants around me, sense their roots pushing deeper into the soil, seeking sustenance, seeking life. I could feel the rabbits sniffing the breeze, tasting for danger, the wolves doing the same, tasting for the hunt; fully alive. This hunger for life was sucked into my body. I felt alert, alive.

The stump I had been resting on had a wonderful moist 'give' to it, a bit like crumbling clods of soft soil. As I broke little pieces off, enjoying the feel of it, I saw insects scurrying off to find new dark places. I thought back to that old dead oak tree that I loved. My tree must be like this too, full of life, hosting a whole new community of vitality. It thrilled me, actually. Life had transformed in this tree, and it was still a part of everything, a perfect component of this forest habitat. Still necessary, still with a role to play. And there, low to the ground, just a few centimetres from the base of the old tree, a small shoot was thrusting exuberantly up towards the light, alive with rising sap and vigour. I stroked down the delicate twig. It was tiny, but full of spring and bounce, unaware of its minute size in this vast forest. It had attitude, and I loved it for that.

I refocused my eyes, and allowed them to travel across to the far horizon. The miles in front of me stretched away. I could see everything. I could see a falcon take flight from a hedge line over a mile off, I could zoom into a distant glade where a shy deer was testing the air before venturing into the open. I quivered – realising that I could hear all the noises of the forest, too – could choose to zone in on one and then another, hearing them as if they were standing next to me.

Even my fingers in the breeze, and my feet on the sodden ground, were telling me things –speaking of changes in the wind, tremors that announced the movement of animals not far off down the valley.

The sensory impact was overwhelming. Like a tidal wave, it crashed over me, and then receded a little while I absorbed it. I was engulfed, consumed, invaded. It was around me and in me, all at once. It was everywhere; it was everything. The currents of it sucked me from my feet, my mind shifting as I lost balance and tumbled in this strange space. And when I was placed back down, the world had changed to me. The flood had broken some barrier in me, something that I had built many years before, that hadn't been sophisticated enough to discern which parts of the flood needed to be repelled. It had blocked everything. These defences had been relics from another age. They had worked well for what I had needed at the time, but their cost to me was high.

The broken pieces of those walls now eddied in front of me, bumping into my legs as the flood sucked them back out. The scratches on my legs cut deep, and it stung. But the water also soothed as it receded.

I faced a new world, the same as it had ever been, but entirely different to me. Life surged through me. I could see with a million eyes, feel with a thousand fingers.

The Craven

It was the hour of long shadows. The time when each entity on the earth was stretched out and extended to its fullest – dwarfed by its own shadow. The trees on the bluff were half in the light and half in darkness, and the darkness would only grow. Night reclaims the land unapologetically – just as the tide comes in to claim the beach. It doesn't steal in; it marches unrelentingly forward. It is not the rumoured thief in the night; it rides in as a dark lord, sweeping all before it. And there is a part of you that belongs to this night, that thrills as he rides in. If you face him without fear, you are gathered up by his dark clouds, and embraced by the night. You enter a new world, a world that you have always been a part of, but had forgotten.

The deep red of their cloaks and their wings alerted me at once. I didn't even need the wave of intense dread that was transmitted to me on high frequency. I was glad of the wind today: Raul needed me up here in the sky, and I knew I still couldn't get airborne without that initial lift. From up where I was flying, I could see for miles, and home in on their movement. I could also feel the change in the patterns of air around me, the scent on the wind.

Some were already beating their wings slowly, working the muscles, preparing for battle. The natural majesty of their wings contrasted sharply with the hideous masks they wore on their faces, alien and anonymous. It was as I scanned them more throughly that I spotted evidence of what Raul and I had spoken of. In among the sea of deep red wings, were the occasional set of white, brown, even purple. An army of lost souls.

I had a sudden flash in my head, a vision: one of the riders rode with dark, glossy wings, flashing with deep blues and turquoise. And then I was suddenly no longer the observer; I became the rider. The mask sat heavy on my face, dark, sweaty, suffocating. Through my eye holes I could see the legions of other riders I rode with, uniform, disciplined, red capes flying out behind them, masks obscuring every face.

"No!" I screamed. "No! I am not that!" My hands pulled at my face to dislodge the mask, but my fingers clawed onto skin alone, scratching rough furrows into my cheeks. The vision was just as abruptly over; there was no mask, nothing to pull from my head. I slowly brought my hands down from my face, shivering in the chill of new awareness.

"The Craven!" I shouted down to Raul and the others. "Large numbers, riding in formation."

Raul immediately circled on his horse, whirling around to face his band. He spoke to them in quiet, direct terms, as was his way. The attention they paid to each word he said had been evident for the whole time I had known him. Today was no different.

"Go for their masks! The masks, Eve!" Raul shouted up at me, surging forward into the throng. I saw them thrusting at him with their broadswords, slashing and hacking. He parried with his own, pushing hard against them, waiting for chances to unhorse them and rip off the masks. Frozen, I simply stared down at the scene below me, feeling as if I was back in one of my dreams, just floating above the horror. A helpless onlooker, I could only observe the death of my friends, impotent up here. No! I wanted to be present here, part of it. I needed that. I rushed back into myself, slamming into my own rib-cage with such force that I shook. I opened my receivers to full volume, and I let the sensations flood in. I was back, I was here, I was now. Noise was everywhere; screaming, grunting, the manual effort of a fight for life. As I saw the Craven unmasked, I saw a flash of their faces before a puff of dark smoke obscured them, and their cloaks sagged empty on the ground. They vanished, turned to ash, blew away on the wind. The sensory input was excruciating, but I took it all in hungrily, gritting my teeth through the disorientation. I fought to focus my mind, to use the information coming in. After an agonising few minutes, a sort of calm came over me. The input was still there, but I was able to regulate the pain a little, think above it, feel it thrumming underneath, bubbling with life. The masks, I remembered. I have to go for the masks. My wings, powerful now, beat the air, caught the gusting wind, and I angled them to allow me to swoop down at speed.

Power surged through me as I rushed through the air, feeling my old friend stroking past my cheek, filling my wings. I could sense which riders were less sure. I could feel out their weaknesses, smell their lack of composure. Their masks could hide a lot, but not that – not now I was plugged into the mains of the sensory world. I slammed on the brakes at the last possible moment, coming at speed between two riders who couldn't track me well enough, constrained by their blinkered masks. As I shot through between them, each of my hands pulled at their masks, willing them to come away. They did, and the two figures slumped into oblivion.

I did this over and over, diving down into the field, pulling off the masks. Occasionally, one wouldn't come away – was too tightly held on to – and I soared upwards again, having failed. Once or twice I experienced the shock of unmasking one who was still human. Rather than the smoke, the ash and the slumping of the cloak on the grass, a person fell from the horse, hitting the ground hard. They looked lost, exposed and terrified. They remained on the ground, looking around, breathing hard and curling up into foetal shapes. They reminded me of hunted animals. Their wings of various colours, dishevelled and weak, hung limply over the ground.

It didn't take very long. Their flight was so poor, hardly any of the Craven left their horses to meet us in the sky. Red cloaks were strewn on the ground, the wind tugging at them as they sagged and flapped. The pitiful sight moved me. Those who had survived were given food and water, and horses were there to take them back to our camp. I wondered what the future held for them, what they would choose next.

My body ached with effort, but my mind bore the brunt of the pain. Raul found me, sat amid the detritus of our battle, my shoulders slumped, my wings tucked in.

"Talk to me," he said softly. He sat down next to me, and waited.

The words wouldn't come immediately, and when they did they were halting.

"I feel the pain of this place, these Craven. I can almost taste it. I never wanted to be near a war again. I might not be attacking them with a sword, but I am killing them nonetheless. I'm not a killer; I can't do this."

"No, you're not a killer; I know. But you are a survivor, and you are fighting a war − whether you wish to or not. You've been fighting a war ever since you lost your family − you never left it. Trying to kill bits of yourself, trying to find ways to struggle through every day. You wake up to a battle each morning. That was your reality. And that was a battle you could never win: trench warfare − designed to last forever. But there is a different way to fight, Eve. A way that can break through for you − can give you back parts of yourself, that can lead you out of war. To peace. To home."

"I don't understand, Raul. Killing is killing. And I can't do it."

"Death is a part of life for all of us. What you were doing out there today was banishing parts of life that sought solely destruction. What we faced today were one group of the Fears − soulless, faceless creatures that can suck you down

244

into oblivion, keep you alive but only in the most limited sense of the word, swelling their own ranks by stealing your mind, stealing what makes you you. And these Craven are the easy ones – the ones that you can simply unmask are the easy ones. You will meet others that are so much more sophisticated, that can steal you by temptation, by false promises, by betrayal. Those are the Riven. They can assume many forms, and you should never underestimate them. Their masks can be so seamless that you are unaware of them: they are the most dangerous.

"But you are also right, Eve, you are not a killer. There is a world of difference between a killer and a fighter. And you are a fighter. Yet you must be prepared to fight for what you seek. And you know about fighting. I'm not talking about what happened to your family – I'm talking about what you've done every day since. Just in a way that damaged you. There are different ways to fight, ways that do not involve these crude weapons," – he glanced down at his sword – "these are not it. The weapons you need are within you already, waiting to be found and used. And the strengths you have within you can cause unspeakable damage, or unimaginable wonder. And you get to choose."

"What do you mean?"

"You have something inside you that can help you. Everyone has it to some degree, but yours is vast Eve; I've felt it."

"What do you mean?"

"You have a well inside you – a vast body of water, just moving there, holding. I've mentioned it before."

"Holding what?"

"Everything that you have lived through, seen, sensed, thought and felt. It has absorbed all the reactions of those around you, drunk it all in. And now it holds it all there inside you."

"What's it there for?"

"It's there for you. For you to draw on when you need it. An unseen strength – a calm place to which you can retreat and examine all you have. Somewhere to look to for answers for anything that life can throw up. It is all in there. It is you. It is the source of all your power."

"I don't really understand."

"It doesn't matter. It doesn't make it less real. Just remember that when you really need it – when you need to hide away, to regroup, or look for new strength – you can look there. It will make sense to you then. It is a wonderful thing."

* * *

I didn't take my earlier vision to Raul. I didn't need him to tell me again that my destiny was in my own hands. The vision had been profoundly unsettling, but I had an innate understanding that it was simply a metaphor, not just of my possible future, but also of my actual past: how I had already chosen to be living. I had flirted with joining those legions, coming closer than I had known. Rejection of that now shuddered through me. I no longer wanted to feel anonymous, confined behind a mask, suffocated by my own camouflage. Perhaps if I had continued in that way, I would have become fully Craven: that rider cloaked in red.

It was what I had always been afraid of – that by stepping out from behind my protective glass wall, I was not only opening myself up to the wonder of life, I was also in the firing line again for all the pain that came with that.

I dreamt such confusing dreams in those nights. Some had me sitting up screaming, seeing blood and destruction all around me; others had me waking in tears of longing, desperate to get back to sleep again, to get back to the dream where I saw them all: my family, playing in our garden at home. Sitting out under the jacaranda trees as we tried to spot the first stars of the night. Licking clean the wooden spoon with my little sister after baking, giggling as she smeared the chocolate all over her rounded face.

I felt desolate on waking. Like those first days of grief – a few seconds of confusion, wondering what this heaviness pushing into me was, and then everything came smashing back into clarity. Pinned to the bed, breathless, wanting to escape back into my dreams. I didn't like this reality – I wanted another one. I wanted to go and find them in my sleep.

That was it, I thought as I lay there. It is what we do. When one reality is too much for us to cope with, we create another, we live partially elsewhere so that we can function and survive. We shield ourselves with other worlds. And yet now I found myself in another world entirely – another reality – and it was forcing me to feel. How many realities were there? Do we create them all? Are they all just fabrications, dreamscapes?

And even as my strength grew in this place, my senses opened, and my wings took flight, I wondered. What was it all for? They all spoke about the great gift it was to live fully realised, but no one had told me just how painful it would be, too.

There was a price to pay in feeling again. Feeling anything meant feeling everything, and some days that was too much. Pain really is the cost of love. The crowning and the crucifixion. The thaw is always yearned for, but it isn't pretty. Like the melting nose of a glacier, out would come a mass of debris that had been locked away, a random army of moraine strewn across the valley-floor.

The next few days were full of agony and doubt. I felt that I had lost my way, and I was frightened. My mood didn't seem a surprise to my friends, and they let me be. In some tiny way, I found some solace in that, as if this was 'normal.' I hadn't felt normal for a very long time. It was a start.

"There'll be many days like this," Raul said, one evening. I hadn't seen him much for the previous few days; he had been busy with scouting out the surrounding land, keeping the camp supplied with fresh food, and finding reliable water sources. And, well, I had been avoiding as many people as I could.

"I like things to make sense. I know where I am, then. I find this a lot harder. I have so many questions – and no one to whom I can address them. No, I don't mean there is no one around who I could talk to; it's just that I know they are questions I am asking myself. I want to answer them. I don't think anyone else could.

"But I miss them, Raul, my family. I miss them so much at the moment, it's like a raw wound. And I feel so angry. I feel this anger in me that I had forgotten was there."

"I know." Raul put his hand over mine, and I was reminded of Marni making the same gesture so recently. Now, as then, I didn't flinch at all.

"It's OK to feel angry. And it is better to know that it is there."

"But what do I do with it?" I asked.

"What if you don't have to do anything with it? Maybe you do, maybe you don't – but you'll know. Maybe it is enough to feel it, and know it is there. It doesn't change who you are. You were already that person – you were already angry. You are just more aware of yourself now. Don't let it throw you into doubt."

"I'm trying."

"I know."

"And what am I doing with Sula! I mean, I can't help her, and she looks up to me. But I'm a mess myself – and I know I am just going to let her down."

"So who should help her then? Someone who doesn't understand where she's come from? Someone who hasn't seen what she's seen? You don't need to have all the answers, Eve – for you or for Sula. But the fact you are still here, still trying, means something to her. It makes her think that maybe she has a future too. That in itself is a great gift. You shouldn't be doing that for her, anyway – just for yourself. You don't have to do anything beyond that, or feel any pressure. Stop thinking you are going to let people down."

"I know, I know! We've been here before. I'm just struggling right now."

"I know. And sometimes things can become clearer only after a struggle. And I'm always here – if that helps at all."

I smiled my thanks up at him, and, sensing I wanted to be on my own, he stood up and left me to it.

That afternoon, with the shadows lengthening, I slipped away into the woods. As I stepped out into a clearing, I caught my breath.

With the sunshine pouring through the trees, Raul sat astride his horse in the clearing. As the light caught him, his features were cast in gold. The hairs of his furs glimmered and his open wings were gilded. The shadows of the trees, the darks of the woods - all served to provide the relief for this glittering spectacle. I stood transfixed. I had never fully understood before that the lights shone brighter when the darks were there: just what magic could be created when they worked in harmony. Like a Caravaggio painting, the scene was infused with life. I had seen all these things before; I just hadn't properly felt them.

I understood a little more now about what Claire had been telling me, what Raul had been nudging me towards all along, what my father had taught me so long ago about the stars needing the dark night to showcase them. Something I had somehow always known inside but shied away from. Light with no shade was a blinding life, parched and sterile.

Hunted

As the creatures swarmed up the hill, any chance of escape was rapidly disappearing. I grabbed my son, shoving a few things that he would need into the little school rucksack on his back. We had all agreed to defend this last central room of the compound until death, but I couldn't keep that promise. Not with my little boy to protect. We had barricaded the front door, but now the creatures were climbing up the steep hill at the back, too. We would be cut off in minutes. No one would listen to me.

We crept out of the back door. I could hear the crack of foliage, and the heavy grunts of the creatures. They were close. Every few seconds, I caught sight of their vile faces as they lurched up the hill. Their faces. They chilled me. Contorted and misshapen; their eyes their master weapon. One beam from those eyes meant incineration.

I looked down the valley as the hill fell away to my left, the creatures coming up on the right. I clutched my little boy, and begged him to hold on tight. I leapt from the ground, to fly out down the valley. As soon as I was in the air, one of the largest creatures locked on to me with his eyes. Then came the shock wave. Intense pain spiked through me. I'd failed.

As I opened my eyes I was back in the central room, panic filling it, and the smell of fear permeating everything. Someone knocked into me as he ran to help barricade the front door. I struggled to understand for a few moments. I was back at the start – a second chance. This time I had two sons, and I had to save them. I filled their rucksacks, and we crept out of the back door.

"Fly, Mummy, fly!" one of my littles ones cried. But I saw the enormous creature coming up the hill. In another few seconds he would be looking directly at us, and would have a clear line of fire. Flying wouldn't work; I needed to hide. If we couldn't be seen, we couldn't be killed. I turned left and ducked into the long grass. The thickness of the cover swallowed us up, protected us. I ran, hunched over, both boys clinging to me. We ran and ran, stumbling through the undergrowth.

There was nowhere to run, but we ran anyway. The Creatures were close. Under the cover of night, we hid in the ditch along the side of a road that ran through the forest. As headlights approached, we shrank back into the mud as far as we could, feeling it cold and sticky on our skin. With our eyes closed, our breaths caught in our throats, we waited to be found. The headlights seared through our eyelids. The engines did not stop, though, and the jeeps drove on through the forest, the Creatures searching endlessly for us.

The bottom of the ditch

We knew the forces of the Shadow Beast were edging closer and closer to where we were – striking now into the heart of Enanti. We had started to talk on some nights about heading for the Straits themselves – the northernmost point of Enanti, where, it was said, the Shadow Realm had split away, all those generations ago.

"Where are the Straits? Are they far?" I asked.

Raul turned to me. "They are – but they are where we need to go. There are no settlements in the Hinterlands around them; no one has lived that far north for many generations. People fear those black waters. But we know of some who have travelled there and returned with stories. And we know of a few who have managed to get over to the Shadow Realm itself, and come back alive. We don't know how, but perhaps they were lucky enough to get in and out undetected.

"But we have differing accounts of how far the Hinterlands are; how many days' travel. It is almost as if they are differing distances for different people; it makes no sense, really. And we know of some who have tried, but have never reached them; they bring back stories of going around in circles. But we can avoid that – we have expert trackers among us."

"Why are the Straits so feared?" I asked next.

"Few have been there, and even fewer have been and returned. That in itself is enough to bring fear. It is said that they start at the very place that Eferon struck the ground all those lives ago – where he cleaved Enanti apart from what became the Shadow Realm. It is a place of death and division; few people want to go there.

"The Straits themselves are said to be wild, tumbling seas, with currents that will suck you down. Two ocean currents meet there; two bodies collide. It is a point of transition and flux. I think the only way we can get across is by flying. And there will be little to sustain us in the Hinterlands, if the stories are anything to go by. The land is sparse and windswept. Everything that remains has earned its place. Things are spare, streamlined, necessary. We need to travel that way ourselves. We will take with us only what we need," Raul said.

"I knew a man who said he had been to the Hinterlands." Silas chipped in. "He was as mad as a brush, but there was something about him that made me believe him. His eyes looked as if they had seen a great deal more than they should. And he kept saying that he would be going back. I think he must have done, because one day he just wasn't there anymore."

I chilled at his words. What had this man been like before venturing to the Hinterlands, I wondered? What had taken him there? How had he got back? Had he found what he was looking for?

Lara, Esker and I left late morning for a hunting trip, and had been going for less than an hour when we reached a ridge-line that gave us panoramic views of our new location. The light was still thin, but shot through with warmth now. I heard a dove calling, and listened patiently for a response. The rush of a stream was not too far distant. Behind us was virgin forest, thick with life noise. The tree line petered out further up the ridge - just a few stubborn trees still heading for the summit. The incline on the other side was too abrupt for anything more than scrub and grass to grow. As the land evened out again, though, little pockets of woodland were sprinkled though the more open, undulating landscape.

Our eyes were drawn immediately to the smoke. Billowing from what looked like a little settlement, huddled in a depression, it was rising high up into the air before the wind shook it to pieces. It was clear that the village had been attacked.

We crept into the ruins. Smoke was still rising from some of the piles of rubble that stood as tors; marking the dead and the depths of human experience. The silence was crushing. I had seen devastation like this before, and I closed my eyes as I felt the horror of what had happened here. As survivors began to emerge from the collapsed buildings. I looked in their eyes, and I saw myself. It was a horrible moment. I could see what they had seen, feel what they felt, know what they had known. And I knew that life had changed forever for them.

Esker, Lara and I rushed to help those still trapped amongst the rubble. One little baby was passed up to my arms as his mother was pulled free, and he looked directly at me.

"Laila." I gasped as this solid little nugget of warmth lay in my arms.

"It's Brecon," his mother said, automatically, reaching for him.

"Sorry, I…" There was no explanation I could give. But I couldn't hold him anymore, and I quickly passed him back to his mother, my arms trembling.

Esker would lead the people we had already found back to our camp. It was late now – the light fading – but Lara and I stayed a little longer, to ensure we had not missed anyone.

When dusk fell, Lara and I knew we had to leave. It was the hour of stalking shadows, where the strident uprights of the trees were in burnished gold on one side, and brushed in black ink on the other. As we walked back through the forest, the night so still, my senses suddenly pricked. I tensed and tried to tune in further. I could see Lara was feeling something too. I felt fear coming from the small creatures that were suddenly running towards us. And behind that, a great wall of desolation and darkness, on thundering feet.

Lara looked over at me. "Craven", she gasped. "Fly, Eve! Fly!"

"I can't! There is no wind tonight! I can't take off. I can't do it. I'm so sorry!"

We turned together, and ran.

The moon was more than half full, but dark clouds raced across its surface, creating constantly changing shadows.

We were illuminated one second, hidden another. The strong verticals of the trees were occasionally backlit, then swallowed up by the night.

We ran deeper into the woods. Tangled roots occasionally slowed us, but the ground was thankfully clear of much thicket and undergrowth. The trees were too tall here to allow much to gain a foothold on the forest floor. I suddenly skidded as we ran straight into a ditch, slipping down the side to its bottom. It ran as far as we could see in either direction, and beyond it, raised up on a manufactured embankment, was an earth road, cutting right through the forest. The road carrying the Craven directly to us.

"We need to get right down, become just like this ditch, Eve. Roll in the mud with me. And keep your eyes closed – they will give us away," whispered Lara.

We covered ourselves in mud, as the whole embankment above us reverberated with their footsteps. They marched in unison: The Craven, hundreds of them. Each stomp of their feet into the ground was a smash on to our shield of resolve. They paused just before they had drawn level with our hiding place, and we saw the arcs of light from their caught-beams searching through the forest. The urge to run was almost overwhelming. I gripped Lara's hand and silently willed us both to resist the impulse. I felt the mud beneath us, cold and pliant, and I squeezed myself in further.

We shrank back as beams were angled down the embankment sides, scanning right over our area. I knew the lip of the ditch would impede their beams to some degree, but the side of the ditch furthest away from the road smashed into clarity. My foot, not pulled in tight enough, lay there, exposed. I pulled in my breath, and closed my eyes, half-hoping in that childish belief that if I couldn't see them...

Lara and I stayed utterly motionless as their beams swept on, and over. We knew the fear of the fox at ground, the stag at bay. A tiny moan escaped her, but I would have missed it if I hadn't been pressed right into her slight frame.

And then it stopped. The lights were all pointed forwards once again, and the marching resumed. The reverberations held a different quality now. The very pulse that had terrified us with its thunder a few minutes before, now made me feel we had a chance. Sometimes things really are just a matter of perspective.

"Your foot! I thought they had seen your foot," breathed Lara.

I could hardly believe it either. One thin layer of mud, less than a few millimetres, really, had saved us. Even down there in a ditch, you can find things to save you.

Fog

When we stumbled into camp that night, the whole place was on alert. Raul ran over and clutched me to him, gripping my shoulders painfully. There was no need for questions. We couldn't stay there. We needed to act.

We rode out early that morning, before the sun was even up, the day just a thin grey promise on the horizon. We went as a group of six: Raul, Silas, Esker, Sorcha, Lara and myself – leaving Koni, Breven, Arno and the others to head up the camp while we searched out the land. We needed to know how pressing the danger was.

We rode in silence, only the gentle rhythmic thump of the horses' hooves could be heard. It seemed unnatural. Where was the bird call that should punctuate this first light? The forest felt full of secrets, shrouded in a heavy fog. The upright lines of trunks loomed out of the mist before us, and I turned in my saddle to see them swallowed up again by the mist behind us. Our visibility was only a few metres, and this closing in pressed hard on my chest, shortening my breath. The horses sensed it too – this strange dawn. My senses felt on alert, and yet dulled by this heaviness hanging in the air. I could only feel ambiguity, and an inching sense of dread. I couldn't read it, and as I looked around, I realised we were all feeling the same way.

Raul shifted in his saddle next to me and whispered low. "Are you getting anything Eve? This doesn't feel right, but I can't pick up anything specific."

"No, I can't either. I don't understand."

Esker joined in: "It's probably just this mist. It's so heavy that it is throwing out our... Shit!" We shot out eyes over to him just in time to see the spear embed itself in his thigh, causing him to jerk in agony and his horse to career off into the rest of us. In a split second, chaos erupted. Other spears followed the first, and we wheeled around, frantically trying to protect all sides. I heard a horse scream as something found a home in its flank.

"Up! We need to get up above this stuff! They can't throw those spears much higher!" Raul shouted urgently, as we braced our shields against another flurry of shots. I knew he was right; it was the only way out; the only way to be free of the cloying ether that swirled around us. I didn't want to leave my horse; the poor thing was utterly terrified, but I knew that it was we who were drawing the attack, that it would stop if we got out of the way. We rose as one into the air, Raul lifting me bodily from my horse to get me started. The forceful strokes of our wings was the only sound over the hiss of incoming spears. Esker rose with us, but with great effort; his leg was badly hurt. We kept going up, and suddenly we broke free of the mist, reaching the height of the canopy. The horses below us were swallowed up into the fumes, and disappeared. We turned west and flew urgently back to the camp, Lara flying close to Esker, expertly encouraging him with her voice.

As we landed, others ran over to see why we had come back so quickly, and on the wing.

Our nerves were taut as we strained to hear anything from outside the camp. The flurry of activity had stilled to a disconcerting silence, as we all listened intently. Nothing. That was wrong. And then, as we waited out the minutes, we heard the wondrous call of a wood thrush – solitary at first, and then another and another. We sank back in relief. The night was retreating, being beaten back by day as the misted air around us thinned, and lifted.

"They've never come that close to camp before," Silas said. "What's going on? Something has changed."

"Yes. We must be getting closer to the Straits. Nothing is going to get easier from now on. We always knew that," rejoined Raul.

"So what do we do with the camp? Shouldn't we keep them further back? Go on with a smaller number? We can't fight our way over the Straits, and look after all these people," Silas said. It was true; the dilemma over whether we should travel as one to the Hinterlands needed to be addressed. Now.

At full light, we all gathered, chastened by the early morning's events. Raul stood to speak.

"The group we formed out of necessity grew as we found more and more of you, dispossessed and fleeing. But over time, we have altered our path to one of confrontation with the Shadow Realm, and we can't risk everyone in that venture. It must be a choice for each of us who can fight, but we also need to protect those who can't."

Others stood to voice their feelings. It was eventually decided that the main body of the camp would return to the relative safety of the central forests. It would be a long trip back, but they would be far further from the Shadow Beast's forces, which, we knew, were amassing here now, anticipating our approach to the Straits. Several of our best fighters would go with them as guards – Arno and Breven among them. If other groups were found, they would join ranks, and any fighters amongst them would be urged to join us at the Straits, to help us spearhead our assault.

Some didn't want to go. We had faced everything as a group, and breaking off felt like a betrayal. But most were aware that they could be a liability if we found ourselves in a full-out attack, and saw the sense of it. We all knew it would be a hard journey to the Hinterlands.

Sula didn't want to go. I saw it in her eyes. I sought her out after the meeting, and hugged her close.

"It's OK, you know. It's OK to not want to go, and it's OK to be scared. But you are going to be safe – and that is the important thing."

She hugged me harder. I relaxed into just feeling her, to hear everything that she couldn't say, and I heard it as clear as day. She wasn't scared for herself. She was scared for me. I kneeled down in front of her and looked right at her, cupping her face with my hands.

"And I'm going to be OK too. I need to do this, Sula. You know that, don't you?"

She nodded. Then she hugged me to her again, and with the tiniest of whispers, she conquered the world. "Yes."

262

The flooded maze

As another thin grey dawn split the sky from the land the next morning, we set off – as two different groups. The great bulk of the Free was heading back inland, as far away as possible from the marauding forces of the Shadow Beast, protected by a few trusted hunters.

Our new, small group comprised just Raul's closest band, Lara and myself. We were far too few, in my view, to achieve our aim, but we took heart from the fact that our departing group would be spreading the word that all fighters from other bands of the Free should head for the Straits and join us there.

We travelled all that day, and then for many more, in the direction of the Straits, but as the days turned into weeks, we seemed to be making no progress. I could have sworn that we were passing the same landmarks repeatedly. It began to feel as if we were walking in eternal circles. Frustration crackled increasingly through our group like an electric charge.

* * *

I knew that tree stump; without question we had passed by this exact spot two days ago. I looked at Raul in exasperation, and he nodded in acknowledgement.

"Shit!" Silas threw himself down on to the ground in annoyance. "What the hell is going on here?"

There is something at work here – something stopping us getting to the Hinterlands – bending this reality into a curve. I've heard of this, from people who have tried to reach the Straits before now," Raul said quietly.

"Let me try?" I suggested.

"What does she mean?" Silas asked Raul.

"I can speak for myself," I snapped, and felt a surge of satisfaction as Silas's eyes flew over to mine.

I continued: "We've been going around the same part of this forest now for weeks, and we keep ending up back here. That's no coincidence. Something is warping reality to make it so. If we keep going in circles when we have seven expert trackers with us, then something is going on. Simply carrying on doing the same thing is a pointless exercise."

"Agreed," Silas said. "But that doesn't explain what you meant by 'let me try'. You have no idea what we need to do."

"No, I don't. But at least I know that. Watching you all crash around in the forest for another circuit isn't exactly the answer. Surely you can see that it's futile? If Lara and Raul think I have a role to play here, then let me try."

"What did you have in mind?" asked Raul.

"Let me try going to one of the Shifting Pools. If they do take me where I need to go, then maybe I will find something we need."

"It's too risky; you'd be there on your own," Raul said immediately.

I'd been in a lot of places on my own. Often surrounded by people, but very much alone.

"I can look after myself."

"You have no idea where you will find yourself." Raul shook his head adamantly.

"Again, that is nothing new to me. And you've told me the Pools will take me where I want to go. If I want to find a solution to this warping of space, then surely they will take me somewhere I can find that?"

"She is speaking sense, Raul." Lara touched his arm gently, but I could see the tension coming off him. I knew he would let me choose for myself, but it would be hard for him. Every fibre of him wanted to be the one to protect me. I knew that feeling, and I respected it. But this was my choice.

"It's surely worth a try," said Silas. "But you are not bloody linking with him this time!" He jerked his head angrily towards Raul.

Raul shot him a look that spoke of his frustration. But it was decided. Tomorrow, we would find a Shifting Pool, and I would enter it alone. Unlinked this time. Perhaps it would be a key I would bring back, perhaps a map – but it had to be something.

***

As we neared a Pool the next morning, I shivered with

265

portent.

"Do I have to go in?" I whispered to Raul. I wanted him to decide for me, to tell me what to do. I didn't want to do this. I didn't want the responsibility of it.

"No," he said – as I knew he would.

I stopped just before the pool.

"How do I know that I won't go back to London?" I asked.

"The water will take you where you choose to go. It is up to you. It always has been. It has always been you driving where you need to go."

I didn't want to correct him now, not here, just before this and in front of everyone. I didn't want an argument. I still knew he was wrong about it; how I had been spat out into Enanti without ever choosing to be, without any chance to control it.

He laughed: "Yes, even that! Something within you did choose to come here, Eve. Something in you needed to come, and you came."

The fact that he could read me so completely was a comfort to me now, I realised. I had never sought that out with anyone, had actively taken steps to prevent it. Yet here I was, utterly transparent to him, completely seen – and I liked the sensations it brought. Security and safety unfurled a little within me, as if they were waking from sleep, and blinking their eyes.

"They've always been there," I think I heard him mutter, but I couldn't be sure, as I focused on the pool before me, shining in the moonlight. My feet were bare: I preferred the feel of that these days - it helped to carry messages to

266

me, helped the flow. The dampness of the grass made me feel clean, and rooted. The mud oozed between my toes as I curled them downwards, relishing the feel. I rested my hand on the tree to my right, feeling the bark, silvered by the moon. I was trying to absorb it all, take all the strength I could in with me, fortifying myself with this woodland glade.

I walked towards the pool, and, crouching, let the water run through my fingers. The inky surface, studded with reflected light, rocked from my entrance, stirred into motion. The impact we have, I thought to myself, from such tiny choices. Raul's gaze was piercing at my back; I didn't need to turn to know he was watching me intently. I breathed in deeply, before regaining my feet. I turned to face them all, smiling a silent farewell, then turned back to the pool to face myself. The water closed over my head as I dived in, claiming me, feeling me, knowing me. I was sucked down, into the cool depths, currents rushing past me as I crossed worlds.

When I became conscious, my eyes opened on a familiar world. I froze; paralysed with fear. My breathing shallow, I allowed my eyes to sweep around, confirming my suspicions. I knew this place. I was standing thigh deep in cool water, stark white walls zig-zagging away from me endlessly, hip-high. The white heat of the sun beat down on my shoulders. Blinding light. No shadows anywhere. My fingernails digging into my palms, my mind forcing my lungs to increase the depth of their intake.

The flooded maze. So seemingly serene and bright, yet possessing such a chilling desolation. Such a masterstroke of punishment. An emptiness; a permanent isolation from life. I knew I would see nothing else alive in here. Of course I wouldn't – why would anyone else even be here? It was my own personal hell.

As I calmed, I allowed myself to visit my well inside. I closed my eyes, standing at the edge of the dark, glossy surface. I dived in, submerging myself in the cool darkness there. I knew that what I needed was in here, so I kicked down. Then I let myself hang, suspended, without gravity in the dark. I didn't have to hold my breath: breathing in this element was as natural to me as sleeping.

The answer was there. I felt it soak inside my conscious mind, seep through my vaults of memory, flow down each of my limbs. An electric current of awareness. Like a sponge, I absorbed it back from where I had kept it safely. I kicked for the surface.

As I faced the stark landscape around me again, I knew what I needed to do. There was only one way out of here. Moving through the water would lead me endlessly through the maze. I needed to pull myself out, be above it. I needed to fly. I wasn't sure whether I would be able to; there was no wind here, in this vacuum. I was more confident that I could do it with the uplift of the wind, but what about on my own?

I strode forward a few paces through the water, trying to get my circulation moving. I unfurled my wings, and let them stretch and open out under the glaring sun. They beat the air. The noise was comforting in this sterile place. The only noise would be one I made. So I made some more, enjoying the ridiculousness of the situation. I shouted out my name, joyfully, and laughed. I noticed tiny, almost imperceptible changes going on around me. The water surface trembled and shook at the changing frequencies created by my shouting and my wings. I revelled in it, speeding up my wing beat. As my feather tips touched the water on occasion, curtains of droplets were rained back down on to the water and the white walls. The flash of feathers in the light was beautiful. The tiny droplets of water running down the white walls were beautiful. They moved; they had life.

I suddenly saw how much I could bring to this place, this desert of life. When I had dreamed of this place I had always felt that it sucked life from me, but it wasn't that. It was simply a blank page, and I had been looking at it all the wrong way. I hadn't considered what I could bring to it; only focused on what it failed to give to me. My ability to use my senses had been so muted that I hadn't seen the possibilities that existed. This was not where I had to live, not how I had to be. In an exultant rush of power, my wings lifted me clear off the ground, raising me higher and higher until my legs were free of the water. The wind may have been absent here, but I could feel the body of air collecting under my wings, giving me lift. I savoured it, felt it, and used it to rise higher.

I climbed up and up, my wings caressing the air, working with it. When I was high enough, I extended my wings to their fullest extent, and let myself soar. It was magnificent – the freedom of it coursed through me. I had been wrong, my doubts had been wrong; I could do this. And up here, there was the lift I needed. With all that sun pouring down, the air up here was warmer and I took full advantage, wheeling and riding the thermals as I sobbed with pleasure.

I hadn't realised how high I had circled until I looked to the far horizon. There, right at the limit of my sight, I saw a line of green. The maze had an edge. I flew on, and the green line became a crowd of trees, and they became the start of an immense forest that stretched onwards to a new horizon. I skimmed lower.

With the edge of the maze approaching, I left my joyful heights in order to gain more detailed information about what was ahead. My mind snapped back into focus, and I allowed the sounds and smells of the forest to reach me. There had been rain recently. The air was pregnant with messages. As I skimmed lower, I saw an immense wall, running as far as the eye could see, at least 100 metres high, which marked the very edge of the maze. Fully confident in my ability to fly now, I decided to land on the maze-side of this wall, curious as to its design. For such a high wall, I had never seen it from the distance when I was down on the ground of the maze.

I stared in astonishment at the wall as I landed back in the water of the maze. It was made of glass, and it was silvered at the back so that it functioned as a mirror. The magnitude of this structure was extraordinary; there were no flaws in the surface, no lines where a new piece of glass connected. One, smooth, seemingly endless structure; the perfect illusion. It tricked the eye into thinking the maze continued forever; fooling a weary heart into believing that there was no point in continuing in this direction. What was chilling is that my reflection did not look back at me from the mirror. In order to maintain the deception, the mirror only reflected back the maze; not anything that was in it. Anything I did, down to splashing the water furiously with my hands, was unrepresented in the fabrication in front of me. As I continued to study the wall, I realised that all the forest sounds I had heard before my landing, all the smells and tastes on the air, were also absent on this side of the wall. It seemed to serve to keep out all other life, allowing only still air, water and light.

"I would have been here forever," I said out loud, horrified.

I shook off the chill that crept up my spine, and primed my wings for flight. As I lifted off once more, I marvelled at how little I had to rise up to start to see the mirror wall for what it was: once the angles changed by being up here, looking down, the illusion was shattered. And as I rose higher still, I started to be able to see over to the teeming forest just beyond.

I alighted in a small clearing on the other side of the wall. The back of the wall was as jet black as if it were carved from obsidian, arching up into the sky. As it swept off to the left, I saw that the forest here petered out into more open country, with the hills falling away and rolling down to the distant coast. I had done it; this was the way onwards.

As I spun around in the other direction, I saw my friends, standing in a group under the trees a short distance from me. I smiled and waved as Lara looked straight in my direction. She simply turned back to the others and continued their discussion. I was puzzled; I didn't understand how she could have missed me. I tried again. The same thing happened. I strode closer, calling out to them. Nothing. They couldn't hear me. I realised that the forest we had all been in, that they were standing in now, had been subjected to the same reality-bending as the water maze. My sound would be blocked to them, and I was pretty sure that what they could see if they looked in my direction was simply a reflection of the forest around them. I needed to reach them in a different way. I concentrated all my energy into focusing on Raul. Once I had him in my head, I closed my eyes and willed him to look at me, willed him to hear me, somewhere inside. I opened my eyes, and I saw him looking directly at me, puzzled. "Act on it, please act on it," I muttered to myself. I kept my focus on him. I watched as he quietly shushed the others with his hand, and then started to walk slowly over to where I was. I put my hand up on to the invisible barrier. Raul was concentrating, I knew I was getting through to him. He reached in front of himself with his right hand, patting the air before him as the others looked on, intrigued. I could hear them.

"What is it Raul?" Lara asked softly, not wishing to break his focus.

"It's Eve. She's right here somehow. Somewhere close. I'm just not…"

Raul broke off to continue touching the air in front of him with his hand. His hand inched closer to mine, and I held mine completely still. Suddenly, his hand brushed over the place mine was, and I saw him freeze, then look straight into my eyes. He smiled, and then suddenly his hand was gripping mine, had broken through whatever the barrier had been, and he stepped through to join me. The others all followed; it must have seemed as if they were stepping into a void, but they trusted the person in front and each chose to follow. Soon we were all standing in the same clearing together, and they were looking back at the invisible wall they had just come through.

"Could you see us the whole time?" Raul asked.

"Once I was out of the maze, yes."

"What maze?"

I pointed at the immense wall of obsidian to our left. "I was in there." And I explained.

"I think the barrier in the forest uses the same trick - you can't see what is behind it; it just reflects back to you. But I think the forest barrier has some way to warp our sense of direction, too – or it wouldn't have fooled you so well. Whenever we got near it, it must have had some way to bend us off over into another direction, without us ever realising."

"We'd have been going in circles forever. You did well, Eve." Silas didn't give out praise often, but he never did it grudgingly – just sparingly. He was the first to say it when it was justified.

The Riven and the blade

We all sensed them on the breeze and through the earth. The unmistakable throb of The Craven on the march.

We grabbed our gear, dashed out into the central small fire clearing that we made at every camp, and listened to Raul. We were going to travel west, and then come in from the side. We would travel as one group, but with some of us in the air, scouting from above, relaying information directly to those travelling on foot below.

"I need you up there, Eve. Can you do it?" Raul asked.

I nodded. I could fly well now, and I felt a new confidence. My senses were sharp, and gaining volume, distance and depth every day. I felt alive.

"Esker, Sorcha – you, too – up in the air," Raul continued. Esker nodded, and smiled over at me. Raul, Koni, Silas and Lara were going to go on foot. Raul was confident that the majority of the army we had felt approaching were Craven. I felt some comfort in this, as I felt I knew what I could do, and how I could protect myself. But we were so few in number now, and we would be stretched to our limit. Our success would lie in using the cover of the forest to our advantage. But the trees made flight difficult, and we would need precision-flying to avoid damage and entanglement.

We had to protect the mass of people retreating back to the interior lands of Enanti. We were their line of defence. As I rose up into the air, I held the image of Sula and the others from the camp strongly in my mind. And the image of another girl, Alette, also came to me. The vision morphed from Alette to Laila, and I shook my head to clear my mind. I needed to focus. This wasn't the time for regrets. I had a role to play here, and I could make a difference. I had chosen to be here.

Raul's plan worked. By travelling far to the west before cutting in from the side, we were able to approach the Craven unseen. They were clearly on the march, alerted to the proximity of our tiny camp, and its easy pickings. With us so close to reaching the Hinterlands now, we knew that we would encounter increasing numbers of the Shadow Beast's forces. They were travelling through the forest, using the first line of their number to cut a path as wide as six men. This allowed the ranks behind to follow without breaking step, their regimented steps at odds with the organic shapes of the woods around them. They were not on horseback, which would have hampered their progress through the trees, and this gave us an advantage.

We fell on them from the right flank, Raul signalling silently to us in the air when the action would start. With one airborne scout always keeping an eye on the horizon, we took turns in swooping down and trying to rip the masks from the Cravens' faces. They hadn't been expecting us – that was clear – but they quickly regained their composure and held their lines. Arrows and spears were launched into the air, and we ducked and weaved as we flew through the chaos.

I saw little snippets of Raul and the others down on the ground. His band was fighting in little snapshots, and then suddenly disappeared, reappearing many metres away, fighting a new foe. I tried to calm my mind and focus strongly on them just before they moved. With great concentration, I managed finally to see Raul move at hyper-speed over the ground towards another member of the Craven. It was a bit like looking at one of those optical illusion pictures – you just had to relax your gaze and allow yourself just to see what your eyes were telling you. The mind then opened, and more things became possible.

I was flying low to the ground. I had just pulled a mask from a Craven who had sighed his last breath, collapsing into ash at my feet. As I was about to regain height, two things happened simultaneously. I heard Raul bellow out my name, just as I felt an immense power pluck me straight out of the air.

I was thrown at least ten metres before I crashed to the ground, wings skidding and juddering across the forest floor. I staggered to my feet, and spun round in time to see a creature I had never seen before moving swiftly towards me. He was horrifying. Over eight feet tall, with skin that flickered and moved with an unearthly torrent of darkness beneath it, like seeing a black river moving under the ice. His face was a mass of metal shards, his mouth a gaping hole with blades opening and closing mechanically. He made a whirring sound as he closed in on me, and I saw that his hands, too, were simply a mass of metallic weaponry, part of his own body. I looked wildly around for something to use as a weapon. One glance told me that the entire clearing was now overrun with these creatures, and each of my friends was tangled up in their own struggle with them. We were utterly overwhelmed.

With the clarity of those near death, I took a deep breath, closed my eyes and went to that dark place. I knew it would give me what I needed; I trusted that now. I walked to the edge of the well in my mind, and dived in. Kicking down through those dense waters, I felt my blood rise, my life-force surge within me. Whatever I needed now, I would find here.

In the inky gloom, I saw the gleam of a blade. I kicked towards it, grasped its handle and then pushed for the surface. As I burst out of my well, I stood there in front of the creature, brandishing a long broadsword, unable to explain not only its appearance, but also my ability to wield it so effortlessly. I leaped forward, holding the blade expertly in my hands. Along its length I saw symbols carved in a language I didn't know, glinting in the shafts of light. The creature saw them too. It stopped dead in its tracks, threw its mangled face skyward, and howled to the sky. It was a horrifying sound, anguished and tortured, and I wanted to block it out with my hands. The other creatures heard the cry, and each stopped where it fought. An extraordinary silence fell over us all as we waited. Slowly, inching backwards, the creatures retreated to the cloak of the trees. I looked towards Raul for understanding, but he looked as shocked as I was. After a few minutes, the entire clearing was emptied of those beasts, leaving only our bewildered band.

'What was that?" I asked finally, still holding up the broadsword in a defensive position. I suddenly felt its weight, and its point dropped heavily to the leaves at my feet.

"They were the Shadow Beast's own personal guards – the highest caste of The Fears: The Riven. They never travel far from him. He must be near." Raul looked pale, trying to take in this information, and work out what it meant for us.

"The Riven? They were terrifying!" I couldn't get them out of my mind. "Why did they leave?" I asked.

"Because of this," Raul said, coming closer and looking in wonder at the blade I was holding. "Where did you get this?"

"I...I don't really know," was all I could say.

Raul looked shocked, as he gently pushed my hands down and persuaded me to let the sword fall from my grasp.

"It was just there! I went down to it, that well...that dark place...and it was just there," I stammered, aware that everyone was looking at me.

"What dark place?" asked Silas, eyes wide.

"Not now, Silas." Raul gently waved Silas away. "Just not now."

Raul walked me over to a large beech, and sat me down by its roots. Then he went around the clearing checking on everyone.

After we had returned to camp, I still felt unable to

process all that had happened. Lara and Raul found me, and I knew they were asking whether I was ready to talk.

"There is a dark place inside me," I whispered. I've tried to stay away; it scares me. I don't know what it is. I have often retreated to its shores, many times over the years, but I've never dived in, until I was here. It helped me in the maze. Somehow I know it will help me – that there will be an answer there. But it frightens me; I don't really know its depths, and I don't know what it will give me."

"Well, it gave you the right thing this time," said Raul. I've wanted you to carry a sword ever since you got here, to protect yourself, and you refused. But this is one heck of a sword. And they seemed to recognise it."

"What are the others saying?" I asked.

"Some of them are a bit concerned. They don't understand what happened, and they didn't like the fact that this sword seemed familiar to The Riven. They are worried whether it is a good thing, or an evil power," Raul said.

I nodded. "I'm worried, too." I gave voice to the concern eating away at me. Who was I? Where had this weapon come from?

"It's OK, Eve. This came from you. This well inside you, some of it will be dark; that's true. You might find things there that you don't like, but it is all you. You needed this protection, and it was somehow there. That's all you need to worry about. If you can find things inside yourself that can help you, then it is OK to bring them to the light. They are stored there for a reason.

"And don't worry about the others – I'll talk to them.

They've heard of this sort of thing happening before, in stories passed down to us. They've just never seen it until now. And just like you, they shouldn't fear it. It saved us today."

He looked down at the sword that I still held in my hands, I had been sitting there, fingering the dark handle, and running my touch along the deeply engraved marks on the blade. He touched it too, almost reverently.

"These are runes," he said, almost to himself. "Protection runes. They were in you all along. And here was I, worrying about the need to protect you! Today you protected all of us."

He looked me in the eye. "Thank you."

The Beast comes

As I prepared for sleep, I still felt the shock of that day's events. Like a moth that beats itself against the glass, right next to an open window, something was trying to seep into my consciousness. All these castes of the Shadow Beast's creatures; the whole essence of this place; how it was all playing out. At the edge of my mind I felt some flickering sense of pattern, of rhythm. But I couldn't hold it. Like the moth, the closer I seemed to flutter near the open window, the less I saw that it was there.

I dreamt of him that night. The Shadow Beast came to me, through the camp protection, through the flimsy material barrier of my tent, and right into my head. He always seemed to have open access to my mind.

He appeared in his beast form, hunched over, colossal shoulders a mass of swirling darkness and power, eyes that seemed like black holes, pulling me into a tunnel from where there was no return.

"It won't work like that the next time you know," he purred into my ear. "The sword. That was a one-off."

"I don't believe you. I saw the effect it had on your Creatures."

"Ha. Yes indeed, but why do you think that was? My Creatures saw something in it that made them retreat, but why should that placate you? Why should that embolden you? You just haven't thought it through..." He chuckled under his breath, then continued: "I know that even some of your friends are suspicious about what happened today, about how you got that sword; about you."

He had touched a nerve. I remembered the look of astonishment in the faces of my friends, and their awkwardness afterwards. What did his Creatures see? Was it something that made me akin to them – just one step away? Is it a fine edge, between walking with the uncontrolled darker urges of the soul, and letting them consume you? Did they see something that made them think I was touched by the Beast – belonged to him?

"I belong to no one but myself!" I shouted at him. "No one but myself!"

I could hear his receding chuckle in the night even as I felt gentle hands shaking me awake, trying to get to me through my nightmare.

Elemental

Morning reclaimed the land. The sky looked as if it were on fire, licked by flames. Daubs of alizarin crimson bleeding into cadmium reds and blood orange, softening out to the palest pink edged by grey. I stared at the sky, absorbing the beauty of this artwork that changed by the minute. Is there beauty in the reflected light only? What about the beauty within? Does it even matter, if we are lucky enough to see it? As long as it is there. Like the pebbles on the stream-bed that shine and glint, illuminated by the sun's rays, does it matter whether that beauty comes from within, or is borrowed from without? Does it not just serve to remind us that it is the sense of connectedness that is actually where the beauty is revealed? That without the grey pebble, without the water sheen, without the sunlight, there would be nothing to remark upon.

"We are now entering the Hinterlands. We need to travel light: we leave everything extraneous behind," Raul announced.

For a man who travelled as light as he did, I wondered what else he could possibly be able to leave behind.

With only passed down stories to guide us, we were just

flotsam on the surf, entering a place where we didn't know the rules. All we took in with us was ourselves – what we knew, what we'd learnt, what we sought. If that would be enough to bring us out again, then we'd be lucky; it was all we had.

We left any extra items – even some food we felt would weigh us down – in a hollow in the root system of an old tree near the edge of the tree line. It was left unspoken, but we all knew that for those of us who made it back, this tree would offer some replenishment, while others may never come this way again. I could see some of us touching the tree lightly, hoping they would be lucky enough to see it again, imprinting its form in their minds.

Each one of us had a caught-beam, strapped onto our backs in a rough leather holder. I also had the dagger that Raul had made me promise to carry at all times. The pouch at my side held my sea glass and Sula's note – I didn't consider those extraneous at all, and I knew that Raul would understand. Other than that I carried some food, some water and a few other basic items. The broadsword was slung across my back.

I felt so different now from the woman who had fallen into that cave. I'd stepped out of the cave, in so many ways, and I felt powerful now; ready. I could stand in the wind, not to touch some form of redemption, but simply because it was where I belonged. It didn't punish me now; it just was. The world was a storm, but I was part of it. I didn't feel pulled into the vortex, I could now ride with the storm at its very centre, sentient and alive.

My body was different, too. My form had purpose. I was

sleeker and more powerful, because I was using my body for what it had been designed to do. It was an honest form, primed with life. My wings, fully developed now, had been conditioned by the journey and what I had learned. I could stow them, unseen, until they were needed, and although I knew I would in time gain even more control over them, I could already outfly everyone around me. I could hold them out fully and ride the thermals to the giddy heights, or I could tuck them in close to my body to achieve near terminal-velocity speeds as I plummeted back towards the earth, angling them minutely at the last minute to swoop out of my fall. I had reached a point a while back, where I had realised that I was no longer simply following the lead of those around me. I had entered a new phase of flying, starting to fulfil some of the untapped potential in me that allowed me to fly higher, fly faster than any of my friends. I had a reached a point where I could only go further alone, had to step out of the shadow of tutelage, and find my own horizons. The liberation had been intoxicating.

"Ready?' Raul asked, after we had all deposited anything inessential by the tree.

We all nodded, wordlessly. We hoped reinforcements would come in time. We hoped we wouldn't be so few to face this trial, as we turned and walked into the Hinterlands.

The land was different here – you could feel as well as see the change. The blanketing of trees was gone. The air itself felt thinner, less nourishing. Each breath gave you less than you expected. Salt hung heavy in the wind, stinging your nostrils with each intake. Yet I found this curiously enlivening. I felt energised by the salted rasp of oxygen, the more urgent need to breathe, the feeling that we were on the edge of what the earth could sustain.

The flora around us had changed considerably, too. Only the hardiest of plants could survive here, but they did so with poignant gusto, clinging on to rocks that concealed the merest pinch of earth within their nooks and crevices. Clumps of sea thrift facing the open water, purple saxifrage sending creeping stems out to find any toehold, and the thick carpets of heather, each flower so tiny, and yet lending a flush of pink to this edge of the world. And they moved in the blasts of air, bending right down to the ground in supplication, only raising their heads once the burst receded. It made me think of the world between the tidelines, it had the same ebb and flow to it, the same dynamism, the same feel of living on the edge of the known. The seaweed beds would dance in the same way in the falling tide, moving with the pulse of the water, until they were left bereft and lifeless, awaiting the next wave.

You couldn't escape the sea here. It was everything. You might like to think that the rocks jutted out defiantly into the water, ruling the waves from above, but theirs was a false authority. The rules of millennia dictated that the sea was in charge, caressing the protruding landmasses slowly to death down the ages. The waves pounded the shoreline relentlessly, crashing into the land. And the sea was everywhere. It came inland on the salted air, it burrowed into the earth, turning it increasingly crystalline, it determined the plants that it would allow the earth to hold on to and display. There were few trees to stem the ravages of the salted squalls that blew in from the sea. Those knotted trees that remained had thrown their branches out beseechingly towards the milder climes of the south.

You could see further here. The lack of tree cover allowed the eye to travel for miles – not only out over the dark waters, but along the empty coastline, too, dotted with sea-pinks and lichens. A free, elemental place. Desolate only in the lack of luxuries and protection it afforded. To me, it represented life at its most fundamental, its most primitive, and yet also its most sophisticated. It gave me the visceral joy and exhilaration that I had always sought by the sea – but had never fully touched until now. My new, heightened senses allowed me to drink in this heady mix in abundance, and I felt almost faint from the onslaught.

And there was the water of The Straits itself – dark and brooding as far as the eye could see. Even in the distance it looked restless, moving constantly, as if looking hungrily for more to consume. It had nothing of the serenity of the sea I had seen further back in my journey. Here, the waters were clouded, concealing their pitch depths with raven-tipped swells. The surface was too rough to reflect any starlight at night, and during the day, the sun was never clear enough for us to see much reflected off this dark body of water, which appeared to suck in, consume and pull the light around it into its obsidian depths.

As I looked down into this churning sea, I saw the life clinging to the walls of the cliffs. Throngs of seagulls nested in this most jagged of havens. Some circled round and round, gaining height on each turn, while others broke out of the holding pattern to attempt a landing that had to be inch-perfect. Their cries filled the air. So many voices working in unison, creating a new sound, a higher sound. I quivered with pleasure as gulls flew over my head, shooting out across the water, wheeling and calling, holding this niche so perfectly as their own, finding freedom in the wind, finding life itself from the water. Everything around me was alive.

"We make camp here." Raul's voice broke through my reverie. We were standing in a slight incline in the land, a bluff to the seaward side, sheltering a good area of ground that was protected from the buffeting wind. A ragged colony of trees had taken hold in this dip, running in a determined line for several hundred metres, sending their roots winding down into the earth for the deepest grip they could find. We had a few tents we were still carrying to allow some of us to sleep protected from the night air – not the luxury of the individual tents we had enjoyed in our larger camp, but enough material to make a rudimentary dormitory tent for most of us.

As the others busied themselves with making camp and getting water on to boil, I went with Raul to see what dry wood we could find in the tangle of trees to the side. The cover was dense here, everything taking full advantage of the respite from the wind, the undergrowth clawing up from the ground in the living tent of the tree canopy. We eased our way through carefully, unwilling to damage the foliage that had worked so hard to hold on here.

"The next few days determine everything," Raul said unexpectedly.

"Yes," I replied. What else was there to say?

"So much," Raul answered, and my eyes shot to his.

"Do you always know what I'm thinking?" I asked.

"Yes. Well, I know what you are feeling, and sometimes the two follow each other. Not always, though."

"How?"

"Because I am tuned in to you. In a different way from how I'm tuned in to other things. I see you," he said simply.

I felt a little electric current travel through me at his words. It was true; he did see me, and it wasn't just because I let him. And why did I let him?

"Because you trust me," Raul said quietly.

"Of course I trust you. You're my friend. You are the first person I met here, all those months ago, and you've taught me so much. That's why we feel connected."

"Partly," Raul responded.

"What do you mean?" The air was even thinner than it had been.

"I haven't just been teaching you, Eve; you've been teaching me, too. I don't like you always putting yourself at the passive end of things; I thought you were done with that. Look at yourself now – I'm not responsible for getting you there. If you hadn't flown on from me, flown past what I could teach, into things that I couldn't, we couldn't be where we are now."

"Where are we now?" He wasn't referring to the Hinterlands.

"We are past friendship, Eve. You know that as well as I do. We are standing on the threshold of something more, and I want to cross it."

He reached for my hand and his eyes shone down at me, glittering with a feral edge. His other hand reached for my face, but I startled and hastily backed away. Immediately, he let me go.

"Don't!" I managed shakily, sounding breathless even to myself.

"Don't what? Don't want you, or don't act on it?"

"Either! I mean, both! Just don't." I was completely shaken.

"Are you offended because I am drawn to you, or are you simply scared by the fact that you are drawn to me?" he said, very softly.

"I am not drawn to you!" I shot back, angry at his presumption. "No! I would never be with a man like you. You are everything I avoid – with good reason!"

"Being scared isn't a good enough reason."

"I'm not scared of you!"

"No. I know it is not me you are scared of."

"I am not scared! Will you stop saying that. I know what that feels like, and this isn't it!"

"Oh Eve, you are so afraid of being scared, that you can't even recognise it in yourself. You stifle any possibility of putting yourself in a position where you are exposed, or could be hurt. By doing that, you are actually hurting yourself – can't you even see that!?"

He was angry now. I thought back to the first time I had heard him speak to his men, thinking then that I wouldn't like ever to hear him angry. I'd been right. The force of his anger, even with his voice controlled and low, blew through me like a desert wind, stripping me and leaving me parched and raw.

So I did what I'd done every time that someone had tried to get too close. I tried to wound him.

"I would never be attracted to you. Why would you even think that? You're not my type − you have no finesse, no charm, you don't know the rules of the game. I thought you were my friend − and all the while you just wanted something else. Something so much more basic. How could you see me that way! How could you! I thought we were friends."

"So sex is just something you do with people you care nothing for?" he asked.

"Yes! Of course! It is easier that way. Easier all around. Why would I want a friend to think of me that way? It's disgusting!"

"Disgusting! Is that what you really think?"

"I thought you were better than that!" I threw at him, sobs lurching through me now. I felt so angry, so betrayed and, yes, so frightened. I was scared of losing him, his friendship, the solidity of him next to me, helping me find my way.

And I knew that I did find it disgusting. I was disgusted in myself when I went looking for sexual relief − and disgusted with the man: disgusted that he would want my body in that way. I found the male sexual appetite overwhelming, but my own even more troubling. It was something that was a means to an end, and I always wanted to get out of there as quickly as possible afterwards, ashamed. And it was never with anyone overtly curious about me. Or trying to be too intimate. Or hoping for more than sex.

And never a friend.

"What rules of the game? This isn't a game, Eve. Life isn't some board game where you can control all the pieces. That's not living."

I tried to get my words out through my tears – mortified that he was seeing me like this.

"I mean that if I am having sex with someone, they know the rules, they know the score –they don't try to get too close. I don't want that; I've never wanted that! It is what it is, and I don't want ever to confuse it with anything else."

"Confuse it with…? Shit, what happened to you..? No, shit… I'm sorry I asked that. Sorry."

I didn't want him ever to see that I had been cut too deeply – cut down to where it can be too painful to pull out the knife.

"I don't need, or want, your pity! I want nothing from you – nothing! I don't need anything from anyone, and if I did, it wouldn't be from you!" I spat the words out, almost choking on their venom. Unable to stop the tears.

"Why did you do this? Why did you have to do this?" And I didn't know if I was saying it to him or to myself.

"Message received." Raul spoke quietly, his face taut. He looked at me, directly in the eye, and his eyes were charged with emotion. I couldn't place whether he looked at me with sadness for himself, or pity for me – but either way I didn't want any part of it, didn't want to feel any connection to it at all. I looked away. I heard the soft crunch of leaves underfoot, and when I turned back, he had gone.

Talking to the Shadow Beast

I stayed a long time in that tangle of trees, feeling sick. This wasn't what I wanted, wasn't why I was here. I couldn't stay. Not now. If some believed I played a key role here, then I wanted to go to do that. Alone. I knew what I would do. Over the next few days, as we moved along the coast, hoping to have our numbers swelled with reinforcements, I would keep my eyes open for some form of Shifting Pool. And when I found one, I would ask with all my being to be taken straight to the Shadow Beast himself. And that is what I did.

* * *

The dense darkness swirled loosely into Beast form, sending wafts of black smoke off into different directions every time it swung its vast head from side to side. These tendrils of smoke would then start to return to the Beast's body, groping back towards their kind; a powerful gravity pulling them back to the centre of darkness.

"What do you want?" I managed to get out.

The Beast looked at me with ancient eyes, his huge head hung low between his shoulder blades like a creature that had just stalked out of the primordial jungle. His brow was heavy and ridged, and a row of horns ran up the centre of his face, gaining in height as they reached the dome of his head. His eyes flashed with a black fire, and he opened his jaws on a sneer.

"Why, you, of course. Your heart and soul. And I will have them. Some day, very soon, I will have them." He leered at me, salivating ribbons of black smoke from his grotesque muzzle. Drops of this hit the floor, sizzled loudly, and then started to waft back up to join with the rest of him again.

He laughed, and then continued.

"But that can be another day. Everything is unfolding just as it should. Soon, you will come to me."

"Never. You are not conducting this orchestra – you don't get to plan my every move. I don't believe in fate."

The Shadow Beast stalked closer. "Ahh, you think you get to choose? How sweet. How touching. Ahh…that's lovely…really. I don't get to see that very often.

"Very well, I will let you choose then: I have a couple of options for you today."

My skin prickled at his words, sensing great danger, and ancient cruelty, perfected down millennia.

"What do you mean?" I asked carefully.

"Well, if you are so keen on choice, then I will give you one. I will give you a glimpse of the enormous responsibility that can entail, and then see if you like it so much."

I didn't reply, as my mouth had run dry and I could feel my pulse pumping too hard though my head. I dreaded his next words.

"So, today, Miss Free Will, I give you this choice: the choice over two different lives. I have Alette – ahh – I can see how much you want her. You believe she is important in all this; you believe that she can somehow provide an answer here. You believe wrong. She is nothing – just a child. I took her to amuse. Your friends are wrong; they have filled your head with ideas of her wonder, but they are deluded. She is a child! Like any other. But it does amuse me to see them flinging themselves at me to try to get her back! And I am getting so many wonderful new recruits because of it!

"Anyway... They believe if they have her back then the war will be over, that somehow I will be magicked away."

He swung his head back towards me now and caught me full in the face with his glare.

"Let me tell you now that that will never happen, Eve. Never. Believe it if you want. But I thought you were smarter than that. You've seen my armies – do you really believe a simple child could stop them from sweeping all before them?

"Well, you can have her, if you want. If you believe that she is that vital, then you can have her. But in return, I get to keep a prisoner that I have wanted for some time now. A token of this pitiful land, a nobody. But, before you decide, I want you to remember that although he is a nobody, he is a person, with family, people who love him, maybe children that depend on him. By choosing Alette, you would be sentencing this other man to death. Everything has a price, Eve – you see? With any luck he might survive the Riving, and then he could be another member of My Craven, flying again on borrowed wings. Or one of my exalted Riven, sworn to protect me. Either way, he would be mine."

The laugh that came from him made me stumble backwards, like the wave of an aftershock.

"How can you do that? That is no choice at all! You have set up the two options, and you want to pretend that that is free choice?" My hands were bunched by my sides, my voice rising.

"That's how life works, Eve. That's how it goes in politics. Ahhh, of course, you can go into it with such lofty ideals – ridiculous, really – but when it comes down to it, it is all about snap decisions like this, made on a warped board of compromise. This player here, or that player there? Sometimes life conspires to focus down to tipping points like this. You sometimes only get one move. What's yours going to be?"

I didn't want to choose. Saving Alette was so precious to me, had become so much of a sacred mission to me that I started to doubt my own reasons for wanting to do it. It was almost too convenient that my own need to assuage my guilt over Laila coincided so perfectly with my friends' belief in the importance of recovering Alette. Was that too simple? Was the Beast correct that she would have no influence over events?

And how could I condemn this stranger to The Riving? Another free man, snatched by the Shadow Beast, to fall into darkness. My mind revolted at the thought. I couldn't live with that on my conscience. I knew what failing Laila had done to me all these years, and I knew his faceless form would also haunt my dreams. And he was an innocent in all this, a pawn being used to push me – and I would be treating him with the same lack of humanity and respect as the Shadow Beast was doing now. I would be accepting that he was a pawn, and, by extension, that we all were.

But my heart screamed at me to save Alette. Here was a chance – the fruit of what we had fought for, for what many had died for. Who was I to take their sacrifice in vain? If this man was part of The Free, then it would have been what he had been fighting for, too. He would have already chosen to lay down his life for this end.

As I stood there struggling, lost in my confusion and moral crisis, I saw plumes of dark smoke leaving the Beast's form and flowing over the ground towards me. They nuzzled around my ankles, as if they were sniffing prey, then crept up my legs, swirling gently around me, under my arms, around my chest, mocking me.

I recalled the conversation where Raul had counselled me urgently to save Alette at any cost. Her safety outranked any other concern, he had said, even if that meant great pain and sacrifice. He had spoken directly, plainly, as was his way. He had made it clear that every one of The Free would die willingly for that end; that I mustn't lose that focus.

God, Raul. What I wouldn't give for him to be standing beside me now, helping to untangle this thicket that was clutching me. I winced as I thought back to the last words we had exchanged, two days ago now. I had succeeded in driving him away. That knowledge was raw pain. I thought I would bury that loss down inside me, and carry on as I had before, but I had found it impossible. I felt like a wounded animal, desperate and in agony.

Although I had seen him on the march the next day, I had refused to make eye contact, even as new fighters arrived to join our cause, and I had kept myself at some distance from him for the entire day. He had eaten off to one side of the main group in the evening, speaking low and urgently with his band, and then they had all stood and left the glow of the fire and moved towards the edge of the camp to set up lookout posts for the evening. I hadn't bothered to look for him as I ate my early breakfast this morning, as I knew he would still be out at the perimeter, guarding. But I would. I had felt devastated since our fight, and I was appalled at some of the things I had said to him. I wanted to explain to him, wanted him to see that what he was asking was impossible. But more than anything, I wanted him back, I needed his friendship in these dark times. I wanted his quiet strength and his unwavering acceptance. I thought I could survive alone, and I could. But, as Raul would say, surviving is not living. And I was ready to live now.

What would he do here? I thought to myself. He would surely save Alette. I knew that without a shadow of a doubt. But I also heard his voice in my head urging me to be true to myself. What would I do? That was so much harder to answer. How could it be easier to know someone else's mind more than your own?

"Maybe because you don't have one..." purred the Beast

in my ear. "Maybe you just always do what you think you are meant to, what you're told to do – never wanting to stick your head above the parapet..."

I knew he was goading me, but it struck home. I felt furious with myself, rage at this situation. What would I do? Who was I now? What did I believe in? When the Shadows ravaged all around me, what values would I hold tight to?

And I knew then what I could, and couldn't live with. I couldn't live with knowing I had sent an innocent man to his death. And I couldn't live with failing Alette. I didn't want to play this game, and I realised that I didn't have to. I didn't want to take part. I had enough awareness to realise that the Beast was in charge of this game – and that he could change the rules any time he wanted to, regardless of anything I said. He would destroy that man, or not, on his own whim. He was just enjoying watching me tear myself apart.

I also knew that he had not harmed Alette up until this point – that something kept him from doing that – and I gambled that this meant we would have another chance.

"I choose neither," I whispered to him.

"What!" It wasn't the answer he had been expecting.

"I choose neither. They are not mine to choose, they are in your power, not mine."

"You can say that? When I was willing to cede some of that power to you? Their lives were in your hands, Eve, and you let them both down! Both!"

"That isn't power. That is seduction. You were ceding nothing to me."

"You are a fool, Eve. And now they will both be mine anyway. I mean, they always were, weren't they?"

He swept past me, scattering his dark tendrils. They hummed and throbbed as they slowly made their way back to him, rippling over the floor. I was reminded of a flight of cockroaches, teeming across a surface.

"Show her what she has done," he spoke to The Craven posted at the doors.

He gestured with his foot towards the door. The Craven turned, and opened one side each of the double doors in unison. There, standing just beyond the threshold, was a little girl, flanked by several more Craven: Alette. My heart thudded painfully, and I heard myself cry out – a strangled, anguished call. She looked so small there, flanked by such an insurmountable barrier. The doorway was such a distance away that I could only really make out her stature and her youth – I couldn't tell how old she was, or whether she looked scared or numb... No...I could, I could. I could tell in the way she stood that she was alive inside. I could feel from the blast of emotion that tore through me as I opened my sensors to her, that she was not afraid.

"I'm so sorry," I whispered to myself – she was far too far away to hear me. "Alette – I'm so so sorry. I'm so sorry, Laila."

The guards then grabbed her arms roughly, and she was stolen from my view.

I turned my anguish back towards the Shadow Beast. I didn't try to hide any of it. It seemed somehow acutely important to me that I hide none of it – that there was something sacred in allowing it space to be seen, heard, felt. Not hidden away. Alette deserved that simple respect. So had Laila, I thought now.

"You think that is it?" sneered the Beast. "You think you have this all worked out, nice and simple?"

My body iced in dread as his snigger reverberated around the Hall.

"Bring in the condemned man," he ordered then, staring at my face the whole time with unconcealed glee.

Another figure flanked by guards was presented at the doorway, and this time he was marched over the threshold, and up the Hall towards us. But I didn't need him to come any closer for the arrow to pierce my heart. It was Raul.

The sound that came out of me was like nothing I had ever heard before. I had nothing left, and I sank to my knees in the middle of that Hall. I thought I had lost everything that I ever could, that nothing could ever hurt me in that way again, that I had made myself impregnable. Lies, lies, lies!

I couldn't do this; I couldn't live through this pain. I started to feel myself drifting away. I saw myself as if from above, heard the strange chokes that came out of my mouth, and then I was slammed back into my body with full force, back into the midst of all that pain. This was where I belonged – here, within this body, feeling these rip-tides of despair. How could I ever have thought I could escape this?

I covered my face with my hands as Raul was marched closer, rocking there on my knees.

"Look at me," Raul prompted, gently. His gentleness only served to fuel my agony, stick the blade in deeper.

"Look at me, Eve," he appealed to me again.

I raised my head from my hands and looked at him, at his beautiful face. A livid cut ran down his left cheek, blood still oozing out from where the edges were failing to knot together. His left eye was partially swollen over, and was horribly purple and red.

"What have they done to you?" I whispered.

"Nothing in comparison to what you've now done to him," gloated the Shadow Beast, revelling in the moment, switching his gaze between the two of us constantly, drinking up the pain in thirsty gulps.

"I'm OK, Eve. I'm OK. This isn't your fault. Don't let him do this to you – it is what he wants. I'm OK." He spoke low, softly, and I knew he was trying to soothe me, take away some of the pain. "Please, get off your knees; you don't belong on your knees. Please, get up."

"I'm so sorry. I could have saved you. He said I could have chosen one of you – I could have saved you." I was devastated, having to force my air over my vocal chords to form any noise at all.

"And I let you down; I didn't save you, but I didn't save her either. I let you both down."

"No, you didn't Eve. Don't think that. Yes, I would have saved Alette; you know that. But who is to say that would have been right? If it had been putting myself in her place, I'd have done it a thousand times. But, if it had been a choice between her and you – god, Eve, I can't imagine ever being in that position. I'm so sorry. Please get up off your knees."

"I let you down. I let you down."

My sensors open full blast now, I let the swarming emotions in the room pound into me, smash through my protection and punch through me. Malevolence, horror, respect, rage, anguish, forgiveness, love, revenge, pride, terror, joy – they were all there in the room. I drank them down, and I rose to my feet.

"What you did was right, Eve. You were true to yourself. Do you remember that I told you once that you could never let me down, if you were being true to yourself?" He gave me such a brilliant smile.

"You were right not to condemn a man to death, however anonymous. Don't let that change, now that you know that it is me. Whatever you had said, The Beast would have taken me anyway."

"Ahh – don't let her think that, and ruin my little game!" The Beast now returned to me.

"You don't know that to be true." He laughed again, the smoke swirling more rapidly in his centre, stimulated by all the pain in the room.

"Eve, please, listen to me. You did the right thing. You did the right thing."

"But he is going to take you to The Riving," I sobbed.

Then I knew what I should do. I whipped my head around to the Beast. "Take me instead. Take me in his place."

"No!" shouted Raul. "No!" He strained at the Craven holding his arms, his whole body rejecting the idea.

"Please!" I cried, "please take me instead." I was frantic now. It was so clear in my head. I had a way to save Raul, and it was all I could think of.

"You said you wanted me, heart and soul – so take me instead!" I was screaming at the Beast now.

His pitch eyes flashed with pleasure, and He stalked near enough to draw His ragged tongue up my side, from thigh to face. I shuddered at the contact, dark spirals swirling on my skin where he had been.

"Stop it!" Raul shouted. "Get off her!"

The Beast roared, shattering the glass in the mirrors that lined the Hall, sending shards flying inwards at us. A few caught my side and I winced. The fragments simply shot through the amorphous form of the Beast, tinkling harmlessly to the floor on the other side of him. He laughed again.

"You have no sway here, human."

He turned back to me. "It's a lovely offer Eve, really it is. You don't know how excited it makes me. You don't know how much it turns me on to hear you offer yourself to me like that." He sniffed close to me again, and I shrank back.

"But the timing isn't quite right, yet. I will have you, but I don't like to be rushed into these things. Let me play the suitor a little longer, won't you? I haven't even got warmed up yet. There is so much more fun to be had.

"And I think you'll agree that one of the first things I need to do is get rid of any other suitors that may distract you; clear the field, if you like. Mark out my territory."

He sneered back at Raul, then. "Get the stench of the losers off the pitch, eh? Didn't you hear her the other day, Hero? She can't bear the thought of you touching her." His raven form shook with mirth. "But she will accept my touch. Be sure of that, Hero, as you die a thousand deaths

304

at The Riving.

"Take him away," he snapped at the guards.

"No!" I screamed as they started to pull Raul away. "Raul, I didn't mean what I said. I'm so sorry."

"I know, I know. It's OK, Eve. It's OK." His last urgent words to reassure me died away as he was marched further and further down the Hall to the doors. He was taken through them, and they clanged shut, making my ears ring.

I whirled back to the Beast, but he had gone too. I was standing alone on the clifftop.

* * *

I made my way back to the camp a different person from the one who had set out that morning. I had lived a thousand lives since then. Pain lanced through me every time I recalled Raul's damaged face; the way he had tried to smile to reassure me. And I was haunted by that flash of Alette – so tiny in the distance, so vulnerable. And I pictured Laila, too. Her warm chubbiness in my arms, clinging to me as her last hope. And what a life-raft she had put her faith into. One small eddy out on the water, and I had let her drown. And now I had condemned Alette and Raul to the same. I raged at my own impotence.

I couldn't accept that Raul was gone; lost. I had heard about the horror of The Riving too many times to find any shred of comfort. I felt as if my entire being was on fire. I'm not sure I was even sane. The enormity of what I had lost, what Enanti had lost in Raul, was too much for me to bear. And he hadn't fallen in battle, but was about to be torn apart – torn from himself, lost into oblivion. I screamed and screamed, and I didn't care who could hear.

And I couldn't forget the way I had rejected him, hurt him, tried to make him believe that I thought he was some base creature that disgusted me. How far from the truth. The man made me come alive. If I had thought that trying to keep some distance from people made the loss of them hurt less, I had been so terribly wrong.

In the midst of my grief, I felt hands shaking me, gently at first, and then more urgently, their voices swelling in my head.

"Eve, Eve, wake up. Please, wake up."

I opened my eyes, blinking a few times to try to comprehend what was real.

"Eve, there's been a raid in the night. We don't know how it happened, but The Craven flew down in the night to our lookout posts – we have no idea how they made it through undetected. They held onto Silas and the others, and made them watch as they took Raul. He's gone, Eve." Lara started to cry: "He's gone. He's been taken. And they didn't even take any of the others. They only wanted to make them watch. They've taken him."

I sat in the bed, stunned. The Shadow Beast had come to me in the night, found me in my dreams to test me. And I knew what had happened to Raul. I haltingly began to tell Lara what had happened that night.

Reaching out

Our focus gone, our camp in disarray, we sat together for long hours over the next few days, talking urgently about what we should do. Although so many fighters had joined us by that point, we felt rudderless with Raul gone, and utterly undone by grief.

As the others sat around on the fourth evening, knowing we had to make a decision either to attempt an attack, or retreat from these barren lands, I walked off alone. I spotted a figure walking towards me, right along the cliff edge. I knew him immediately.

I couldn't help myself. I didn't even have time to think. I threw myself at him, desperate for contact. I clutched at him and felt his arms band around me, gently at first, and then with increasing pressure. I didn't care, I needed that pressure. Rather than making me feel trapped, I needed it to feel safe – as if I had found some unexpected source of refuge in the storm. And it was a storm that crashed through me. I clung on as it whipped around my entire being, catching me up in the vortex. I clung on as he found my face and took my lips in his. I had never felt this urgency, never this need to get closer, get deeper. I didn't

307

understand it, but I allowed myself to trust it. I gasped as I felt his wings enfold me, marvelling at the little sacred space that he had created around us, within me. I felt his hands moving across my body, and I shuddered, then kissed him back with a hunger that I hadn't known was there.

In the dark of that night, as we lay gazing at each other, I asked him how he could be here, how he had survived The Riving.

'How did you get away? How are you still whole? What happened?"

"I'm not exactly sure. It was pure agony. I could feel myself being pulled into a thousand pieces; about to split apart. I could start to feel where the crack lines were going to open up along my body. It was so dark there, I couldn't see where I was, or what else was there. I started to think of all the things I love, have loved, through my whole life. I thought of my parents, my brothers, my friends. And I thought of you. I held you all in my mind, and it felt like some kind of sacred rite. I just held you all there, and loved you. And I felt so glad – so glad that I had known all that, whatever was to come now. So grateful. I thought of your face when I'd been taken out of the Hall, and I felt so moved that you had tried to save me – that my life had meant that much to you. It gave me more comfort than you can imagine.

"I didn't want my life to be over – I wanted to stay so much. But I also felt so grateful for all that had been in my life. My parents are long gone, but I held them in that space, and I was honouring them. I don't know how to describe it, really – it was as if I was more fully connected to the whole of my life, than I had ever consciously been – both now, reaching back into the past, but also beaming out into the future.

"And just as I was drifting in that feeling – almost a moment of bliss – I dropped suddenly. The density of the darkness lifted around me, and I was just crouched on the clifftop, completely alone. No great Hall, no Craven, no Beast.

"I guess they let me go. I'm not sure why. I don't know what else they have planned. But they let me go for now."

"What?" I asked. Raul looked unsure.

"No, nothing, I don't want to think about it now. I just have an uneasy feeling that it was too easy – that they let me go for a reason – that maybe by holding those things I loved so strongly in my mind, I gave them some ideas I don't want even to think about."

He shuddered, and dragged me closer to him, taking care to tuck the cloaks in around me to protect me from the night air. I reached for him. It was enough for him. His eyes smiled, then he closed them, buried his face in my hair and breathed me in.

When we rose to dress and get ready to move on, there was no sense of the shame I had always felt before with men. There was no defiance, no aggression in me – I felt calm and even joyful. But I also felt shy, and tried to cover my nakedness as I dressed. I'd never felt shy before, because no one had ever actually seen me – only my body. Now I felt a new sense of identity with my actual body and it felt a little confusing.

Raul smiled at me, before snaking his arms inside the

cloak I was trying miserably to use as cover.

"I'm not going to look unless you want me to. Ever. OK?"

"Ok." I smiled back, feeling faintly ridiculous. But he didn't force the issue, just kissed me gently on the mouth, and then stood to go.

"I'll wait for you by the fire, with the others. Hell, I'd have waited for you forever!" He grinned at me, and left me to get dressed.

The many paths we have

"What happens to us if I leave this place, and can never get back?" I was almost too afraid to voice the concern that had been eating away at me since Raul returned. "Will I lose you? I can't lose you." I bent my head into his chest, feeling the warmth there.

"You'll never lose me. Not if you don't want to. I can be anywhere you are. I can be a part of anything that you can be a part of. Don't let yourself be limited by place or time – not when you've seen all this."

"But I don't mean in some weird, cerebral 'we'll always have each other in here…' [I struck myself in the heart] bullshit. I mean really with you."

Raul laughed. "I know exactly what you meant! And I mean it – you'll never lose me if you don't want to. I can be anywhere with you. And you can be anywhere."

But I can't imagine you out of the woods. What about your wings? What about this life?"

"So many questions. Stop worrying about it. The woods are everywhere, the earth is everywhere. I can be at home anywhere because of it. These clothes, and these woods don't define me. I can be anywhere – I am just me. And you can be anywhere; you are just you.

"You won't see my wings in your world. But they'll still be there. You just use them in a different way. Yours have been there too – when you went back there." He smiled at me as I shook my head and started to contradict him.

"No, they…"

"They have, Eve. But they stay unseen, and you can't use them as you use them here."

"Then what is the point of them?"

"There are so many different ways to fly."

"What?"

"It is only when we can't do the obvious with them, that our trust can be shaken. Don't let that happen. Once we trust in them, it opens us up to so many other ways to fly. If you trust in them here, you should trust in them there also. Never think they are gone. We are all born with wings, Eve, and don't believe the fairytales of childhood. Wings are what we grow into, not grow out of. This is no Puff the Magic Dragon. Worlds are not closed off to us as we get older – they are opened up. But only if we allow them to be."

"OK." I didn't fully get what he was talking about, but I knew him well enough now to know that he was telling me the truth, and that he was sharing something important with me.

"Enanti can show you the extreme of a sensory way to live – how to live fully realised. And once you have tasted it, you will know how to seek those paths wherever you are, use those gifts. You may not be able to breathe underwater there, but you will remember how that feels – and you will find new things you can do that you never believed you could."

He stroked the side of my face.

"But I have to stay here until we have Alette. You understand that? I would love you to stay until then too. Still, that is your choice. It is a choice we each have to make for ourselves."

I nodded, knowing the importance of his having chosen this path, and needing to see it through. And I knew I would stay here to fight for Alette, too, for my friends, for this beautiful man, for this strange land, for myself.

To go in the dark with a light is to know the light.
To know the dark, go dark. Go without sight,
and find that the dark, too, blooms and sings,
and is traveled by dark feet and dark wings.

Wendell Berry

Summoned

That night I went to dark places in my dreams. A shadowed figure approached through the gloom, and as it came nearer I recognised the dark blood red of one of The Craven. It was silently holding something out to me; words burned into parchment. A summons from the Shadow Beast. I was to come alone, and we would talk. This way, hundreds would not have to die.

As soon as I woke, I told Raul. We were sleeping alone, outside, protected slightly from the elements by the thorny grove of stunted trees by the camp.

"Are you sure? Is this what you want to do?" Raul asked.

I nodded, feeling the quickening, the pull towards this crisis. I couldn't explain it, even to myself, but I knew it was everything – it would decide all. But for that evening, I still had the security of Raul's arms. I needed it that night. I didn't know who I would be the next day, or if I would even survive it.

"Hold me?" I asked. He let out a breath, and gathered me in close. His arms were so tight that they allowed my body to sag, and I relaxed into him.

"You don't need to do this you know. There will be

another way, a more straightforward one. This is too risky. This is...uhh, fuck this, I can't lose you, Eve."

"This is as straightforward as it gets. The Beast has given us a chance to meet – to discuss terms – to see Alette. We can't pass up this opportunity."

"But why just you? It is too risky, far too risky. You'll be in there alone, entirely at his mercy. And I won't be able to protect you."

"You can't always protect me, Raul; you know that. And you also know that I can protect myself. I learned from the best." I smiled into his chest, and heard the snort of acknowledgment from inside him.

I continued: "What you've given me will always protect me, because you've given me back parts of myself. Some parts of me were still functioning, but others were starved of oxygen; still there, but stunted and gasping. I know I have further to go – but, for the first time, I've started to believe that I can. That is an incredible gift – and you helped me to unwrap it.

"But I am scared to cross this water. I sense something. Night is coming, and it is an older night, a longer one, with no certainty of the sun rising again."

I sent my soul through the Invisible,
Some letter of that After-life to spell:
And by and by my Soul return'd to me,
And answer'd: 'I myself am Heav'n and Hell.

Omar Khayyam

Adrift in the darkness

I needed to trust in myself. When the Shadow Beast visited me in my dreams that night, he knew he had my acceptance. He had told me to come alone. Told me what would happen to the others if I did not. His voice was silky, seductive – I was tumbling through the night. He held me in my bed and opened his vast wings around me. In them I saw a million worlds. There was the sensation of flying, being carried off, and then I was dumped abruptly on a cold stone floor. In front of me was a heavy wooden door, which was open to reveal stone steps leading down into the earth.

I climbed down and down the steps, spiralling down into the darkness. As my legs started to burn with the effort, I reached the gates at the bottom. They were incongruous here, down this deep under the earth. They could have graced any palace with their grandeur. They appeared to be made of metal, but were so smooth that they could not have been beaten into shape. Around the edge, and down the centre, precious stones nestled in intricate settings, as if a thousand rings had been set here, suggesting promises made. As I pushed on them, the gates swung open.

Light flickered around me in the gloom of the chamber I had entered. It was vast, and I couldn't properly see across to the other side. It was built in the design of a full gladiatorial arena. No pillars were in evidence, to hold up the ceiling that I knew must be there. From the number of steps I estimated I was at least half a kilometre underground. The aisle led gently down to the circular area in the centre. Around this, terraced stone seating sloped upwards, staggered up the slope. Set at exact intervals along the stone seats were stubby, lit candles, thousands upon thousands of them. The light they gave off flickered and wavered, sending an eerie glow throughout the chamber. They reminded me of the stands of candles in church, remembering the dead. It should have been beautiful, and in a way it was, but the room felt numbingly cold. I wondered what the creatures that dwelt here would have to commemorate: what peace they were searching for.

"The same as you." The voice was everywhere, deep and sonorous, running right through me and stealing my breath.

"Where are you?" I managed, hoping that my voice held firm.

A snort of derision. "I am everywhere, Eve, haven't you worked that out yet?" Each word sounded as if it had come from a different corner of the chamber, and I spun around trying to keep up with them until I realised the futility of my efforts.

'If you want me to reduce myself to something you can simply see, if that would give you a false sense of some parity, then I can, but I had hoped for better from you."

That voice, so honeyed and rich. As it spoke it seemed to create harmonies with itself, pitching each word at myriad different notes simultaneously, chiming so melodically.

"I'm not afraid of you!" I shouted into the gloom, and the force of it sent the candles closest to me flickered madly.

A deep chuckle followed, and then a silent pause.

"Oh Eve, you do amuse. Of course you fear me. How can you not – when you don't understand what I am? And the amusement continues; because if you did fully understand what I was, you would be even more afraid!

"You are afraid of some things that you know – but above all, you fear those things that you know are out there, but you don't understand. Out there in the dark. That is me, Eve, the one that is out there in the dark, always there, and waiting."

"Waiting for what?" I asked.

"For you."

My heart ran cold as I heard the truth in his words. "What do you want from me?" I asked on a whisper.

"I want all of you Eve, your strength, your heart. I want your soul." These last words were whispered, but they reverberated around and around the room, like an echo that had been trapped underground.

I shivered violently from the frost in his words.

"Look around this chamber. See all these candles? You were wondering what creatures from this land would be commemorating, yearning for. Oh, we yearn, Eve, believe me. The power of our longings would leave you appalled. I know what yearning is – just as you do. Yes, I know how much you yearn, Eve; it rolls off you in waves. And I can help you. All you need to do is surrender to those feelings, give into them, and come back to me. Come back home.

"With me, you would satisfy those longings, you would take vengeance on those who have wronged you, you could rain fire down on your enemies. Wouldn't you like to see them writhe in agony? I know that you have fought those feelings, but I also know they have been there. And I can show you such dark magic that your family would live again."

I could feel myself leaning into the seduction in his voice, wanting the release that he hinted at. His voice was warm, delicious, spreading through my body. I shook.

"Eve, Eve," he breathed. "I am unbridled power, I can answer all your heart's desires. You have become very powerful, but this is nothing compared to what I can give you. You have always thought that darkness was simply the absence of light, haven't you? Oh, Eve! That was never true – there is a whole world out here in the darkness, seething with life. The shadows are where the real power lies. The true passions of mankind lie here, waiting to be harnessed. I can show you worlds."

"What of Alette?" I demanded.

"She is mine. You will never have her. And soon you will be mine, too."

As he spoke, a vast darkness entered the room. I can't explain it fully, but it felt as if it misted down from above and made the very air heavy and hard to breathe. Some of the dark mist even seemed to flow out of me, or through me. The candles all flickered and bobbed, throwing crazy patterns on the nearby stones. As I struggled to drag in enough air, the darkness seemed to collect in one area, swirling around with a deep vortex at its centre. As I watched, it became denser and denser, until it finally took the rough shape of a creature – a massive horned Beast that walked on four legs. Its lizard-like tail dragged along the ground behind it as it prowled along a line of seating several metres above me.

"Perhaps you can only cope with seeing me in this form," chided the Beast, as he stalked along the stones. "Disappointing."

I felt a pang of shame. I wanted him to be impressed with me for some reason. I wasn't sure now whether that was because I wanted him to fear me, or a simple need for him to find me special, worthy.

"I can cope with a lot," I spat back at him. "And I am not the person I was when you first started to stalk my dreams. "We have fought with your armies, and we have cut you back in many places. I can fly now, and I can sense things that I couldn't before."

"Yes, you have pushed back my armies, but Eve, can't you see? The Fears are infinite. There will always be new recruits to my ranks, there will always be an army in your way. You can't win! It was all engineered so, so that you would be standing here, as you now are, talking with me. At my mercy.

"And oh, Eve, I want to be merciful! Yes – you have grown, and you are wonderful, just wonderful!" He spoke as if to a young child who had just produced a rather adorable drawing.

I smarted under his honey laced with disdain. Without

a conscious thought from me, my wings unfurled, and spread around me.

The Beast threw back his head and laughed. Black ash and smoke whirled to keep the edges of his form intact as he moved.

He looked me dead in the eye then – at least, insofar as something without true form can stare. His eyes were devastating. Pools of darkness that were ancient and knowing, that spoke of malicious rage, unbounded lust, manipulation and secrets. They swirled and thrashed; bottomless chasms that pulled you in.

"You don't need wings to fly, Eve. That's a truth that none of The Craven realise – so they are bound to me.

"Now, you will know. You will see the truth, and you will know. And after you have seen, you will not reject me. I see them in you: shame, guilt, sexual longing, the desire for vengeance – and the rest. You think you are so different from me?"

He opened up wings of his own, dark and eternal. The chamber felt too small to contain him. It had always been too small. He rose above me, his form now becoming less distinct around the edges, his eyes pinning me where I stood. His wings grew and stretched, and then they reached for me. They drew around me, and I was lifted off the ground. I crossed that threshold of consciousness. In his wings, I was in free fall. I fell past stars and galaxies, my mind unable to take in all that was shown. I tumbled past palaces that were simultaneously filled with life and joy, but also death and despair. I saw images of the Shadow Beast copulating furiously with prone members of The Craven and writhing members of the Riven, and I saw worlds cracking apart and colliding together, taking new forms, in the blink of an eye. Time had no place here, place had no time. I was in a different Realm altogether. I drifted down.

His voice reached me in this abyss.

"And here I will keep you, until you know – until you realise that you are mine. You will see the truth of everything, Eve – see it well. And you will know that you are mine. In a while, I will call to you and you will give your answer.

"You will let me touch you; you will ask for it. And the funny thing is, that is all you needed to do to get Alette back – just get close enough to touch her. And you were always just too far away."

The voice rocked me, seduced, tempted. The beauty I found in his wings was mesmerising. The possibilities were infinite. I could feel his presence moving through me, making me restless, making me ache for him. His wings caressed me, held me. Everything else seemed so distant, so remote from here. I had lost my footing.

I may have drifted for a thousand years – it didn't matter; nothing seemed to matter. I had the sensation of falling lower, but I had no way of telling in the density of darkness that surrounded me. If he had only held me in a dark prison with damp walls and a bone-deep chill, I may have stood a chance. But it was warm here in the darkness, velvety and rich. I wanted to stay.

I saw lost worlds, dying worlds, worlds made again, and still I kept falling. Visions of my parents appeared in front of me – my sister and my brother. Their smiles told me that they were glad I had come. I was returning to a ship I had once abandoned. I had left them there in their grave of rubble and I had walked away. I had betrayed them. I felt as if I now walked in communion with them once more; they were not lost to me. I knew that I had found the world that Claire had spoken of: the mythical land of the dead. I felt I understood this world. I had to stay.

I saw paths shooting off in all directions, millions of paths, millions of possibilities. On some of them were small, unformed beings, some more developed than others. They all turned to look at me in turn, and in each case I stared back into my own eyes. I felt revulsion and compulsion battling within me.

"Don't fight," murmured that voice of ages all around me. They are all versions of you; you can't fight that. Nascent beings that you wouldn't allow to be fully born; the unfulfilled. You can bring them to fruition, Eve – you have that power."

I looked again; some revolted me, twisted and deformed. Others were strong and lithe, and I was drawn to them, rather proud. I watched as one of them, sensual and magnetic, drew someone in for a kiss. Deepening the kiss, she rubbed herself against the faceless man, and he sank helplessly to the ground with her. I felt a surge of female sexual power within, and revelled in it.

On another path I saw myself again, powerful, with a drawn sword. In front of me stood the soldiers who had taken my life away. This version of me grinned back at me, powerful in her vengeance, then turned and cut the soldiers down, one after the other, with sadistic glee. I was shocked that a thrill of exultation went through me.

So many pathways, so many versions of me that I saw. I watched them all, saw myself in every possible constellation.

When my hand brushed past my hip, I felt it. The small nugget in my pouch, that I took with me everywhere. My sea glass. My hand went to it instinctively, and I drew it out. A piece of light from above. It glowed in my hand, soft and gentle. Not a blinding light, but a soothing one. If someone had shone a torch through this inky darkness, I would have turned away, averted my eyes. But this was the right amount of light. It spoke to me of stormy skies, crashing waves and the world above. It called to me, calling me back to the sea and the free air. I gasped a breath in. I hadn't realised how cloying the air was down here, how it seemed to drug as much as it maintained life. I started to push against the velvet air, feeling trapped in the swathes of material. It was strangling me like jungle creepers.

As I thought this, I felt my feet touch the bottom. There was a limit here, and that relieved me. The words of the Shadow Beast leapt into my mind: "You have always thought that darkness was simply the absence of light, haven't you? Oh, Eve! That was never true – there is a whole world out here in the darkness, seething with life."

I now knew that to be true; I had seen what power lives in the darkness. There are things that live and breathe there – and they ooze with potential. Simply keeping the light on will never keep them at bay. They just move backwards, out of the way of the beam, and then regroup behind you. You need to walk out into the darkness, and meet with them. Only once you have done that can you walk through the night without fear. I had lived long enough to see the same things with different eyes.

And a torch will only help you so much – what you really need to develop is night vision. I remembered back to a flash of my childhood; my father teaching us to see better in the dark. He would make us close our eyes, then turn off the light suddenly. After counting slowly to ten, we could open our eyes, and they really had adjusted to the dark. It was like a magic trick, and we made him do it night after night when he came up to kiss us goodnight.

I recalled the words that Claire and I had shared, a different world ago: that both the darkness of the night, and the glare of the sun can blind you. You need a careful balance of the two to see clearly.

But the Beast had also got it wrong. I could never live down here in this velvet lair. It was as much of a prison as the one that I had been trying to escape; seducing you into captivity. I could never live without the sky arching over me, the waves crashing into me. The bracing of one's feet to withstand the impact was a simple testament to life. Without Raul to love, explore life with, without my friends, without my Marni. They had grounded me as much as they had given me flight – giving me an anchor point to return to again and again. A home. They were my counterpoint to this dark inner world. From the pouch, I also withdrew Sula's words.

But I could see parts of the darkness that had a home in me, too – had a place there. This wasn't a strange dark land; this was me. My inner lands. It was intimidating, but it was the truth. The sensual pleasure I had felt with Raul had scared me, but I accepted it now. The anger in me for what my family had suffered, what I had suffered, was part of me, too. I had met with these parts of myself down there: the desire for revenge, the desire to kill, the cowardice, the guilt, all of them – and I had spoken with them. Some of them weren't pretty; some were tortured and disgusting, hard to look upon. But they were there. My darks to my lights. Shame, such a potent foe, seemed to step away from me now, and I was able to look him in the eye.

I had been so taken up with the parts of myself that I thought I had lost, that I had been unaware of how many parts of myself I had voluntarily hidden away, stuffed under the carpet of my shame.

This is why Raul survived The Riving! I suddenly understood. Like a dream that I had had an eternity ago - before I had come here, before I had grown wings, before I had ever encountered the Shadow Beast – I had seen him in my dreams. Only those who allowed it could be Riven. I felt a rush of power surge through me. It was true; it must be true! Only those who allowed it could be Riven! The Shadow Beast's power lay in suggestion, manipulation, temptation and seduction. He played expertly on fears, pulling you in. But if you didn't want to fragment into a thousand pieces, you couldn't be made to. It really was that simple. Raul had held firm and survived, not because they had let him go, as he had assumed, but because the very core of his being rejected any idea of fragmentation. He knew who he was, right down to the darker parts of him.

He would also have held firm in the furnace. He hadn't been allowed to 'escape' for a more twisted purpose. They were not planning to use his love against him; they simply couldn't. The Shadow Beast had seen it there, and realised that he could do nothing to Raul. The Beast had had no choice but to let him go; Raul wasn't his prisoner any more.

When his voice came down to me through the ages, I was ready.

"Eve, I have come for your answer. I am waiting for you."

I was instantly back in the candle-lit arena. As the darkness began once again to coalesce in one area, I waited for the Shadow Beast to show himself. My hands were fisted, and in my right hand, I clutched my sea glass; in my left, Sula's note. I marvelled at the power of this little frosted fragment and this tiny paper scrap. My wings were out, but unopened, relaxed and folded.

I had surfaced with a different understanding of reincarnation. I myself was an embodiment of past lives, each one stacked within me as an infinite series of Russian dolls. I myself had died many deaths, but those parts were still in there, still essential parts of self. I felt as if I had uncovered a treasure; taken gold from this time of Shadow.

I could sense immediately that I was not as the Shadow Beast had expected. He prowled along the stone lines, stepping down a few rows towards me until I struggled to keep him fully in the limits of my vision. I somehow knew without a glimmer of doubt that he could attempt to eviscerate me, and he would fail. The knowledge thrilled through my body.

"My answer is no." My voice rang strong and true

through the chamber. In it I heard the chiming chords that The Beast had used on me yesterday. My voice was richer, more multi-layered and tonal.

"You sought to take me, heart and soul. You have failed. I know now that you can't take me. You can't take anything. You can't take anything until people choose it. All you have the power to do is to trick people into choosing it.

"Oh, I so nearly chose it all. It was so beautiful..." I paused as I remembered the worlds I had seen in his arms, the pleasures hinted at.

"You work through deception and temptation. I don't want that. But there is some truth in what you showed me. Rather than you taking me, I saw to take parts of you. All you are is parts of me. Nothing more."

At this, the Beast hissed violently, and retreated rapidly up several lines of stones. I couldn't be sure, but it seemed as if I could begin to see the candles that flickered behind him, the vapour of his form thinning. He appeared angry and unstable. The inky density of him in this form started to look patchy and ethereal. More like smoke than form. He hissed again, baring his teeth, and the dark cloud started to break up and dissipate.

"You will have all of me or nothing!" he screamed, as he vanished from view.

Flower

I was in a huge room, and there were flowers all along the sides of the walls. As I looked closer, I saw they were all sewn on to long long pieces of fabric that stretched off into the distance. These pieces of fabric were as tall as a small hedge. They were an expression of grief. Rather than a story, or an explanation, they symbolised the reality of living with grief. Each flower or decoration was an approximation of each time you had thought of the person you had lost. A floral mind-map, building up into a thing of such beauty. It was more poignant than I can say. A real, living memorial of the best kind. It was simply an account of when that lost person was thought of. Sometimes it was clear how they were thought of – that is, a happy memory, or a painful one, a scar or hole in the material with a different-looking flower.

It felt real. It felt true. An honest account of how it is to live with grief each day. An expression of grief that held true to just how much that person was still part of your daily thoughts – however many years later, however much the world around you had forgotten. It was a memorial that was added to, re-created in some way, each day; a visual journal of love and loss.

How painfully, beautifully right. It was a breakthrough – how to express this kind of pain authentically, powerfully. It was open, honest, visible but not sentimental, not asking for anything other than just to be witnessed. It was not packed away, hidden, ugly.

There was pain; that was obvious. But it was stated and presented so simply. So unaffected. It was the most beautiful, intense expression of grief, and living through grief, that I have ever seen.

There was no big empty strip of fabric stretching off into the future. The whole thing would just grow naturally each day; a real thing, grounded in today. The flowers were not in a set pattern, but ran, bustled, nestled beautifully in random truthfulness across the fabric. Some days were so dense, so full of flowers and pain; in other places there were stretches of white fabric showing underneath, then a brief posy of flowers – and so on. So honest. An ECG of the grieving heart. As I watched, new flowers gently appeared on the strip. They weren't sewn on - they were each alive, never fading, sustained by something beyond.

An immense chronological strip, decorated with each thought as it happened. A blossoming. A testament. Not a shrinking, but a growth.

Tonight we fall through our dreams forever
And reveal our secret way ahead
Trading every stone we've thrown for feathers
So we can fly awake instead.

Stefan Mørk

New dawn

I flew all the way back to the camp. I was alive with this new knowledge that I had risked so much for. I also knew that Raul and the others would be frantic at my lengthy disappearance, and I hoped he would understand. I hoped they had not been rash – tried to launch some rescue party, that would more likely have led to their deaths. I had no idea how long I had been away; it had felt like many lives that I had drifted for in those dark wings. I urged my own wings to work faster, cutting through the night with great strokes.

I was flying over the sea all the way. The Straits between the Shadow Realm and Enanti were bleak and restless, waves heaving upwards in the night and throwing spray onto my wings. I didn't care. I knew that I could just as easily dive down into those depths and swim my way back to Enanti. I had no fear of that sea – a wide chasm that the Shadow Beast had always intended to intimidate and separate us from ourselves.

I came upon the camp sooner than I had realised. My concerns had been founded – the entire body of the Free had moved from the forest, right up to the empty shoreline that marked the very edge of Enanti. Beyond that lay the sea, and beyond that the desolate wastes of the Shadow Realm.

I could see that they had dug themselves into defensive positions, in anticipation for an invasion of the Craven. I spotted Raul with his men around a rough training ground, hunched over the ground, drawing out their strategies with long sticks.

My landing wasn't exactly under control, so great was my sense of urgency. Then I ran to Raul, who clasped me to his chest.

"We were just about to leave. Three of us. We were about to come over the sea for you," he managed eventually, into the top of my head.

I didn't know how to explain all that had happened, all that I had learned.

"I'm OK – I really am OK!" I beamed up at him, my smile coming from a different place than the million smiles that had come before.

"Did he let you go? God, Eve, you should never have gone. You should never have gone alone. It was too risky…"

"It's OK. I had to go. You know that. It was my choice."

"How are you here? What happened?"

I wanted to share my treasure with him, the gold that I had taken from the Shadow.

"He can't destroy us, Raul, not unless we choose it ourselves. He just doesn't have that power. His power is in mirage, sleight of hand and tricks with mirrors. He makes you believe things are one way, but they are not!

"He is immensely powerful – but not in the way we

335

thought. We have always had the power to end this, to reduce him, but we've never been able to see it."

I talked low and urgently, giving them a tiny glimpse into what I had seen in his wings, and they all listened. I spoke of the worlds I had seen, the birth and death, the paths shooting outwards that whispered unfulfilled possibilities. I even spoke about the versions of myself I had seen down there, and Raul squeezed my hand as I revealed so much of myself.

When we had a chance to speak alone, as the others continued their conversation, I said to Raul, "I belong to no one but myself. The Beast works by making you think that by thinking certain things, feeling certain ways, you belong to him. You don't. You never did – unless you let those darker sides of yourself control you. Then you are lost."

Raul nodded his head quietly, taking it all in.

"I know I have those darker urges in me Raul – I think now that we all do. And I think in some strange way they give this strange blade power that I don't really understand." I gestured to the huge broadsword that I had somehow pulled from myself.

"But I also think it is important how I choose to use this blade. Whenever I clasp its handle, I can feel the energy pulsing through it – I can almost feel the streaks of light pulsing out in every direction, illuminating the infinite number of paths I could choose to go down. And sometimes it feels as light as a feather, and other times I can hardly lift it. I don't understand this sword; it feels like redemption and temptation all rolled into one – but I do now believe that I am the one driving it; not the other way around."

Lara came over: "I need to speak to you about the sword." She looked concerned.

My heart sank. I hadn't wanted to think that Lara, my friend, would be holding onto the same concerns and suspicions about me that had been circling the camp like vultures since the sword had appeared.

She caught my expression. "No! It's nothing like that, Eve. I had some information for you – you need to hear it." She placed her hand firmly on my hand, willing me to feel her belief. "I know that there is nothing to be afraid of, with you finding that sword. It is a good thing. A part of you. And I know you, and I don't have the slightest concern that you have that sword. But I need to talk to you about it." She glanced around, and then: "not here. Any talk of the sword out here will just get tongues wagging again, and that's not going to help anyone. I want to talk to you first – then I will talk to the rest."

We walked off to the edge of the camp, far enough from the fire to have the night largely claim us, with just the faintest flickers of occasional light dancing across our faces when the fire spat brightly.

"I had a vision in the night, Eve. I spoke to the main Oracle. My mind was stumbling towards some truth, and the Oracle must have sensed that, and wanted to help me.

This sword you have – it is a protection sword. It was pulled from you, by yourself, at a time you needed protection. And that is crucial. It is not an attacking sword. They are very different things, although they look exactly

337

the same. It is the manner in which you found it that is the important detail. If you had sought a sword at a time of anger and hatred, you would hold an attacking sword. With an attacking blade in your hand, you can't protect yourself; you are lost to the Shadow Beast in fundamental ways. You can only kill. And likewise, a protection sword isn't meant for aggression. If you try to use it in that way, you are lost. Remember that, Eve, when we go into battle. You get to choose how you use that sword. Remember what it is meant for. Don't forget that – even when it feels so tempting; even when it feels like the obvious thing to do."

Each word made perfect sense to me. My own mind had been half aware of this, had already had some sense of knowing that how I chose to use the blade was important.

"Yes," I said. "You are right. I can feel that. And I won't forget how to use it. I can feel the power it has."

Reclaiming the land

The starved light of dawn prompted us to seek our beds. We would need our rest before the night ahead. We had talked through the past night, carefully birthing our plan.

We had to cross the sea – all of us together – to the Shadow Realm.

Some would fly out over the sea, some would swim, and we would land on the shores of the Shadow Realm at dusk. We knew that many of us would be killed. There was nowhere to hide in the desolation of the Shadow Realm – no tall forest cover at all. We knew that creatures roamed the wastes unconfined, sating their appetites on anything they could find.

Our strength lay in knowing the limitations of the Shadow Beast. Once seemingly so omnipotent, a chink in his armour had been revealed. No, not so much that, as a diamond-plating of our own shields and hearts. A sword or an arrow could still kill us, but we no longer had to fear a perpetual death, a rendering of our entire being. Living while dead.

It was an astonishing sight – seeing the Free take flight as one. Our numbers had swelled to more than 200 over the past few days, and all were ready for the night ahead. Some chose to plunge into the silvered waves. The sea and the sky thickened with life as we headed out over the Straits. As far as I could see in either direction, I saw us, the Free, all on the wing or gliding through the water beneath me. We flew in on a cloud of expectation.

A dark smudge thickened on the horizon, taking form as we drew closer. From our height we could see much of the littoral, and glimpses of the interior. In the centre was the Great Hall, with its arching buttresses and glittering domes. It was an astonishing structure, of flowing lines and pinnacles. It looked as if it had been carved from one block of obsidian, so flawless were its languid curves. It was seamless, jointless, perfect. And it shone. Not a glittering, sharp, refracted glow, but a smooth, seductive dark luminosity – like an opulent black pearl. It was an unearthly beauty, a menacing pull that drew you in. One end of the Great Hall launched out over the sea, taking full advantage of the towering cliffs. A tiny door up there opened out directly onto the clifftop, using it as a balcony.

The front side of the Great Hall was an extended stretch of thicket and thorns, reaching all the way down to the sea. We couldn't see beyond the Hall, but we had heard that this part of the Shadow Realm was covered in thick, low jungle creepers, with plants that moved and could devour a person whole, and where the dreaded Glades of Truth were said to be dotted – picking apart the seams of your sanity. Once trapped in there, you may as well face The Riving, so mad could you be driven. Shattered into a million pieces, blown away on the wind.

We landed as the sun began to spill the blood of that day onto the sea below. The day was gone, and we must enter the night.

It had to be that way. The cover of the night would aid us against The Craven. With their stiff masks blinkering them, we could use the dark to our advantage. The Creepers were our main fear – creatures who could camouflage themselves by assuming human form, then self-detonate when they got close enough. But because of the nature of their attacks, we would have been equally hampered in the daytime. We just had to trust that our lookouts and scouts would pick up on them. We would only face The Riven once we were close to the Shadow Beast, we knew, and I hoped that the talk we had had before we set off would retain its influence once we were actually face to face with the Beast. Knowledge can be one thing, but feeling something and trusting in it, quite another.

"You OK?" Raul asked, to my right.

"Yes. I'm ready. I really think we can do this."

"We can. And we will. What are you taking in?"

I relaxed my mind, and allowed everything to flow in – the crashing and draw of the waves behind us, the suck of the water back over the pebbles, causing some to tumble back down the incline, the shallow breathing of the men and women all around me in the dark, the rustle of feathers and the uneasy shifting of feet. I knew that the decision to do this at night had been strongly resisted by some in the camp. Raul, Silas and I had explained why it was our only option – that the cloak of night could be used to our advantage, taken back as a valid strategy from the very Realm that had commandeered it.

I let my senses stretch out further, beyond our company. Tucked into the night and coming closer on our left flank I felt the unsettling slide of something approaching. A Creeper.

"A Creeper, to our left." I breathed to Raul. "Coming closer."

I felt the second that the Creeper came out of cover and changed form.

We ran over to the left of our group, and saw a man wandering slowly towards us, smiling and gesturing apologetically.

"Sorry, just needed a comfort break."

I felt the waves of bitterness and malevolence rolling off him – completely at odds with his friendly persona. His disguise was so perfect, anyone would have mistaken him for one of our band.

"Shields up!" I cried to the people closest to us. "I know you!" I accused the Creeper, as I ducked behind my own shield. He snarled, suddenly abandoning human form and rushing towards us on all fours, snarling and slavering. Then – boom! – an almighty shockwave sent us falling backwards as The Creeper detonated. He had taken none of us with him. But we knew he would not be the last that night.

We all lived through many lives in those long, dark hours. Many thousands of The Craven were unleashed upon us, but we were well-skilled in confronting them, and we suffered few losses. After a night of confusion, effort and courage, we saw a thin edge of grey lighten the horizon, splitting the sky from the sea. A crack of light coming in.

We had fought our way around to the part of the Great Hall that was closest to the coast, where the turret hung out precariously over the cliffs. With The Craven largely defeated, we now faced The Riven. I steadied myself with a deep breath. I had seen these creatures before, but they still sent a shiver through me. Most were foul-faced, grotesque forms – the distillation of the very worst in us. Formed by rabid, murderous intent, they were strong, ruthless and killed blindly. A few were shockingly beautiful. Their dark faces were alive with sensual promise, and their skin sparked and glittered as they moved. They were the hardest to bear, the hardest to fight. The male versions of these Riven were the embodiment of physical masculine perfection, and they wore little to hide it. The female ones did likewise, and a momentary hesitation from an adversary was taken full advantage of. In close contact with one of these, you were hit by such a shock of sensual awareness, that your mind was not your own for a few vital seconds. And that was their greatest weapon. Some, I was told, took on the perfected form of a lost love, even slipping in details such as a favourite necklace or arm cuff. I had myself seen the hesitation in one man as he gasped with recognition of something he had lost in the Riven in front of him. His sword had come down, his eyes full of longing as she had stalked towards him. He was completely undone. He didn't see the dagger glittering in her hand, probably didn't even feel the sting of it as she slid it between his ribs, cutting his heart.

As the light swelled, the wind picked up. Dark clouds

were tumbling through the sky, racing in from the north. Bullets of rain started to sting our cheeks, driving into us from the side, and making our footing less sure on the shingle.

More Riven flooded towards us from all directions, but we were holding our own. I flew up and down the lines of our people, shouting reminders to them that the Riven were not as they appeared, reminding them to see through it all.

Suddenly archers took up positions either side of us on the shoreline, sending shafts of death flying towards us.

"Shields up!' I heard the scream, and quickly twisted in the air, trying to avoid the deluge. One arrow hit me in the wing, piercing through, but not causing any real damage. I tore it out as I struggled to find space to land, finding a spot at last in our squeezed position. We were all trapped on the ground now – pinned down by the sheer number of their archers. It was far too dangerous to take flight.

"Up off the beach!" I cried, just as Raul, Silas and the other leaders urged the people nearest to them to do the same. "We must get off the beach!"

We started to push our way up towards the hinterlands of this Realm – leaving the shingle for the deepening thicket. Brambles and creepers clung to our legs, forcing us to slash and cut with every step, slowing us down and making us vulnerable. The dagger that Raul had insisted I take for protection was being well used now – and with gratitude. My sword, too, seemed to slice through the tendrils like butter.

Suddenly a huge throng of the Riven were in front of us.

344

We skidded to a halt, completely outnumbered, with more creatures coming at us from the sides. I swung my head around to catch the faces of my friends, all too aware of the desperateness of our situation.

"The sword, Eve!" I heard Raul shout. I knew he was right, but I was so afraid to use it in the wrong way, that I had been failing to use it in the right way either. I raised the sword in both hands and thrust it out in front of me. It seemed to glow with a hidden promise, and my heart surged. I could see the impact on the Creatures immediately. They froze, and stepped back. Each step forward that I took, they retreated. I felt almost giddy with the power of it. And I felt I had it under control.

But then I saw them. Standing right in the front row of this mass were three figures with faces that cut right to my core. They had the faces of the soldiers who had abandoned Laila to a hideous death, who had raped me, and they were leering at me now. I screamed, and started to race towards them. I was oblivious to the fact that all the Riven were now standing with their arms raised – the universal signal of surrender. I was half aware of the look of one of their faces as they exchanged a glance that seemed to be a pre-arranged signal, backed with a smug smile.

"No, Eve!" shouted Lara from behind me. "Don't do it! Don't do anything else! They are surrendering."

"Kill them, Eve! It's a trick! They are not really giving up – you need to kill them now while we have the chance," screamed Silas on the other side.

I gazed around wildly between the two of them, the

sword held high and pointed towards the Riven.

"Eve, no, please!" Lara cried more beseechingly. "Yes, it is a trick – but it is one that is meant to trap you. Don't fall for it. Remember that whatever you are seeing in them, isn't real. Whoever they are appearing to you as, is just to try to control you. Don't let them do that… Remember what that sword is for: what it can do and what it can't. Please."

I looked into the eyes of those who had attacked me when I was so small. My whole body shook with my desire to cut them down. As Silas kept roaring in one ear, it was the silence that Lara now maintained that was the thing I heard the loudest. She was letting me decide this moment, allowing me the space to feel what I should do. Time seemed to freeze. The raindrops seemed to linger in the air for longer. The arrows raining down on us from the beach sides seemed pathetically slow and easy to parry.

And I knew who I was. I knew what I would do. I screamed loudly as I dropped the sword to the ground, and dug its tip brutally into the earth. Drawing a blunt line. Let them come. Just let them try. If I cut them down in anger, it would take me ever closer to being a creature like they were.

Everything still seemed to be in slow motion as their pretence of surrender was shown to be the farce it was. They rushed towards us as one, snarling and snapping with their contorted faces. I didn't move. And as I had known would happen, as soon as they got within a few feet of the line I had drawn, they bounced off some invisible barrier that had been created. They howled in frustration as they scrabbled and slipped on the nebulous surface that was keeping them at bay. And I knew what I could do. I gripped the sword hard again with both hands, and without raising its tip from the clodded earth, I dragged it along as I ran around the outside of our band, back down onto the beach, around the perimeter of every one of our group who was under attack. Running back up the other side, I completed the circle by returning to where I had started. I knew the line would hold as long as I was in possession of this sword.

"Look, Eve!" I heard Raul shout over the throng, and I turned my head immediately to the right position to pick him out.

"Look – look up there! He shouted, pointing wildly up into the sky.

I followed the line of his fingers, and suddenly stilled.

"It's her, Eve – it's Alette!"

It was. Even from this vast distance I knew that truth.

Completion

I saw her up there, a tiny figure right up on the cliff-side. She looked so inconsequential against that backdrop. Yet that was why we were all here – for this precious scrap. I could see the Beast approaching her, trying to take her out of view. I redoubled my efforts, slashing with renewed vigour at the living tentacles that were beginning to wrap around my legs once more. I couldn't fly up there; it was too exposed. I was aware that any flight on my part would see me shot down in a storm of arrows. I wouldn't get the chance to touch her. My wings, primed and powerful on my back, shuddered with agitation. What, then?

Shaking my head to clear my mind, I fought to focus. I knew we had a just a moment of time before this opportunity was lost to us. I stared wildly up at the cliff-top again, and caught my breath. She had wings! I had never noticed them before. A tiny set of dark wings adorned her back, visible only now that she had turned to face the approaching beast. It crept along the cliff-top towards her, certain of its prize.

"Fly!" I screamed up to her: "Fly down to me!"

The wind must have carried my words to her. She spun

around, and looked towards me. The gusts whipped her dark curls about her head, and she smiled down at me. Her features were too far away to be distinct, but I knew she smiled. I felt it. It was as if she had been waiting for my invitation. That somehow the invitation itself made her invulnerable to the arrows stinging through the air. She stepped towards the edge, and for a prolonged moment she appeared to lean out towards the drop. I held my breath. She leapt, and everything slowed down. As she fell through the air, I willed her to open her wings, willed them to be big enough to carry her back to me.

"Use your wings. Open your wings," I muttered through gritted teeth. She spiralled down and down, impossibly small in the buffeting wind. I thought she would smash on the cliff-face. Two, five seconds, ten and still she fell. Finally, finally her wings began to open, and caught her wild tumble. She descended more slowly now, gracefully, soaring down towards me. I felt the strangest sense of a memory, just out of grasp, but urgent, and growing. A shaft of light pierced the storm clouds. As it hit her wings, I gasped, and stumbled to my knees. Flashes of brilliant turquoise and indigo – a kaleidoscope of colour, image, knowledge and memory. I felt the world change. She glided slowly down and landed lightly, so lightly, in front of me. She smiled, tenderly stroking my wet cheek, as I reached for her.

"Hello, you," I whispered.

"Hello, me," she replied.

* * *

I am all I've ever seen. I am all I've ever been.

I am the avenging angel, I am the poet, the healer, the soaring eagle. I am the air, the endless sea, the earth, the fire. I am the dove, the raging tiger, I am strength, I am tenderness, I am the lover, I am the mother, I am the child, I am life.

I stand in the wind, and I am.

Acknowledgements

There are many to thank, and little space to do them justice. This book would be just a manuscript in my study at home were it not for Dan Hiscocks, and the whole team at Lightning Books. Thank you for feeling this story from the very first read, for having faith in it, and in me; for making it become a reality, and for allowing me to be as fully involved as I have been. I am very grateful. Huge thanks must go also to my editor, Clio. She has done a magnificent job in polishing up this story with her wisdom, her expertise and her honesty. It is far better for her contribution, and I shall be running to her with my next one.

Thanks, too, to my wonderful friends who read early versions of it, and were so generous with their support: Caroline, Jo, Emma Jane, Patrice, Charlotte and Stefan.

To my boyfriend Chris – who has put up with my rather obsessive mind while I've worked on the book, my scattiness, my woeful technical abilities and my limited time. Thank you – your support means a great deal.

I want to thank my family, my parents Bruce and Toni, and my sister Hannah, for always being there – not just for this. And my wonderful children, Raphael, Lochlan and Meredith: the centre of everything for me. Their support is the world. Their pride in me for creating this book has been unexpected and very precious to experience. While I have tried to limit the impact of all this work on them, I know they have had to put up with my slightly preoccupied mind at times, as well as some rather substandard dinners on occasion... Thank you x

Citations

List of works cited, with grateful thanks to the copyright holders:

• **Christina Rossetti**, Echo, first published in *Goblin Market and Other Poems*, 1862, Macmillan

• **Edna St. Vincent Millay**, excerpt from a letter to Witter Bynner (October 29, 1920), from *Letters of Edna St. Vincent Millay*, edited by Allan Ross Macdougall. Copyright 1952 by Norma Millay Ellis. Reprinted with the permission of The Permissions Company, Inc., on behalf of Holly Peppe, Literary Executor, The Edna St. Vincent Millay Society, www.millay.org

• **Thomas Moore**, *Oft, In The Stilly Night* (Scotch Air), 1815

• **Lisa Hannigan**, We the Drowned, from her album *At Swim*, released 2016, www.lisahannigan.ie

• **Kahlil Gibran**, *The Prophet*, 1923, Knopf

• **Kathee Miller**, Imaginal Psychology, lecture series, 2008, Pacifica Graduate Institute

• **Jill Mellick & Marion Woodman**, *The Art of Dreaming*, 2000, Conari Press, www.jillmellick.com and www.mwoodmanfoundation.org

• **Viktor Frankl**, *Man's Search for Meaning*, 2004, Rider Press. Reprinted with permission of The Estate of Viktor Frankl, Vienna, Austria, www.viktorfrankl.org

• **Kahlil Gibran**, *Sand and Foam*, 1926, Knopf

• **Carl Gustav Jung**, Psychology and Religion: West and East, 1938, from *Collected Works of C.G. Jung*, Volume 11, Routledge, www.routledge.com

• **Omar Khayyam**, *The Ruba'iyat of Omar Khayyam*, 1981, Penguin

• **Wendell Berry**, To Know the Dark, *The Selected Poems of Wendell Berry*, 1999, Counterpoint, www.counterpointpress.com

• **Omar Khayyam**, *The Ruba'iyat of Omar Khayyam*, 1981, Penguin

• **Stefan Mørk**, Dreams Fall Through, 2016, www.stefanmork.com